A SOUNDING
BRASS

A SOUNDING
BRASS

SHELLEY BATES

AUTHOR OF

Pocketful of Pearls

WARNER
Faith®

New York Boston Nashville

Warner Faith
Time Warner Book Group
1271 Avenue of the Americas, New York, NY 10020
Visit our Web site at www.twbookmark.com.

Warner Faith® and the Warner Faith logo are trademarks of Time Warner Book Group Inc.

Printed in the United States of America

First Edition: June 2006
10 9 8 7 6 5 4 3 2 1

Library of Congress Cataloging-in-Publication Data

Bates, Shelley.
    A sounding brass / Shelley Bates.— 1st ed.
        p. cm.
    Summary: "A sheltered young woman is torn between a magnetic evangelical leader and a nonbelieving cop out to discredit him"—Provided by publisher.
    ISBN-13: 978-0-446-69492-6
    ISBN-10: 0-446-69492-4
    1. Evangelists—Fiction. 2. Radio broadcasting—Fiction. 3. Police—Fiction.
I. Title.
    PS3602.A875S68 2006
    813'.6—dc22   2005034424

For Jeff

ACKNOWLEDGMENTS

My thanks and deep appreciation go to the following people, who unstintingly shared their knowledge and experience with me.

Louise Steck, general manager of KKUP 91.5 in Santa Clara, California, the last listener-supported radio station in the country, brainstormed numerous creative methods of embezzlement.

Jackie Loken, DJ of "The Moonlight Trail" on Thursday nights at KKUP, hosted me during her show and explained how the studio works.

Amelia Rose Kelly (retired, Corrections), answered my questions about court procedures.

John Langholff and Jennifer Leonard explained the complicated maze that is the commercial banking system and gave me some nifty plot points along the way.

Bruce Redding of the Spokane office of the Washington Human Rights Commission clarified Washington employment law, particularly in regard to discrimination and at-will termination.

My parents, Dan and Carol, and my husband, Jeff, continue to support me as I follow my dream and forget to clean the house.

And as always, my thanks go to Jennifer Jackson, Leslie Peterson, and Holly Halverson, the best partners a writer could wish for.

I love to hear from readers. Visit me on my Web site, http://www.shelleybates.com, or feel free to drop me a note at shelley@shelleybates.com.

Though I speak with the tongues of men and of angels, and have not charity, I am become as sounding brass, or a tinkling cymbal.

—I CORINTHIANS 13:1 (KJV)

"This is Luke Fisher, coming to you live from 98.5 KGHM in Hamilton Falls, where we rock for Jesus!"

—LUKE FISHER AKA BRANDON BOANERGES AKA RICHARD BRANDON MYERS, DOB 4-13-74 OCTF SUBJECT FILE 06-17033

So then faith cometh by hearing, and hearing by the word of God.

—ROMANS 10:17 (KJV)

A SOUNDING
BRASS

Chapter 1

"JUST AS I AM, without one plea."

Willie Nelson's voice filled the car, and Claire Montoya gawked at the radio as if it had suddenly started speaking in tongues. The man in the farm truck ahead of her slammed on his brakes for one of the three traffic lights in Hamilton Falls, Washington, and Claire whipped her attention back to the road before she ran into him.

"Just As I Am"? What on earth was Willie Nelson, a worldly entertainer, doing singing one of the hymns of the Elect of God? Had he run across one of their privately printed hymnbooks?

Or was it a sign of something bigger? Lately KGHM's programming had changed from farm reports that nobody listened to, to gospel music, call-in shows, bluegrass, and Christian pop. An even bigger change was that everybody in the Elect—well, the young people, anyway—listened to KGHM, even though listening to the radio was technically a sin. It filled the mind with worldly noise, which caused the still, small voice of God to be drowned out.

Or so said the Shepherds, the itinerant preachers who gave up all natural expectations such as home and family to minister to the souls of men, and who were the final authority on all things natural and spiritual.

But how could "Just As I Am" fill the mind with noise when they had sung it just last week in Gathering? At least Willie Nelson was easier on the ears than Alma Woods, who on a good day sounded like a raven with its tail caught in a gate. During that very hymn last week, a woman had risen to her feet, indicating her willingness to serve God with the Elect, their community of true believers scattered throughout the state. Claire wasn't sure how valid the woman's profession of faith was, though. At the moment, they had no Shepherds to oversee the flock, and a person couldn't enter the fold and find salvation without one.

She turned into the parking lot of their plain, unadorned mission hall and parked her car, feeling very visible and solitary as she crossed the lot alone, went into the hall alone, and chose a seat halfway up on the right side, where the young people tended to sit together. There weren't as many as there used to be. A year ago she and Julia McNeill, her best friend, would have come in together after having spent the day together or with the gang. But Julia had left and married Outside their fellowship. Unlike someone who had been Silenced, people could still speak to and about her, but they tended not to. What would be the point? Her soul was lost for all eternity. And besides, she and her husband lived in Seattle.

Lucky Julia.

Claire could have sat with Dinah Traynell, if she still lived in Hamilton Falls. But Dinah's mother, Elsie, had sold the home place where people had been going to Gathering for a hundred years or more and had bought a cozy house in Spokane. At the same time, Dinah had left town and gone to California.

It hadn't taken long for the reason the whole Traynell family had moved away to leak out. That reason—Phinehas, former senior Shepherd of the flock—was currently spewing fire and brimstone in the county lockup at Pitchford while he waited for his trial, which was scheduled to begin tomorrow. Much to everyone's shock and dismay, their leader had been accused of raping two generations of Traynell women. It had taken all these months for Claire herself to come to the slow acceptance that their leadership had been seriously flawed.

She sighed and stared sightlessly at the open Bible in her lap while she waited for the service to begin. Dinah would be back to testify, but it wasn't likely she'd get much of a welcome. She'd gone Outside, too, and was engaged to be married to her former hired man. They were going to Cornwall for their honeymoon.

Claire had never been farther from home than Seattle. Cornwall seemed like a magical place, full of Celtic ruins and brilliant light and flowers—at least, according to Matthew Nicholas, Dinah's intended, who had spent fifteen minutes on the phone the other night long-distance from California rhapsodizing about all the childhood haunts he was going to show his bride.

By the time Dinah got there, she was going to need a good dose of light and flowers. Claire didn't see how her friend was going to get through the next few weeks. Or how she herself was going to manage it. She hadn't been deposed yet, but there was no guarantee she wouldn't be called upon as a character witness. Or so said Investigator Raymond Harper of the Organized Crime Task Force, who was camped out in Hamilton Falls and Pitchford for the duration of the trial. She'd met him on her last visit to Ross and Julia's when he'd dropped in at dinnertime. He was Ross's partner, and frankly, he made her uncomfortable. Maybe it was his size or maybe it was simply the knowledge of just how ugly human behavior could get that lurked in his eyes. Whatever it was, the less she saw of him, the better.

Owen Blanchard left his seat and made his way to the microphone at the front of the hall. He was Elder of the church that met in his home—or had met there. After the Traynells' departure, Sunday Gathering had been moved here to the hall because not everyone could fit in his rec room. Gathering could only be held in the homes of one of the favored families, which was problematic now since there was only one, and Owen couldn't be expected to shoulder the burden indefinitely. He had two children and the principalship of the local high school to think about.

Face it, Claire thought, *the Elect are in total disarray. Julia started it, Dinah finished it, and now we have to pick up the pieces.* She hoped Owen had come up with some kind of solution. These stop-gap Gatherings couldn't go on forever. She also hoped she could grab a private moment with him after the service. She needed an answer, and the waiting was killing her.

Owen announced a hymn, and after they had sung it in

tolerable four-part harmony, he led them in prayer. Claire expected testimony time would happen next, when all the men took turns speaking on a verse or confessing struggles or saying what their wives told them to say. But Owen stayed at the microphone until everyone stopped wiggling in their seats and whispering.

"You all know what's going to happen tomorrow," he said. The overhead lighting glinted on his hair, which had been a vibrant reddish gold until recently, but was now a sandy gray. "Phinehas's—I mean, Mr. Leslie's—jury has been chosen, and his trial is going to begin. It's up to you folks whether you go or not. Some of us have been deposed to testify." He sighed, and then went on. "Folks, we have to come to some kind of decision, here."

Mark McNeill, Julia's father, whom Claire had hardly ever seen speak outside of his duties as former Elder, stood up. "I heard from Spokane this morning. Melchizedek is still at the Grotons' place. He had a nervous breakdown and is completely unfit to lead the flock. The family is on suicide watch."

Melchizedek, the younger Shepherd over the congregation in Hamilton Falls, had practically worshipped the ground Phinehas had walked on. At the news that Phinehas had been sexually abusing the females in the Traynell family for thirty years, he had cracked and gone to his sister's place in Spokane. The other Shepherds, scattered throughout the state of Washington, were in as bad a condition as the people in Hamilton Falls when they'd heard the news about their leader. Some believed the accusations; some did not.

Some tried to carry on in their faith; some had gone Outside and had not been heard from since.

"Why is God punishing us?" Derrick Wilkinson, the man sitting on Claire's right, wanted to know. "Have our sins been that bad?"

God isn't punishing us, Claire thought. *He's punishing Phinehas, thank you very much. And just because you don't get to marry into a favored family and become an Elder, let's not take this personally.* It was a well-known fact among the local Elect females that Derrick had pursued first Julia McNeill Malcolm and then Dinah Traynell because they were daughters of the two favored families. Without one of them as his wife, he would never realize his career aspirations to be Deacon and, later, Elder of his own house church. The position was hereditary—and now there was no one left to inherit.

Poor Derrick. Maybe he'd have to move to a new town and find another favored-family girl to date—unless the Shepherds had told him what they'd told her.

"There is a solution," Owen said. "I'm putting it to you all tonight in hopes that we can take heart and move on in strength, particularly in view of the days ahead."

"What's that?" Derrick asked, speaking for all of them.

"I'd like to introduce a guest speaker." Owen waited for the murmuring to die down. Claire glanced at Rebecca Quinn, her landlady, on her left. Other than the Shepherds, who were anointed of God to speak, and the Elder, whose job it was to administer the flock in the Shepherds' periodic absences, guest speakers were unheard of. Who else could bring the Word of God to his people but the anointed ones?

"Maybe the Shepherd from Richmond has come to help us," Rebecca whispered.

"He's gone," Claire whispered back. "My folks got the word this morning. Left without a trace. They think he joined the army."

Claire would have said more, but a man got up from the front row and bounded up to the microphone as if he owned the very earth.

Wow. Claire blinked and forgot the rest of what she had been about to say.

The man was tall and had the kind of presence that natural leaders possessed. His shoulders were broad and strong, in contrast to a trim waist and athletic grace. Chestnut hair glinted under the lights, and when he turned to face them, she saw that his eyes were brown and long-lashed. He smiled, and a long dimple cut into his cheek.

Claire heard a rustle as all the single women in the crowd sat up and took notice, including a few of the widows.

"Now, that's a fine-looking man," Rebecca murmured.

"If he's a new Shepherd, it won't matter," Claire said. The Shepherds were homeless and celibate, the better to go wherever the gospel led them. Free of natural ties, their lives were consecrated to God's will. Most of the Elect's rules about women's dress, Claire often thought privately, were designed to make it easier for the Shepherds to make this sacrifice. If a man couldn't see a woman's skin, if her hair was pinned up modestly, the Shepherds were less likely to be reminded of what they had lost from a physical standpoint.

Theoretically. This, of course, had not proven to be the

case with Phinehas and his thirty-year persecution of the Traynell women.

"I'd like to present Mr. Luke Fisher," Owen said, "evangelist from our very own KGHM radio, right here in Hamilton Falls."

What?

People turned in their seats to stare at one another and gaped at Owen as if they couldn't believe their ears. A worldly evangelist? To speak to them? Someone who wasn't even Elect?

"Is he completely mad?" Rebecca asked aloud, forgetting to whisper.

No one heard her. Everyone was busy talking, speculating, wondering the same thing.

"Please, folks, listen to me." Owen's voice rose above the noise, and out of habit, the congregation quieted enough that he could be heard. "We've all been praying without ceasing that God would save us in our hour of need. And I believe the reason He hasn't is because we've strayed away from Him. We've put our trust in our leadership—in man, in human frailty—and the result has been a disaster. We've looked inwardly to ourselves instead of looking outwardly at what God is doing in the world."

People murmured, and Claire nibbled her lower lip, wondering where on earth this was going.

"It's been revealed to me that perhaps God speaks to people outside of the Elect, that maybe we might have something to learn from Mr. Fisher, who has led congregations two and three times this size and who, I'm convinced, has his heart right with God." Owen looked around at them all.

"I'm not saying he's a Shepherd. I've only invited him to be a guest speaker. Our fundamental beliefs remain the same— but I think it would do the people of God good to embrace the Holy Spirit in others, as well as in themselves."

Mark McNeill, Owen's father-in-law and a retired Elder, stood and cleared his throat. "Owen, I don't think that's right. You know the Holy Spirit is only given to God's people. His grace is only poured out on us through the gospel spoken by the Shepherds. Only they have the authority."

Owen nodded respectfully. "But at the moment we don't have a Shepherd. Mr. Fisher is just a guest speaker, Dad."

"You or I could speak in the Shepherds' place."

Owen began to look uncomfortable at having a disagreement with his father-in-law in public. "I've had a revelation," he repeated, "and I believe it was from God."

It was hard to argue with that. Since the downfall of Phinehas, Claire had wondered if the Elect put their leaders on a pedestal, to the point where perhaps they blocked the light that came from God. Some, such as the McNeills, catered to their every whim, bringing out the best china, the best food, making even a bowl of cereal or a cup of coffee an event. Others, including her parents, treated the Shepherds like visiting relatives whenever they came to stay. Hospitality to the Shepherds was part of their sacrifice, but the danger lay in making a show of their service in order to impress the leaders.

"Folks," Owen pleaded, "let's listen to Mr. Fisher's message and then do what Paul exhorted us to do—try the spirit and see if it's of God."

He yielded the microphone to Luke Fisher and returned

to his seat. Every eye in the hall was riveted to the front. Claire drew in a breath as Luke Fisher began to speak. That melodious voice—which had sounded in her car, announcing songs, exhorting people to come to God, talking with people who called in—filled their humble meeting place with his particular brand of music.

"Those of you who listen to the radio," he said, "may have heard a number of your hymns being played and wondered how it could be that worldly artists could sing the music and words that mean so much to you."

He paused, and all the young people in Claire's row looked at each other, eyebrows raised. Obviously they'd thought the very thing she had. Maybe some of them had even been listening to the radio on the way to Mission and had heard "Just As I Am."

"Well, here's the thing." He paused, then said, "I grew up in the Elect."

An audible gasp swept through the room.

"I did, and when I went Out, I lived a life of sin and suffering, brought on by my own headstrong will. But God had a plan for me, and do you know what that was?"

Claire found herself shaking her head, as though he had spoken directly to her. She wished he would. She wished those eyes would seek her out in the midst of this crowd and see that there was a mature, reasonably attractive woman who was currently single and very much available, right there in the seventh row.

"God's plan was for me to preach the gospel, but not as a Shepherd. No, His plan for my life reaches farther than that. It's been revealed to me that radio isn't a sin, my friends. It's a way of reaching the hearts of the sick, the shut-in, those who aren't as fortunate as we are in this hall tonight. It's a way of bringing cheer to your soul as you drive to the supermarket, of focusing your mind on Christ while you work in the office. It's a way to reach the soul on the other side of the cube divider who doesn't know which way to turn in a life that looks like a maze."

The crowd was utterly silent.

"God gives us all our talents, my friends. And what have we been doing with them? Have we been burying them in the backyard of our own little group? Or have we been lending them out to others?"

"Backyard," Claire heard someone say. Six months ago, no one would have agreed with such a thing unless Phinehas himself had decreed a change in doctrine. Just a few months ago, the Elect had been sure of themselves and sure of what they believed. Things were different now. They were all shaken and a little uncertain about what exactly was right.

"Nonsense," snapped Elizabeth McNeill, Julia's mother, and then blushed scarlet at having actually spoken aloud in a Gathering, where it was forbidden for women to raise their voices except in song.

Luke Fisher smiled, and Claire lost her ability to breathe. *If only someone would smile at me like that.*

AFTER GATHERING WAS OVER, Claire hung at the fringes of the little group that had gathered around Luke and Owen. It was hard not to watch the newcomer, what with that smile and that charismatic presence.

"Don't go making eyes at that worldly preacher." Alma Woods shook Claire's hand in her abrupt way. "Enough of you young women have lost your salvation by chasing ungodly men."

Claire choked down a defensive retort. Not by any stretch of the imagination could Ross Malcolm or Matthew Nicholas be called ungodly. And she'd never chased anyone in her life. "I'm not making eyes at him," she said with dignity. "I'm waiting to speak with Owen."

Alma ran a critical eye down her dress and coat. "Been ordering from catalogs again, have we?"

"Yes, as a matter of fact. There are some pretty things in—"

"Vanity, all is vanity." Alma looked her in the eye. "You should be a better example to your mother. I saw her in Pitchford, you know, traipsing around in a pair of pants, worldly as you please when she thought no one was looking."

Shame flogged hot color into Claire's cheeks. "My mother's choices are her own," she said. "Excuse me, Alma. I need to speak to Owen."

Please let him help, she begged the Lord. *I have to get out of this town.*

Owen broke away from the little group at last and she stopped him with a hand on his arm as he glanced around for his kids. "Owen, could I speak to you a minute?"

His smile was open and warm, and she took heart. "Sure. What's up?"

"I—I wondered if you'd heard anything from any of the Shepherds about whether I could move or not."

His smile faded. "Claire, we've been over this. Your place is in Hamilton Falls. Besides, you did move. To Rebecca's."

That didn't count as a move. More like an aborted flight that crash-landed. She'd received notice that she'd gotten the position she'd interviewed for at one of the bank's branches in Seattle. She'd given her notice, packed her things, and was practically on the highway when Phinehas had stepped in to ask her what she thought she was doing.

"There are plenty of young people in Seattle, Claire," he'd said with that gentle smile of a man who controlled people's lives with absolute authority. "And not so many here in Hamilton Falls. I need you to be an example to the younger girls."

The younger girls hardly looked at her—why should they? Nobody needed her, really, with the exception of her manager at the bank, who'd been delighted she was staying and had offered her the new accounts position. She hadn't wanted it. She'd have been a mail clerk in the Seattle branch if that's what it took to get out of Hamilton Falls.

But no. Even that had been denied her. So, when Dinah had declined it, she'd rented Rebecca's suite and put the best face on the situation that she could.

"You know what Phinehas said," Owen reminded her now, with a little of Phinehas's own gentleness.

"But with him on trial tomorrow, maybe we should look at my situation again."

"Claire, the Elders have a lot to think and pray about right now. Please be considerate."

Her desire to move away and have a real life was inconsiderate? Tears burned the back of her throat as Owen stepped around her to shake someone else's hand.

She should be used to it by now—the bitter flavor of unwillingness.

INVESTIGATOR RAYMOND HARPER of Washington State's Organized Crime Task Force ran his fingers through his hair and gripped his skull as he read through his notes early Monday morning. The district attorney's assistant detoured around the desk temporarily on loan to him and dropped a pile of papers on the corner of it.

"Your depositions came back from Transcription," she told him. "George thought you might want a look."

Great. One more thing to do, one more thing keeping him in beautiful downtown Pitchford instead of back in Seattle doing what he'd signed up to do.

Sexual abuse wasn't his bailiwick—organized crime was. But two things had prodded him into taking the case: the fact that this religious group was statewide, which put it in the OCTF's purview, and Tamara Traynell's big brown eyes and the depths of pain he had seen in them as she'd told her story. He'd left Ross and Julia Malcolm's dinner table that night if not a changed man, then certainly an angry one. He had at last understood why his partner and best friend had made busting bent religious groups his particular mission. Trust wasn't Ray's biggest fault, but it was in plenty of people—people who gave their faith and their money to a group and got nothing but abuse and a bunch of happy brainwashing in return.

Which is why it puzzled him to see Ross and Julia and their daughter Kailey tripping off to church as if Ross's daily disillusionment about human nature never happened. The guy must have superhuman powers of denial. Or a bigger capacity to love and forgive than Ray himself possessed.

With a sigh, he closed his notebook and laid it on top of his file on Emile Johan Rausch, who thought he was going to get away with running cocaine over the line into Canada in the guise of horseback-riding trips, and the frustrating case of Brandon Boanerges, the invisible fraudster with the beautiful voice who had been driving him nuts for a year. He opened the deposition file for the rape case.

This Philip Leslie guy—aka Phinehas, aka the senior minister of the group Julia, Dinah, and Tamara had belonged to—was a real prince. As his arresting officer, Ray had been delighted to be subpoenaed to testify against him. As far as he was concerned, the prosecution's case was open and shut, but he still had to show up on the stand and say his bit about the arrest.

He had no doubt young Tamara would hold herself together while Leslie gave her the hairy eyeball from the defendant's chair. Her sister Dinah, who was also on the prosecution's witness list, had lost her fear of the man, too. He glanced through the young woman's deposition. Her answers had been clear, concise, and full of damning detail, just the way Ray liked them. In Prosecution 101, this girl would get an "A."

TRAYNELL: Phinehas is an itinerant minister, so he stays in the homes of the Elect. He would come to my room at night and have sex with me against my will, telling me that I was a vessel filled with love and my purpose was to give love to him so he could have the strength to go on preaching the gospel.

HARPER: For how long did this go on?

TRAYNELL: Ten years. It started when I was fourteen.

Ray's stomach turned over. Justice was supposed to be blind, but the people in her service didn't have to be so impartial. It was a stroke of luck they'd pulled Judge Eleanor Keaton—a woman, the D.A. had told him, who was particularly hard on sex offenders.

The D.A.'s assistant stopped by the desk a second time and tapped her watch. "It's time, Investigator."

He was one of the first witnesses on the schedule, so he hustled down the corridor that connected the county offices with the courthouse. It sported all of two courtrooms, one for municipal cases and one for superior court, housed in a modest brick building facing a green space that formed an old-fashioned town square.

By nine-thirty he was sworn in and on the stand, with Judge Keaton on his right and a sea of people dressed in black in front of him. Tamara had told him the Elect dressed in black to symbolize the charred remains of the burned offering of their human nature. Weird. He wondered how many still supported their former leader, and how many were here to see him condemned, if that turned out to be the verdict.

The accused, Philip Leslie, his spine straight and his face calm, sat at the defense table next to John Ortega, the public defender. Phinehas was dressed in a beautifully cut black wool suit. Ray suspected that none of the flock knew he would be strip-searched each time he changed into and out of it. For a man as fastidious as he'd learned Phinehas was, each time he had to submit to the search would be a fine kind of torture.

Ray smiled inwardly.

The D.A. ran Ray through his testimony with concise competence. Name, rank, and serial number. How long he'd been with the OCTF. The circumstances of the arrest. The contents of his depositions and the lab reports that had proven both Dinah Traynell and her younger sister's child, Tamsen, were both the daughters of Phinehas. The D.A. sat alone at the plaintiff's table; he'd remain alone until Tamara and Dinah were brought out of the private room in which they sat until it was their turn to testify. Personally, Ray was just as happy he didn't have to watch the teenaged Tammy's face from the stand. He didn't want to give the impression he was emotionally involved.

Because everyone else in the courtroom certainly seemed to be. Nobody talked, but the intensity of their gazes and their focus on every word of testimony was eerie. It was like their survival depended on the verdict.

For all he knew, maybe it did.

The defense had a few questions on cross-examination about the chain of evidence, but Ray had made sure that everything having to do with the lab and the DNA results was airtight. Then it was time to put Tamara on the stand.

Ray could have made his way into the gallery to watch, but he decided not to. He had all the gory details in the deposition if he wanted them, and watching her say the words was not going to help his peace of mind or the case.

Tamara's mother, Elsie, sat directly behind the railing dividing the audience from the active members of the court, and as he slipped out the door, Ray saw Tamara reach over it and clutch her mother's hand for a moment before she took the stand to be sworn in.

Good luck, princess.

A fast walk took him back to the D.A.'s office and the desk where his paperwork sat. He folded himself into the chair and reached for the phone.

"Harmon," his sergeant barked when the call rang through.

"It's Harper."

"Are you finished dazzling that hack D.A. out there in the sticks?" Harmon and the D.A., George Daniels, had been partners back in the Dark Ages, before Daniels had dropped out of the force to go to law school.

Ray grinned. "He sends his love, too."

"So, when can I expect to see you back here doing some real work?"

"I finished giving my testimony just now. I can head back tomorrow."

"What's wrong with this afternoon? You think my budget has endless nights of hotel rooms built into it for you?"

It was a good thing Ray knew Harmon's bark was worse than his bite. "I have a couple of things left to do. And I want to check out a lead on this Boanerges thing. One of the lonely hearts he ripped off gave me a tip he might be over this way."

"Sounds pretty vague."

"It *is* vague. The whole case is vague, and you know how I hate that. But if he's crossing county lines, that puts him in my case load, so I'll do what I can."

"I'll expect you back tomorrow."

"Sooner or later."

Fortunately Harmon hadn't pressed him on his "things-to-do" list. There was only one thing on it of a personal nature. Julia, his partner Ross's wife, had asked him to take one of their framed wedding pictures to her former landlady, Rebecca Quinn. He'd met her at their tiny wedding, but he hadn't seen her in the courtroom. Not surprising. The lady apparently ran her own business, and driving ninety miles to hear the trial proceedings wouldn't make her a living.

He'd do pretty much anything to make Julia smile, and if that meant playing delivery boy, then that's what he would do.

Then he'd blow this popsicle stand and get back to work.

Chapter 2

NUMBER 1204 GATES PLACE was a big, sprawling house with Craftsman lines and Victorian sensibilities that had been built for a railroad executive back in the twenties, when the town of Hamilton Falls had been founded. It could have housed a family of twelve comfortably, and had at one time, but now all that was left of the original Quinn family in the area was Rebecca.

Rebecca was not the kind of woman to sit back with nothing to do but dust the sepia photographs of her ancestors. She had braved the storms of both gossip and disapproval and, after her brother Lawrence's death, taken over management of his bookstore. Over time, Quill and Quinn had gone from being a dark, dusty place for boxes of used books to a tourist's delight, stocking wholesome new novels and books of local interest, and featuring the odd piece of art or craftsmanship by local artisans. The shop was bright, welcoming, and full of plants and Rebecca's practical, cheery personality.

The suite on the top floor of the house had long been converted and rented to a succession of single Elect girls, the most recent of whom was Claire Montoya. When she'd learned that Dinah wasn't interested in moving in, Claire had comforted herself with the fact that at least she was going *somewhere*, even if it was just across town. Not that she was desperate to get out of her parents' house or anything.

Well, okay, she was.

Her folks were great people, and she loved them, but the fact of the matter was that they were what Alma Woods liked to call "half-and-halfers." Other, nicer people might say "Elected but not perfected," implying that there was still hope. No matter what the expression, Claire always cringed. Her folks had come to the Elect later in life, after she and her sister, Elaine, were born, and instead of embracing the lifestyle and traditions of godliness with a whole heart, they had maintained some outward appearances and not others— and told no one about the television on a rolling cart in the bedroom closet. Late at night Claire could hear them laughing at some program, and it became like a canker, sitting in the heart of the house like a great big lie.

Maybe that was why she tried so hard to live up to the standards the Elect set. So okay, she wore up-to-date outfits, but they *were* black. And she worked in public, which not many of the Elect women did. But no one worked harder than she did at schooling her words, keeping her temper, saying nice things to Alma Woods when all she wanted to do was snap back something that would silence the old crow for good. She always had a smile and an offer of help, even when she didn't want to give either one.

Maybe deep down she thought these things would offset her parents' behavior in the eyes of the congregation. Maybe they'd think, *That Claire, now, she's really got it. She's a hearty one, being such a good example to her parents.* Or maybe they wouldn't, but at least it made her feel as though she were doing her best to serve God.

In any case, at least Claire was nominally on her own. The furniture might be Vintage Garage Sale and the dishes her grandma's second set, with prim little rosebuds that were the last thing Claire would have chosen had she had any money, but the space was hers to do with as she would. She could jump on the bed if she felt like it. Eat cereal lying on the couch. Wear colored pajamas.

No, scratch that.

A woman could wear color in the privacy of her own bedroom, but for Claire, the sacrifice had to be complete. Her nightie was black flannel, and every night she put the desire for red silk pajamas on the altar of sacrifice, where it belonged.

Tonight, though, she was down in Rebecca's suite, dressed in black as usual, with Dinah soon-to-be-Nicholas and her sister, Tamara Traynell. They were both staying with Rebecca until the trial was over, making the ninety-mile commute to Pitchford every morning and evening in Rebecca's car. Claire and Rebecca drove to work in Claire's car, one going to the bookshop and the other to the bank across the street.

"But where's the baby?" Claire asked Dinah as they finished their dessert. Court had gone right to five o'clock before the judge had dismissed everyone, and after driving an hour and a half back to Hamilton Falls, the Traynell girls had been starving.

Dinah licked ice cream from her spoon with relish. "I thought it would be better to leave her at home, with Matthew," she said. "If I'm on the stand, there's no one to look after her, and we thought this whole thing would be emotional enough for Tamara."

Privately, Claire wondered how on earth Tamara could have given up her daughter Tamsen in the first place, but she'd never say that out loud. After all, what did she know? If she were in Tamara's situation, knowing that her daughter was the child of rape, could she be the kind of mother the child needed? Maybe Tamara had been right to place the baby in Dinah's custody. To make a new life for herself up in Seattle.

"Besides," Dinah went on, "Matthew adores her, and she loves him right back. He's teaching part-time at a junior college until we're married, and his friend's wife has a newborn so she looks after Tamsen while he's in class."

"Good for you," Rebecca said with a smile. "And I'm looking after your other babies."

Claire grinned.

"You were so kind to give them a home," Dinah said affectionately, speaking of her beloved flock of hens. "I could take Schatzi and the five most senior, but it was a bit daunting to find a place for twelve. One of the perks of staying here is seeing them again."

"It's not just six anymore," Claire said. "She made the mistake of going to the feed store and looking at the little peeps."

"I only brought home two." Rebecca's tone was virtuous. "We had chickens around here as children, but I'd forgotten how much fun they are. I'm having a little difficulty establishing that the rose bushes are out of bounds, but I'm sure I can convince them eventually."

Dinah laughed, but Tamara looked far away, as though the mention of Tamsen earlier had been hard for her. Claire was dying to ask how it had gone in court today, but outside the courtroom both girls were sworn to secrecy.

The doorbell rang, its gentle peal shivering into silence. Rebecca put her napkin on the table and got up to answer it. "Why, Mr. Harper," Claire heard her say in welcoming tones. "Come right in."

"Harper?" Dinah straightened in her chair.

"Hey, Ray," Tamara greeted him as Rebecca led him into the dining room. Claire wished she could be as casual. The guy was a couple of inches over six feet, with the kind of controlled power that no doubt came from chasing down criminals in dark alleys or arresting drug lords. His wavy brown hair flopped into eyes that didn't miss a thing and only believed half of what he saw. They softened when he looked at Tamara.

"Tammy," he said. "How'd you make out today?"

"Good," she responded. "Nice job with the defense counsel. Mr. Daniels said they couldn't get a thing past you."

"Sounds as though you were playing hockey," Rebecca said. "Mr. Harper, have you eaten dinner?"

"I grabbed a burger in Pitchford."

"Then please have dessert with us. I never met a man who could say no to my apple pie."

"I'm afraid I'll have to, Miss Quinn. I can't socialize with the other witnesses. Conflict of interest. I just stopped by to ask Dinah a few more questions and to drop something off for you."

"For me?"

"Julia sent it." Ray handed Rebecca a package. "It's their wedding picture. She thought you'd like something besides snapshots."

Rebecca's faced flushed with pleasure as she tore the wrapping off. "Oh, isn't this beautiful." She held up the eight-by-ten frame.

"Look at that dress," Claire breathed.

"She'd never be allowed to wear something like that if she were still Elect," Tamara observed. "Good for her."

In the photo, Julia sat with her wedding bouquet in her lap, Ross behind her with a hand on her shoulder. His other hand rested on the back of his daughter Kailey's neck, and all three beamed at the photographer. Julia's dress was a simple waterfall of cream silk that puddled on the ground at her feet. Her arms were bare from the elbows down, and she wore a string of pearls around her throat. She looked more beautiful than Claire could ever remember seeing her, and she regretted now that she hadn't gone to the wedding.

But how could she have gone? That would entail telling her folks and the people in Gathering where she was going. That might work when she could camouflage a visit under a business trip, but to go to a worldly wedding? It would be impossible to explain. Their own were sober affairs. A bride didn't even wear a white dress, because there was nowhere she could wear it afterward. Her wedding outfit was a practical black.

Cream silk and pearls. Claire sighed. Clearly, clothes were the cross she had to bear.

"I appreciate this so much, Mr. Harper." Rebecca set the picture on the sideboard and returned to the table. "Are you going to be with us long?"

"Nope, I'm done. Should be heading back to Seattle after I make my final report tomorrow."

"Is it too late to say thank you?" Dinah asked. "After all, you interrupted the Testimony of Two Men that night and saved me from being Silenced for seven years."

"I have no idea what that means, but no, it's never too late." He gave her a smile that, to Claire, seemed out of place on the face of such a dangerous-looking man.

"Dinah was about to be shunned for telling the truth about Phinehas," Rebecca explained calmly while Claire tried not to choke on the last bite of her pie. Dinah was to have been Silenced? How come she hadn't heard a word about it? "Fortunately the only people who know about that besides her mother and Owen are right in this room. And it will stay in this room."

She glanced at Claire, and her blue eyes and cloud of silver hair reminded Claire of the steely flash of a sword.

Claire cleared her throat. "Absolutely," she said.

Not that this news mattered, anyway. Dinah had gone Out of the Elect, forsaking their fellowship, and now most of the Elect simply treated her with the casual formality they'd give to, say, a gas-station attendant.

Claire had always been taught that an Elect person

couldn't have fellowship with someone who was Out, that there would be no freedom of spirit between them. But for some reason this didn't seem to be the case. The more she knew of Dinah, the better she liked her.

Ray Harper was a cat of a different color, though. He stood behind Claire's shoulder, making her entire right side feel sensitized somehow, as though he was putting off a force field and her skin was tingling from it.

Right, Claire. The man is here to do his job. You mean as much to him as the chair you're sitting on.

Not that that was a bad thing.

"Would you like to use one of the empty bedrooms for your business with Dinah, Ray?" Rebecca asked.

A glance at his witness told her she wouldn't be very comfortable doing that. "Uh, no. Maybe we could go outside."

"It's quite cool out there in the evenings. We're at nearly a thousand feet in this part of the country."

"It's too bad you can't just relax and hang out with us for once," Tamara said. "You never know. You might learn something."

He gave her the kind of big-brother look that made Claire's lips twitch. "What, the latest tips in hair care?"

"For a start. Yours is long enough to braid."

"It is not." A little self-consciously, he fingered the hair that brushed his collar. "I'm undercover most of the time. If I had a regulation cut, the bad guys would see me coming a mile away."

"My kingdom for a regulation cut," Claire heard herself say, and then wished she could grab the words back.

Dinah laughed, and even Rebecca smiled. "You said it. I haven't had the guts to cut mine yet. It seems . . . irrevocable somehow."

"Oh, come on, Di." Tamara ran a hand through her short-cropped brown curls. "It grows back."

Ray had glanced at Claire after her remark, a look that took her in from crown to chin. "Why would you want it off?" he asked. "Your hair is pretty like that."

Don't blush. Don't. Oh, dear. Urgghh!

"Aw, now you made her blush," Tamara said with teenage insensitivity. "You're such a charmer."

"But think of the hours of agony it takes to produce that look," Dinah said calmly, making him look at her instead of at Claire's scarlet face. "I would estimate twenty minutes just to get the front to behave, never mind the coil in the back."

"You would estimate right," Claire said. *Breathe. Don't think about it.*

"So wear it down," Ray suggested.

Married women took their hair down for their husbands in the intimacy of the bedroom, but she wasn't about to say *that* to a hard-bitten cop she hardly knew. "It's part of our sacrifice," she began, but Rebecca interrupted her smoothly.

"Women in our church traditionally wear their hair up. Come on, you kids, leave Mr. Harper alone. He needs to speak with Dinah."

"Why don't you go upstairs and use the kitchen table at my place?" Claire suggested, then wished she hadn't. Good grief, when was the last time she'd cleaned? And were there items of clothing lying on the floor? At least she'd done last night's supper dishes, but the bathroom was probably—

"Thanks, Claire. Good idea." Dinah's soft voice clinched it, so Claire had no choice but to help Rebecca clear the table while Ray followed Dinah up the outside staircase.

Twenty minutes later, they heard light footsteps on the stairs and Dinah came in. Alone.

"Claire, Ray wants to ask you a few questions, too."

"Me? What about?"

"No idea. Go on. Don't look so scared. He's not going to arrest you."

Being arrested was the least of her worries. Being alone in her apartment with a man who gave her goose bumps definitely was.

She thanked Rebecca for supper, said good night to everyone, and climbed the stairs. She found Ray sitting at the yellow Formica kitchen table that had been Julia's when she'd lived here. She imagined a more appropriate backdrop would be a black leather couch, or at the very least a nice, manly corduroy chair. He probably lived in one of those loft apartments in the warehouse district, over a nightclub or something.

What was it to her, anyway? He was out of bounds, an Outsider, and she had no business speculating about a life that was practically on a different planet from her own. If she were going to think about anyone, it would be Luke Fisher and that smile that could light up an entire mission hall. Now, there was a man worth dreaming about. Equally out of her league, but at least he had been accepted by Owen Blanchard and he had grown up Elect.

Luke Fisher would know what the ground rules were— the expectations between men and women. He would know that a dating couple could never be alone in a room with the door closed, or that sharing a hymnbook was a sign of an approaching engagement. He would know that engagement rings were worldly and a godly man gave his intended a wristwatch instead. Luke Fisher would understand the sacrifice behind the clothing and the hair, where Ray Harper probably just thought they were all weird.

"Thanks for letting me use your space," he said when she pulled out the other chair and sat down opposite him. He finished making a note in his notebook and glanced up. "Julia sends her love. I should have told you that before."

"Thank you. I guess the baby is due pretty soon, isn't he?"

"About a month. But you can't tell that to Ross. He has two cell phones. One for work and one for Julia to call with baby updates. The guy is obsessed."

"Babies will do that to you." As if she knew anything about it, really. She'd held lots of them and done her share of cooing and patting other people's, but other than the arrival of her nephews a few years ago, she hadn't had much experience.

She was a bit of an anomaly among Elect women, choosing a career at the bank over home and family. But there seemed to be a sea change afoot among the Elect lately. Maybe in a few years she wouldn't stand out so much. Then again, if a person could get a date in this town, she wouldn't stand out so much that way, either.

"I hope you don't mind my saying so, but you and Julia sure seem different."

Claire glanced at him in surprise. "Of course, we're different. She's left the church. I haven't."

"No, not that way." He waved a hand, as if trying to catch the right word out of the air. "It's not the external things. She's a happy person."

"And I'm not?" Oh, great. Now perfect strangers were making judgments about her. And here she thought she only had Alma Woods and her bevy of critical cronies to worry about.

"I don't know whether you are or not. None of my business. She says you were best friends. Almost like sisters."

"Yes, we were." Still were, on Claire's side. But Julia had a family and a home and a new life to fill her heart. It wasn't surprising that time and distance had amplified their differences instead of minimizing them.

Suddenly Claire felt lonelier than ever. *Thank you, Mr. Harper. Talking to you has just brightened up my whole day.*

"Tell Julia I send my love back, doubled," she said. "So, you're heading back tomorrow?"

He frowned at his notebook. "Maybe," he said. "Maybe not. I've got a case with a connection in this neighborhood. I might follow it up, or I might take a couple of days off."

"What kind of a case?"

He glanced at her. "Sorry. Can't say."

Of course not. How silly of her. "Did you have some questions for me?"

"No, I just wanted to let you know we wouldn't be needing you as a character witness. Dinah and Tamara are pretty convincing."

"Oh. Thanks." She hadn't expected to be asked to testify, and in fact, other than an initial contact by an investigator from the D.A.'s office, she hadn't heard a thing.

She waited, but he only frowned at his notebook as if he were trying to decipher his own handwriting. "Um, would you like something to drink?" she asked. "Tea or coffee?"

Her apartment seemed unusually quiet. She couldn't even hear the girls talking with Rebecca on the floor below. A breeze moved the branches of the oak tree outside the window, and they tapped on the pane as though trying to get Ray's attention.

He looked up and shook his head. "No. Thanks."

"I'm not a witness. It wouldn't be a conflict of interest."

What are you saying? You want this guy out of here, don't you? Or would you rather just sit here and listen to him breathing?

"That's nice of you, but I have to go."

But he made no move to get up. Just when she was about to do so herself, to give him a hint that maybe a person would like to have her shower and curl up with a book, he looked up and she froze in his gaze.

He had hazel eyes. Funny she hadn't noticed that before.

"Hey, you work in the bank, right?" When she nodded, he said, "There's only one?" She nodded again. "So, you're pretty familiar with new people in town, then, coming in and opening up accounts and whatnot."

"I'm the new accounts rep, as a matter of fact."

"No kidding." He leaned forward. "How many do you get?"

She shrugged, trying to figure out where this was going, then gave up. "A couple a week. The southerners from California and Oregon are discovering us. The dot-com people are buying up the acreages, like the one Dinah used to live on. Plus a big discount store is opening up on the edge of town, so people are moving in because of that."

"The name Brandon Boanerges sound familiar to you?"

Claire thought back through a couple of weeks' worth of new-account applications. "No. It's an odd name. I'd have remembered it, especially since it's biblical."

"Biblical?" He flipped open the notebook and clicked his pen.

"The disciples James and John were named Boanerges. It means 'sons of thunder.' "

He wrote it down, and the frown lines between his eyes grew a little deeper.

"Can I ask why you need to know this? Is this guy a witness in Dinah and Tamara's case?"

Snapping the book shut, he got up, then reached across the table and shook her hand. "No. Something else. Thanks for the info and for letting me work up here. Good night."

She watched him thump down the stairs and climb into his truck. As he drove off, she found herself shaking her head. Why on earth was the strong, silent type so popular in those romances in the used-book section in the back of Rebecca's bookshop? It was completely impossible to hold a conversation with one.

RAY HARPER TOSSED the backpack with his case files in it—he wasn't a briefcase kind of guy—onto the small, round table in his motel room. He toed off his boots and fell on the bed in a tired, loose-limbed heap.

Could he have acted any dumber or failed to impress any more . . . impressively?

With a sigh, he punched up the bag of wood chips the motel called a pillow and stared at the ceiling, where Claire Montoya's wide green eyes and flawless jawline seemed to be superimposed over the light fixture.

It wasn't like he was a total zero as far as ladies were concerned. He'd had his share of girlfriends and had even managed to sustain a live-in relationship for two years before she got disgusted with all the double shifts and left. So, why had he reverted to Mr. Neanderthal when he'd been alone with Claire? Not that he was interested or anything. But hey, it was natural for a man to want to impress a pretty, intelligent woman, and she was certainly all that.

Too bad she belonged to this whacked-out religion Julia had come out of. Julia was the nicest person he knew—a woman without a malicious bone in her body when, in his opinion, she had good reasons to bear malice. Claire seemed to be cut from the same fine cloth, which was probably why he'd tanked in the good-impressions department. He just couldn't think of a thing to say. For Ray Harper, who had a reputation in the OCTF for having the fastest comeback in the department, that was just plain ridiculous.

This motel room was way too quiet. He needed something to distract him until he was ready to reread the files to see if a clue to the whereabouts of either Emile Johan Rausch or Brandon Boanerges popped out at him. The clock radio on the nightstand picked up a grand total of one station—KGHM. Some guy on quaaludes was reading stock reports—did people still care about the price of pork and beef? He supposed out here in ranch country, where the grassy foothills rolled up to break against the Rocky Mountains, they did.

The guy's voice was like listening to a history professor drone on about the factors contributing to the Boer War, a class Ray had suffered through on the way to his degree in justice administration. The OCTF didn't take anyone without a four-year college degree, and five years as a street cop hadn't cut it with the recruiting officer. So, Ray had gone back to school at the ripe old age of twenty-six. Funny how different an education looked on the dark side of twenty. He'd never regretted it.

At eight o'clock the stock reports ended, and an electrifying bass voice said, "Good evening, Washington! This is Luke Fisher coming to you live from KGHM in Hamilton Falls, where from eight to midnight, we'll rock and God will talk!"

Something screamed in Ray's head, and he reached automatically for the off button on the radio. If there was anything he couldn't stand, it was "Jesus rock." He could tolerate a nice hymn sung in four-part harmony at somebody's funeral, the way he tolerated history lectures and any attempts to explain modern art, but Jesus rock? *Run away! Far away!*

"We're lucky tonight to have a new CD from Sixth Hour, who as you know, takes bluegrass where it's never been before—straight to the throne of grace. Here's the first cut, 'Holy Grail.'"

Ray's hand froze on the radio dial. Hang on. The alarm signal in his head wasn't about the music, it was about the DJ's voice.

And now he had to wait three minutes, or six or nine, before he heard it again. Instead, he heard a very talented guy fingerpicking a banjo, an instrument he'd always liked because his grandpa had played it at family hoedowns.

Ray yanked his cell phone out of his jacket pocket and hit the first number on speed dial. His partner, Ross, picked up on the second ring. "Hey, Ray."

Ray didn't waste time on opening remarks. The DJ might come on again, and the band was already into the second verse. "Are you at the office?"

"No, at home, but I'm logged in to the interface. I wanted to get some stuff ready for the wiretap girls tomorrow."

"Can you get on the server and e-mail me one of the .wav files in the Brandon Boanerges folder?"

"Sure, but can't you log in from there?"

"Nah, I'm in this tiny motel where there's only a dialup. I don't want to take the time to drive down to the local PD and use their connection."

"With the dial-up at a motel, it's probably faster to take the drive than wait for it to download. But yeah, whatever you need."

Briefly, Ray tuned him out as the bluegrass song came to an end and something schmaltzy and slow came on. That was good. Another three minutes.

"—it going?"

"Sorry, what?"

"I said, how's it going with the rape case? The papers here aren't picking it up, and Julia's going nuts waiting for news."

"I'm wrapped, but the girls still have to testify. The D.A. tried to cut this Phinehas guy a deal—twenty-five to life—

but he turned it down. He honestly believes these women were making some kind of voluntary sacrifice to keep him preaching. Has no belief he's committed a crime. The guy puts the *i* in *twisted*."

"Is the defense going to put him on the stand?"

"I suppose, if Ortega doesn't get fired first. I wouldn't put it past this Phinehas guy to believe he can defend himself."

"More likely he'll use the opportunity to preach. You might warn the D.A. that this kind of personality likes to grandstand, particularly if the gallery is full of good folk wearing black."

"Which it is. I'll give him a call tonight, after I listen to this file. Is it on its way yet?"

"I just hit Send. Give it a minute. It's less than a megabyte."

"Thanks, Ross."

"Any hints what this is about?"

"I just heard something that rang a bell, that's all."

"Your bells are as good as other people's fire alarms. See you."

Ray hung up and pulled his laptop out of the backpack. In a couple of minutes, he had downloaded the sound file of Brandon Boanerges, whom they'd picked up on the phone during his last con job. Ray had a good ear for sounds, whether it was music, birds, or people's voices. Some people remembered names, some visual details, but he was a sound guy.

"Send my love back, doubled," Claire's husky voice murmured in his memory. Ray shook his head, as if to dislodge it.

Boanerges had made a brief career of conning women

into relationships or even bogus marriages, being added to their bank accounts, draining said accounts, and skipping town. Unfortunately, the ladies were too embarrassed or too shy to press charges. One of them, however, had been senti-mental—or cynical—enough to tape a number of their con-versations, and being the kind of guy he was, Ray had converted one or two of the files to digital format to keep on the OCTF server. You just never knew when you might need something like that.

The third song ended and the DJ came back on the air. "That last track by Jars of Clay was dedicated to Linda Bell, who runs a terrific Christian daycare right here in Hamilton Falls. She has a price far above rubies, and I'm not talking about her rates. Now we'll take a break and hear from our sponsors."

Ray flipped the radio off and opened the sound file.

"I can't wait to come home to you, Barbara," Brandon Boanerges crooned into the phone in exactly the tone Luke Fisher had used in talking about Linda the daycare lady. "You're the woman I've been waiting for all my life."

Exactly the same tone. Ray didn't need voiceprint soft-ware to tell him what his ears had already confirmed.

His informant hadn't been far off. Brandon Boanerges was alive and well, and playing Jesus rock in Hamilton Falls.

AT PRAYER MEETING Wednesday night, Claire was thrilled to note that Luke Fisher was seated right in the first row. She also noted that on the other side of the aisle, the first row was packed with single women and widows.

Mentally rolling her eyes, Claire took her usual seat seven rows back. When Derrick Wilkinson slid in beside her, he elbowed her in the ribs.

"Everyone who's on the market is up there in front," he whispered. "What's wrong with you?"

"Pride," she whispered back. "I hear it's a sin. If you want a wife without any, go sit up there yourself."

He grinned and sat back, opening his Bible to a random chapter. She'd known Derrick her whole life, knew his weaknesses and his strengths. Among the former was his ambition to be Elder. What a shame the Wilkinsons hadn't been among the families who, at the turn of the last century, had first accepted the gospel in the valley and given food and shelter to the itinerant Shepherds. If they had, Derrick might have been an Elder by now. As it was, his social aspirations had pretty much come to a screeching halt.

He could always offer to go out as a Shepherd, and Claire often wondered why he didn't. He had a dead-end job as a paralegal at the only law firm in town, and he wasn't getting any younger. He was a decent guy, but this single-minded pursuit of the favored family girls hadn't done his reputation much good among the singles. Who wanted to go into a marriage knowing she was just a consolation prize?

After the first hymn and a prayer by Owen Blanchard, the congregation drew its collective breath as Luke Fisher got up and made his way to the podium.

"People of God, thank you for allowing me to come back and talk to you again." His smile was like that of a child at Christmas. Or at least Claire thought so—the Elect didn't celebrate Christmas, so she couldn't be totally sure. She'd seen plenty of happy kids at birthday parties, though, and Luke Fisher looked as though he'd been given the very best gift of his life.

"I feel as though I've never left. That sense of oneness is still here, giving me confidence that the Spirit is working among us.

"I give thanks today for those of you who called me at the station to encourage me, and even offered song suggestions. I can tell you right now that your participation in that ministry has borne fruit. In one hour alone, callers pledged almost a thousand dollars to help in God's work."

Joyfully, he gestured as if to encourage applause, and people looked at one another uncertainly. No one applauded in Gathering. It was worldly. The gathering of God's people wasn't like a rock concert, now, was it?

"Now, I know we've been taught that the right hand shouldn't know what the left is doing, and our giving should be in secret so our Father can reward us openly," he went on. "But I'm committed to keeping this ministry open to the scrutiny of everyone. Anyone can give, and anyone can know where the fruit of people's generosity is going. So I'll tell you now that the money is going straight back into the ministry, for music and equipment, to start. Our goal is to buy a van for a mobile station, so we can take our message on the road, to county fairs and other places, so that others can hear the Good News we know in our hearts to be true.

"My friends," he went on earnestly, "we can no longer minister to ourselves. The world is crying out for help. We can no longer be in this world but not of it—we need to mix with the publican and the sinner as Jesus did, and tell them His joyful message."

He paused, and the congregation waited breathlessly. "I've spent a long time in prayer over this," he said, "and so have your elders, Owen Blanchard and Mark McNeill. It's been laid on our hearts that God's people need to lower the barriers of separation between themselves and the world. By this we mean things like our appearance."

"What?" Derrick murmured, and Claire gazed at him with the same question in her eyes. This was impossible. Their clothes and hair were counted unto them for righteousness. If that were taken away, wouldn't they be in danger of a lost eternity?

Who were they going to believe—the Shepherds who had shown them the way and the truth, or Luke Fisher? In the next moment, that question was answered.

"Phinehas, as you all know, has been the senior Shepherd in Washington for nearly forty years. He has always made sure that God's people upheld the external standard. But folks, if what the police believe is true, Phinehas has been deceiving us about his character for just as long a time." The audience shifted uncomfortably, and a quick glance to the side told Claire that Derrick was on the point of speaking out in protest. "So, if Phinehas's character and service has proven to be faulty, who's to say that his insistence on the traditions of men aren't equally faulty? How much of Phinehas's ministry can we trust?"

Derrick could stand it no longer. He leaped to his feet. "Phinehas has not been proven guilty! Until he is, God's people should stand by him. And by the standards he upholds."

Claire frowned. One of the women accusing Phinehas of rape was Dinah, whom gossip reported Derrick had hoped to make his wife. Was he now accusing her of lying? He couldn't have it both ways. But of course, there was no way Claire could stand up and say that, because women were supposed to keep silent in the church.

Luke looked down at Derrick from the microphone. "God's people should try the spirits. That's all I'm saying. Would it please God more for us to reach out in brotherhood to others, or to spend our time worrying about how we look?"

Which is exactly what Claire thought every time she fought with her hair on a Sunday morning. But oddly, she didn't feel comforted that their temporary leadership had voiced her unspoken thoughts. Instead, she just felt uneasy.

Change was a disturbing thing.

Chapter 5

AT THE TAIL END of her lunch hour the next day, Claire saw the newspaper lying on the table in the break room. She turned to the County section, where Phinehas's case was being reported in all its shocking details. A quick scan of the two columns told her Tamara and Dinah had both held up steadily under the defense's questions, and it was practically a foregone conclusion that Phinehas would go to prison. But apparently he was to go on the stand himself today or tomorrow, so who knew what would happen.

Personally, Claire thought Phinehas was as guilty as could be and no more deserved his congregation restored to him than Dinah had deserved his abuse all these years. But she was keeping her thoughts to herself. The Elect were taking sides—and so passionately that just having people over for dinner was becoming a risky proposition.

Her manager stuck her head in the break-room door and Claire closed the paper hastily. "I was just coming."

Margot Emerson glanced at the paper. "Reading about the court case?"

"Yes."

"What do your people think?"

"My . . . people?" The topic of her religion never came up at work. Claire did her job well, got along with her coworkers, and always had a welcoming smile for the new clients. The bank wasn't entitled to know or ask about her faith.

"Yes." Margo walked beside her back to her desk, which faced the street door. "The folks in your church."

Was this some kind of trick question? "It's pretty clear he deceived a lot of people for a long time," she answered cautiously. It was safe to say something like that to Margot—she wasn't likely to turn up at the dinner table of anyone Claire knew.

"Can I talk to you for a minute, Claire?"

Claire glanced at her desk, where a couple of new-account applications sat ready for processing. Her workload hadn't been very heavy lately, and with all the customers in the line, she should really put her old teller hat back on and give the other girls a hand. "There's a lot of traffic today and—"

"Just for a moment. Five minutes."

Well, Margot was her boss. It wasn't like she was going to write her up for slacking off.

Claire followed her into her office and closed the door as the other woman went around the desk and sat. Then she sank into the guest chair in front of it. "What's up?"

Margot folded her hands and took a moment, as if she were arranging words in her head before she said them.

"Claire, you know you're a valued member of our team, don't you?"

She didn't, actually. She hadn't been in her new position all that long, so she hadn't seen an evaluation yet. "Thank you. I'm glad to hear it."

"Your numbers are good, your rapport with the customers is good . . . for the most part."

"My rapport with them is always good," Claire protested. "Why, has someone complained?"

Margot looked at her hands again, still clasped on the desk, then raised her gaze. "How committed are you to the . . . how should I put this . . . external standards of your religion?"

The way she looked on the outside was a natural outgrowth of the sacrifice that she was making on the inside, but that was a little difficult to explain to an Outsider. "What do you mean?" she said at last.

"I mean your dress and the way you have your hair styled."

Claire touched the smooth chignon at the nape of her neck—the one that had taken thirty agonizing minutes to beat into submission this morning. Talk about sacrifice. She didn't know a single Elect woman for whom her hair wasn't as heavy a cross as any Jesus had had to bear.

Which took her back to what she'd heard at Gathering last night. After Luke Fisher had dropped his bomb about the possibility that the standards for appearance might change, people had gone away in little groups, talking a mile a minute. Nothing would happen right away, of course. It would take prayer and fasting and probably several levels of discussion among the elder Shepherds.

In fact, she probably wouldn't see changes like that in her lifetime. Unfortunately.

But Margot was still looking at her. "Would you consider changing your look a little? Wearing something other than black, for instance, and getting a stylish cut?"

She stared at her manager, for once in her life completely speechless. This conversation was illegal. You couldn't reprimand someone for how they looked. Besides, it wasn't as if she were wearing a nose ring and flaunting her midriff in public. She wore business suits and high-necked blouses, for goodness sake. What was going on in Margot's head?

"Why would I do that?" she asked at last. "No one has ever remarked on how I look."

"Maybe not, but since this Phinehas person went to trial over in Pitchford, surely you've noticed the slide in our new accounts."

Claire's eyes widened as she connected the dots. "I would think that had less to do with my clothes and hair than with the branch's ability to market to the new residents."

"It's the black, you see." Margot unclasped her hands and laid them flat on the blotter, as if to suppress what she'd just said. "Folks have been reading about your group's customs in the papers, and you're being associated with this man Phinehas by the way that you dress. He's clearly a criminal. Not only that, there was a child abuse case in the papers awhile ago, and this is bringing that up again. It's bad for the bank."

"But I have nothing to do with Phinehas or the other

case!" she protested. "I just told you, I think he deceived everyone."

"Yes, but prospective investors with our bank don't know that. In the last few weeks I've had four prospective clients tell me they'd rather bank ten miles away in Plum Valley because they don't want to bank where the employees belong to a group that harbors criminals. One corporate account has pulled out and another is threatening to go to Pitchford. I know it's harsh, but I need to ask you to modify your appearance. To keep people from making the connection they're making."

"Margot, I don't think you can ask me to do that. It's not legal. If I were from India, you couldn't ask me not to wear a sari. The principle is the same."

"Yes, but if you were wearing a sari it wouldn't associate you with a rapist and a group that is clearly supporting him in large numbers." Margot's voice had lost its usual smooth calm. "I don't want to do this, Claire, but the success of this branch is on my shoulders. The law clearly states that if an employee is creating an undue hardship on the business, that employee can be terminated."

"Terminated?" Her own voice was a terrified squeak.

"Please. Tell me you'll go shopping and get some new things, and you'll do something different with your hair. I won't insist on makeup or jewelry. Just those two things that will break the connection. What do you say?"

What on earth could she say? Suddenly Claire knew what the Christians must have felt like when the Romans demanded they recant or be fed to the lions. How many sermons had she sat through where the Shepherds had urged the congregation to turn the other cheek, to take rejection for the gospel's sake, even as Jesus did? Well, here was her opportunity, but somehow the feeling of being uplifted in righteousness was missing. She just felt flattened and scared and misunderstood.

"Can I have some time to think about it?" she asked.

"Why would you need time? A simple yes or no is all I need."

She needed counsel. She could talk to Owen or Rebecca. She couldn't just make a decision like this on her own. It was a matter of her example, and that meant her salvation.

Maybe she could talk to Luke Fisher. He would know all about being between a rock and a hard place, and he would certainly know how Owen and the other Elders felt about—

"Claire, I need an answer," Margot said sharply. "My regional manager is breathing down my neck on this one."

"Let me finish out today," she said desperately. "I need to talk it over with—with our leadership. I'll let you know in the morning."

Margot gazed at her through narrowed eyes. "You have to talk your clothes over with your church's leadership? I have to say, I'm a little surprised. I had you pegged for moving into an assistant manager position sometime in the next year, but that calls for initiative and decision-making skills that I'm not seeing here."

First her job was at stake, and now her future? The first flutterings of panic began to beat around Claire's heart. "Please, Margot, it's just twenty-four hours."

"And then what happens? Either you can, in which case you would probably know that right now, or you can't, in

which case I'm going to have to start termination proceedings. Work with me, here, Claire. Give me a yes."

"I can't," she said miserably. You couldn't just throw your
entire example out the window for your job. What was a job
compared to your eternal salvation? And did she really want
to work for someone who would put her salvation at risk
like this? First clothes, then hair, then what? Next thing you
knew, she'd be going to a casino for a team-building event,
or taking an overnight trip with a male colleague.

No, an Elect woman's example was directly related to her
salvation, and that was that. No chipping away at it, no slip-
pery slope of giving in.

"I'm sorry, Margot, but I can't change the way I look for
the bank. It's a principle I can't give up."

A muscle in her manager's jaw flexed. "I don't have to tell
you how sorry I am about this, Claire. And you do realize
that under state law, you have no grounds for a lawsuit over
your termination."

Claire took a long breath. As if she would ever stoop to
such a thing. "I understand."

"We need to act quickly on this to stop the client trickle.
Give me your keys to the cage and your access badge, and
pack up any personal items as discreetly as you can. I'll give
you the two weeks of vacation you have coming, as well as
two weeks' pay in lieu of notice. Okay?"

"That would be fine." She couldn't wait to get out of
here. She could hardly look Margot in the face.

Her manager stood and held out her hand. Claire took it
in an automatic reflex, but there was no enthusiasm in the
handshake. "Good luck, Claire. I really am sorry."

"I am, too," she said, and walked out of the office, acutely aware of Margot's gaze on her back. She avoided the puzzled and annoyed glances of the two tellers when she made no move to give them the help they needed on the early lunch rush. Instead, she kept her gaze resolutely on her desk. Not many personal things there. A family picture, a neon-purple stapler an account rep had given her, a framed "employee of the month" certificate.

She didn't even need a box.

CLAIRE HADN'T DRIVEN much more than a block when her hands began to shake so much she couldn't manage the gear shift. She pulled over and rolled down the windows, then tipped her head back against the headrest and tried to breathe long, calming breaths. On the sidewalk, people strolled past the movie theater or lined up outside the ice-cream shop, and down the street the coffee bar was doing a roaring trade in iced lattes.

Kids were back in school, the town was basking in an Indian summer, and she was unemployed.

She'd never been in such a position. She'd earned her two-year degree in accounting and had gone straight to work, first for a landscaping company and then for the bank. And to be fired—well, she couldn't very well say that when people started asking. She'd have to say she'd left on her own, which was true in a way. She'd stood up for her principles and chosen to leave rather than cave in and stay.

The executives used the phrase *spin doctor*, and she'd always wondered what it meant. Now she knew. She was doing it herself—putting the least embarrassing spin on what had happened. But the rent still had to be paid and you couldn't eat off your principles, so since she couldn't leave town, she was going to have to find another job.

She'd been stupid to take the bank for granted. Instead of being practical and buying bonds or something, she'd spent her money on great clothes and designer shoes, although every item that she purchased was black. Even if no one else in Hamilton Falls could tell an Ann Taylor from a Raggedy Ann, she knew. She supposed it sprang from the fact that her mom slopped around at home in T-shirts and jeans, clothes an Elect woman wasn't supposed to wear. Her mom gave way to earthly desires in private, but Claire upheld the Elect standard in public with style, feeling somehow that she needed to even up the accounts.

What if you can't get work here?

Of course she could. There was always Quill and Quinn, where there was still an open position, but that was a step backward career-wise. The only other options were to join the flood of people interviewing for jobs at the discount store, or get married.

Since most of her dreams since graduating from high school had involved getting out of Hamilton Falls and starting a real life, Phinehas's decree that she had to stay had nearly crushed her spirit. But a person just didn't tell a Shepherd to mind his own business and then call a moving van. No, an Elect woman took "bend and blend" seriously. She bent her will to those in authority over her, and did it with a smile full of grace.

Even if in private she pulled a pillow over her head and cried long into the night.

She comforted herself with the thought that if she left town, she'd be even more alone than she was already, without the security blanket of familiar streets that held friends and acquaintances on every block. If she moved to Spokane or Seattle she'd find Elect, but it would take months to get to know people and in the meantime, there she'd be in an empty apartment with a phone that didn't ring.

At least here people cared enough to call. And since she was going to stay, even if the frustrated longing inside her was practically eating her alive, she'd simply have to find a different job.

Soon. Right after she'd had an iced latte.

She climbed out of the car and walked back down the block to the coffee bar, where she got the latte and shook chocolate sprinkles on the top—strictly for medicinal purposes. Out on the sidewalk, she took a long sip of the creamy liquid and let it fill up her senses as the sun warmed her face.

> *Roll up the scrolls of time*
> *Eternity is mine.*
> *I'm gonna do just fine*
> *Safe with the Lord.*

Five Wise sang their hearts out in a cross between swing and pop—two genres of music Claire was becoming more familiar with the more she listened to KGHM.

> *Say what you want to me,*
> *I know where I'm gonna be.*

You don't control me.
I'm with the Lord.

If only she could say that herself. With a sigh and another sip of coffee, Claire leaned against the warm bricks of the building and realized the music was being piped over speakers onto the street.

Of course. The radio station was next door to the coffee bar.

"That was Five Wise, a quintet of talented ladies singing 'Safe with the Lord.'" Luke Fisher's beautiful baritone washed over Claire's ruffled emotions the way the coffee had over her tongue, soothing and sweet. "They'll be coming to the county fair," he went on, "so if you're in the neighborhood, be sure to check them out. Who knows—we at KGHM might even be there ourselves. Our listeners have been so generous that we could have our mobile station by then and could catch the girls for a live performance and an interview. What do you think about that?"

From somewhere among the tables on the sidewalk outside the coffee bar, someone said, "Yeah!"

Sipping her latte, Claire considered the storefronts along Main Street. Clothing stores. A hobby shop. The bookshop, the ice-cream shop, and the coffee bar. The lawyer's office. Hmm. Lawyers billed by the hour, didn't they? Maybe she could ask Derrick if they needed someone. There was the hospital's accounting department, too. Only as a last resort would she consider retail or being a checker at the supermarket—no employer of the kind she wanted would look at her if that appeared on her résumé.

With a sigh, she turned away and caught sight of the bulletin board near the door of the coffee bar. She knew what was on it—business cards, ads for tree trimmers and massage therapists. Part-time jobs, such as delivering flyers. No real employer would post—

WANTED: Full-time bookkeeper. Must know spreadsheet software, be detail-oriented, meticulous. Two to three years' experience and two-year degree. Sense of humor mandatory. Send qualifications and résumé to 98.5 KGHM, 254 Main Street, Hamilton Falls, WA. Attention: John Willetts.

Claire stood as if rooted to the sidewalk, her latte cooling her hand. The card was a little yellowed, as if it had been pinned there in the sun for at least a week.

Yellowed or not, it was a sign.

She leaned over and dropped her cup into the nearest trash can, adjusted her purse on her shoulder, straightened her skirt and her spine, and marched into the station.

THE ROOM WHERE Luke Fisher played the music faced Main Street and had a large picture window so passersby could see him behind his console. Inside, there was another large window between the entry hall where Claire stood and what looked like a library, where the walls were covered in bookshelves holding records and CDs. Most of the records looked as though they hadn't been moved since they'd been shelved sometime in the sixties.

She looked through the window a little uncertainly. This wasn't her world at all. She had gone from listening to the radio to walking into the station, all in a couple of weeks or less. A year ago, even a few months ago, she'd never have believed she would do such a thing.

Luke waved at her, and it was too late to back out.

"Use the door." His mouth moved, but she couldn't hear his voice—maybe his studio was soundproof. She pushed open the door next to the window and walked into the library. At the same time, he came out of the studio, shutting that door carefully behind him.

"Hi." He offered his hand, and she shook it. "I'm Luke Fisher, and you're clearly one of my sisters in God. I remember you from Gathering. What can I do for you?"

You can stop thinking of me as a sister. "My name is Claire Montoya. I—I was reading the bulletin board next door and saw the ad about the station needing a bookkeeper." She wished her voice wouldn't wobble when she needed to appear professional and competent. But it was hard to be professional when Luke Fisher was standing directly in front of her, still holding her hand, wearing his Dockers as well as any L.L. Bean model and smelling of some yummy cologne.

He smiled and let go of her hand. "Come on back to the booth, Claire." At the door to the studio, he looked over his shoulder at her. "There's only one rule in here. You talk when the music's on, and you don't when I'm talking. Otherwise everyone in a five-county radius will be able to hear you. Okay?"

"Okay." Wow. She hadn't realized this little station could broadcast that far.

Luke sat in front of the console, slid some CDs into slots with his left hand, and with his right chose a switch from about a dozen on a board and slid it down its track to the bottom. "There." He made some notes on a sheet of paper. "We've got ten minutes until I back-call these."

Ten minutes to land herself a job. Well, she'd lost one in about the same amount of time, hadn't she?

"Let me tell you how it works around here," Luke said. "My show is eight to twelve, mornings and evenings. We sign off at midnight. Toby Henzig comes in at six A.M., turns the system on, and reads the early reports. Then he comes back at noon and hosts the open mic, reads the stock reports, plays what he wants until eight. You'd work during business hours, of course." Luke leaned back in his chair as though he had nothing better to do than to gab the afternoon away. "Do you have a résumé?"

"No, I was passing by and decided on the spur of the moment to come in. But I can bring you one later today."

"No problem. Give me the condensed version."

Claire took a deep breath and told him about her education, her career—or what passed for a career for an Elect woman in a small town. It was better than a résumé that held nothing but, say, assisting at Linda Bell's daycare, which is what the womanly ideal seemed to be. "I was employee of the month recently," she concluded, "and I passed the Management Potential course in Seattle with flying colors."

He was silent for a moment. She noticed that he hadn't made a single note on his sheet of paper, though he'd been rolling his pen between his fingers the whole time she'd been talking. Maybe he was just killing time in between songs. Maybe she was fooling herself that she was any kind of prize on the job market. Maybe—

"Why'd you leave the bank?" he asked at last.

She'd known she'd have to field this one; she just wished she'd had a little more time to prepare. As in, more than an hour after the event. But Luke was Elect—or had been—or was going to be. She was a little confused on that point. But it seemed that he would understand. She'd always been honest with herself so there was no point in whitewashing anything now.

"My manager said our new-client metrics were down because people were associating me with . . . with a court case going on in Pitchford right now."

"With Phinehas."

Of course, he would know all about it. Probably better than she did. "Yes."

"You know that's illegal, right?"

"Apparently not. There's a provision about people who cause an undue hardship to the bank. It doesn't matter anyway. Everyone signs an 'at-will' agreement when they're hired. You can be fired at any time for no reason at all."

"And you can be hired at any time for the best reasons in the world. When can you start?"

She blinked at him. "Sorry?"

"I'm willing to wait if you wanted to take a few days off." He clicked his pen into action. "Give me a start date, and I'll have your office cleaned up by then. At the moment, all the offices are full of crates and farm magazines and thirty years' worth of dead spiders."

Claire finally got her mouth closed and her brain in gear. So what if he didn't need to see her résumé or check her references? He was obviously a man of action—look at what he'd already accomplished. She'd be crazy if she did anything but jump at this opportunity—and who knew how far it would go?

"I can start right now, if you'd like," she heard herself say.

"Perfect. I'll ask John Willetts, the owner, to put you on the payroll while you go home and get out of your Bank Lady suit. Come back in something you can take on the dead spiders in." The song that had been playing finished, and with his left hand he took the CD out while his right slid the switch back up its track.

"That was U2 and 'Still Haven't Found What I'm Looking For,'" he said into the microphone. "Fortunately, I can't say the same. Folks, God is good. KGHM now has an accounting expert to keep us on the straight and narrow. If you were planning on moseying down here to apply for the job, you're too late. But don't despair. I hear they're still hiring at the discount store."

RAY HARPER PARKED his truck on Main Street across from the radio station and shut off the engine. The other night he'd discovered the station had no Web site, and therefore no way to figure out its programming and when Boanerges aka Fisher might be on the premises. He could call and ask, of course, but he'd rather not do that in case Fisher was as good with voices as he was himself.

The one call he'd had to make yesterday was to Sergeant Harmon, after he'd listened to all four hours of Fisher's show the night before and fallen asleep with Fisher's voice echoing in his ears. Unfortunately the good sergeant hadn't been all that keen on him hanging around in Hamilton Falls.

"I've got a guy here killed by a falling object, Harper. I think that investigation is more important than your hanging out in Hick Central, listening to the radio."

"What kind of falling object?" Knowing Harmon, it probably wasn't a random tree branch.

"A refrigerator. The Skulls are feeling cranky about their guy finking on them on that cocaine case, and we have to shut 'em down."

"Biker gangs aren't my assignment. Teddy Howitz has that detail."

"You telling me my job, Harper? Teddy Howitz needs a boatload of help, and you have some empty spaces on your dance card."

"Sir, you know how long I've had that file open on Boanerges."

"I don't know why. None of those women would press any charges."

"So, he's getting away scot-free to do whatever he wants. I don't know what the deal is with this radio gig, but something tells me he isn't saving his money to go back to college."

"One week," Harmon said. "I'll give you one week of motel bills and meals, and if you don't scare up anything on this guy, leave him alone. We've got bigger fish to incarcerate here."

Ray had to admit the truth of that. He slouched in the driver's seat of the truck and contemplated the picture window behind which the DJ sat. If this really was Brandon Boanerges, Ray could see why the ladies had gone for him the way geese go for bread. Even though he sat there all by himself, you could tell he was putting on a one-man show. Animated movement, pantomimed conversations with passersby, and once in a while, a little air guitar when he got carried away by a song.

Ray turned the key one degree in the truck's ignition and turned the radio on.

"—find this and all kinds of other literary gems at Quill and Quinn, our local headquarters for quality fiction. And speaking of quality, here's Casting Crowns with 'Voice of Truth.'"

Truth? Yeah, right.

Did Christian musicians ever play the blues? Probably not. Christians probably didn't *get* the blues. He'd been listening to Fisher's shows for almost twenty-four hours now, and apart from U2 and that bluegrass band whose name he couldn't remember, he hadn't heard one song about poverty or unrequited love or relationships gone bad. It was all happy stuff, praising God for who knew what. Unrealistic and probably delusional. How was a guy supposed to relate to that?

And just what was the deal with the Christian radio gig? How did a man jump from ripping off lonely women to spinning CDs? Unless he really had found the Lord and turned his life around.

Ray slouched even lower. He was never going to be able to bring Fisher in if he'd seen the light and gone straight. What if he'd settled here in Hamilton Falls to get a new start? The guy could find a nice girl, buy a house with a picket fence, and start having babies. Ray would never get the chance to face him in the courtroom and balance the scales for those silent, lonely women and who knew how many other people he'd ripped off during his exciting career in fraud.

Ray watched as a middle-aged man walked into the station with a sheaf of papers in his hand. A few minutes later, at noon, the stock reports began.

A man could only stand so much. He flipped the radio off.

Now what? Follow Fisher home? Yeah, an address would be good. An address and a license-plate number would be a nice start to a case file. Then he could toddle over to the sheriff's office and run a warrants search against Fisher's name and if he was lucky—

The door of the radio station opened and Ray sat up. Sure enough, there was Luke Fisher, jacket slung over one shoulder, looking as cool as a model in *Esquire* magazine. But who was that with him?

Black shirt, black skirt, sensible black pumps. Dark hair twisted in a classic Greek chignon.

Oh, no. Ray's mouth hung open in dismay as Luke Fisher put a gentlemanly hand on Claire Montoya's back and guided her down the street to the Chinese café.

If Fisher and Boanerges were one and the same, she didn't fit his profile of women to scam. She appeared to be neither middle-aged, wealthy, or lonely—at least that he knew of. So, what was a nice girl like her doing having lunch with a slimeball like Luke Fisher?

One way or another, Ray was going to find out.

Chapter 4

LUKE SLID INTO the booth opposite Claire and gave her the kind of grin that dreams were made of.

"What's good in this place?" He glanced at the menu. "Szechuan beef?"

"This is Hamilton Falls, not Seattle," she reminded him. All the young people knew the menu by heart—she didn't even need to open hers. "Here we get broccoli beef and sweet-and-sour pork, and chili peppers are those dried flakes you sprinkle on your pizza."

"Good thing I like broccoli beef." Luke leaned on his elbows as if he were prepared to spend the afternoon getting to know her. "Nice job on the cleanup. Only a couple of days, and you've made the place look like a business instead of a barn."

She shrugged modestly. "It looked worse than it was. Once the crates were out of there, the rest of it was just housekeeping."

"Which wasn't what you were hired to do. On Monday, you'll start scrubbing our numbers instead."

"What are you doing with everything in the meantime?" There was a computer in one of the offices, but to Claire's knowledge, no one ever used it. She wasn't even sure it worked. "Do you have a bookkeeping program to track the receipts and expenses?"

"Yeah." He chuckled. "It's called Sticky Notes."

Claire toyed with the chopsticks, sliding them in and out of their paper sleeve. "I haven't heard of that one."

"Yes, you have. You tear 'em off a pad and stick them on the cash box. Yellow sticky notes are for receipts, and blue ones are for expenses."

Clearly, this was not a numbers guy. Equally clearly, Claire had her work cut out for her. As soon as lunch was over, she was going to get a handle on the expenses before a financial disaster occurred.

"I'll need to get on the signing card for the station at the bank," she said, "so I can make the deposits and write checks."

"No problem. Give Willetts a call after lunch, and he'll go over there with you. But in the meantime, I'm off shift, and I'd rather talk about my new colleague than about boring things like expenses."

"They won't be boring when the power company shuts down the station because someone forgot to pay the bill."

"Toby Henzig looks after all that basic stuff. I don't have the time for it."

The waitress came and took Luke's order, then glanced at Claire. "The usual?"

"Yes, please." The woman scribbled a line on her pad and then left for the kitchen.

"You always eat the same thing?" Luke asked. "No sense of adventure?"

"Eating here is hardly adventurous. The pot stickers are good, and so is the hot-and-sour soup, so that's what I have. Getting back to Toby, he seems to be a nice guy."

Luke poured himself a cup of pale green tea and filled hers, then lifted a shoulder in a shrug. "He gets the job done. I'd go nuts if I were stuck with the news and the stock reports myself."

"He doesn't have quite the delivery you do, that's for sure." Toby's voice was soft and tended to put you out after five minutes. It was rumored that someone had even used that as a defense to the insurance company after they'd run off the road.

"He's been around here since the mayor was in diapers. A fixture that can't be replaced, according to Willetts." Luke's normally upbeat tone held disapproval, then lightened. "He's also an assistant pastor at one of the churches."

"I heard what you said Wednesday night about us looking outside our familiar boundaries. Maybe Mr. Willetts isn't ready for that. I don't know if the Elect are, either."

The soup arrived, and Luke dug into his as if it were about to disappear. Claire liked to see a man who appreciated his food. She wondered what his favorites were. Roast beef and potatoes, or shrimp and tofu? She entertained a brief fantasy of herself dazzling Luke with her competence in the kitchen. Like most Elect girls, she'd learned to cook at an early age. Skills like that didn't seem to matter to worldly men, but to an Elect man, a woman who could cook had the edge over one who had to be taken out to eat all the time.

And what makes you think he has any interest in you at all, much less how well you cook? Careful, Claire. You don't want to look desperate.

"With the leadership in the shape it's in, change is inevitable. And in my opinion," he said, "it might as well be positive if it's going to happen. Now, I know that these things get decided at the Shepherds' gatherings, but at the moment Shepherds are a bit scarce. If we want to avoid losing our folks, we need to make some changes and welcome others in." He dropped his spoon into his empty bowl with a clink. "I have some experience there, fortunately."

"Really?" The oval dishes of food arrived, and Claire spooned rice onto her plate, then handed the bowl to Luke.

"Yes. When I was the assistant pastor at Lakefield Central in Downey, it was almost defunct. Maybe twenty-five members, and those were considering disbanding. By the time I left, we had just passed the one-thousand-member mark, and they were in the middle of building a bigger chapel."

"Wow. Well, you won't have to worry about that here. We all fit in the Gathering hall with room to spare."

"Ah, but if the Elect make themselves attractive to seeking souls, you might need to expand. And as I said Wednesday, the first thing to work on is appearance."

"So that people don't get fired from banks anymore," she clarified in a wry tone.

"Exactly. By the time we're done, Claire, your ex-manager will be begging for time on your appointment calendar."

Claire laughed and promptly choked on a piece of broccoli. She gulped water, and when she could speak, she said, "I'd buy a ticket to see that."

But Luke wasn't laughing. He handed her a napkin and said, "I'm not kidding. Soon our deposits will be so big that the bank will roll out the red carpet for you. That woman who fired you will be scrambling to bring you a cup of coffee and take your coat every time you walk in the door. Just watch."

"You sure have a lot of confidence." It all sounded like something out of a novel. Things like that didn't happen in real life—and as for deposits, if she didn't make one to her own bank account soon, Rebecca wasn't going to get her rent check.

"It's not confidence," Luke told her. "It's faith. God has always provided for me beyond my wildest imaginings, as long as I let Him do the leading. I mean, look at you. Half an hour after you walk out of the bank, you see our need for an accountant, and there you are on the doorstep. If that isn't God's work, I don't know what is."

Claire wasn't used to thinking of God in those terms. The Elect didn't believe that prayer should be used for everyday things. Prayer was for special occasions, like the good china. Tidal waves taking out entire cities. Earthquakes. Wars. You could pray for people in those circumstances, but you'd certainly never pray that God would send you an accountant, or success in your business ventures. That was . . . selfish. And everyone knew that selfish prayers came to a bad end—unless you were praying for the cure of some kind of spiritual defect in yourself. Claire prayed for willingness on a daily basis—willingness to sacrifice her vanity and put on yet another black blouse. Willingness to stay in Hamilton Falls and believe that she was needed there. Willingness to smile at Alma Woods and ask about her health without noticing that critical up-and-down gaze that always made her feel as if she had a run in her black stockings.

"Yes, but how do you tell the difference between coincidence and the answer to a prayer?" She forked up the last of the sweet-and-sour sauce onto her rice.

"Timing." Luke reached for the teapot and filled the little handle-less cup in front of her. "God operates on a different schedule than we want Him to, sometimes, but He definitely operates. For instance, getting back to change in the Elect, look at how He sent me just when Phinehas was arrested and Shepherds all over the state are paralyzed because they don't know what to do. Is that perfect timing or what?"

"How did you find us, Luke?"

He smiled at her again, and something inside her melted. That was the smile she had wanted turned on her from the first time she'd seen him, and now there it was. Did that count as an answered prayer?

"The Elect aren't that hard to find in Washington . . . especially when a person has grown up inside and knows to look for the marks of Christ. I moved here a few months ago trying to find the peace I'd lost running a huge ministry in a big city. The radio station needed a shot in the arm, and I had a business plan they couldn't resist. Then God led me to Owen in the bookstore. We got to talking and before I knew it, he invited me for supper. He sure has a great little family."

"Everyone loves the Blanchards. I just wish Madeleine would get better."

"That's in the hands of God. Anyway, four or five hours later I felt as though I'd known the man my whole life, and the rest is history."

"If you can induce change in the Elect, *that* will make history. I know you cautioned us about Phinehas's leadership, but people still count their appearance as part of their salvation."

"We'll see how God is able to work in their hearts. Owen agrees with me, and he's the closest thing we have to a leader right now. Whatever happens, God's will is going to be done, isn't it?"

The bill came, and before she could make a grab for it, he'd handed over his credit card to the waitress without even glancing at the total. "This is your official 'welcome to the staff' lunch," he said by way of explanation. Which was fine. It wasn't as though it was a date or anything.

Once they were back outside, he put both hands on his hips and surveyed Main Street the way Alexander the Great must have surveyed the Indus Valley. "This is a great town. God's going to do great things here."

"I'm sure He— Hey, isn't that—"

Claire craned her neck. She'd seen that sleek, granite-gray truck before. In her own driveway a couple of nights ago, as a matter of fact. It was parked across the street, and a shape was slouched behind the wheel. She leaned over a bit more and waved a little hesitantly. Maybe he was waiting for someone. Or taking a nap. Maybe he thought she was the world's worst conversationalist and was even now thinking, *Oh no, she wants me to talk to her again.*

"Um, never mind." She turned back to Luke. "So, I'm going to go back and tackle that computer and make some sense of your yellow and blue receipts."

"Want me to play you a song when I come in tonight?"

"Sure." She grinned. "How about Willie Nelson? 'Just As I Am.'"

"You got it. And hey, I'm going to launch a couple of new gigs. People can phone in, and for a gift toward God's work, I'll broadcast a prayer for them. I'm going to start a book club, too, maybe next week. What do you think about 'Hamilton Falls for Books'? Catchy, huh?"

A reading club sounded relatively normal, but Claire's views on prayer were getting all stretched out, like a picture from the Sunday comics impressed on Silly Putty. Payment for prayer? Sure, it would be used for God's work, but prayer was supposed to be private. Certainly not something to be lowered to the level of a transaction. "I—um—"

"Promise you'll call in a prayer. It's bound to be a little slow at first, so I could use some help. Owen and the kids said they'd call in."

Owen was treating this as though it were normal. Maybe outside the Elect it was and she just needed to get with the program. "What would I ask for?"

He shrugged. "Anything you'd pray for in private. People. Things. Attitudes. Anything."

What, and spill her most closely held secrets and needs on the radio? Not likely. "I'll think of something. Maybe I could—" A cat's paw of a breeze tickled the back of her neck, and goose bumps spread across her shoulders.

"Hello, Miss Montoya."

At the sound of that controlled baritone, Claire turned around and looked straight into the narrowed hazel eyes of Investigator Raymond Harper.

Who seemed to be deeply unhappy about something.

RAY KEPT HIS TONE polite and noncommittal, in contrast to the slow boil of emotions rolling around his solar plexus. He could hardly believe his own eyes, but here she was, standing on the sidewalk chatting with Luke Fisher after a cozy lunch *à deux*. Whatever happened to the rule Julia had told him about the Elect keeping themselves separate? "In the world, but not of it," was how she put it. What a crock.

It was just plain bad luck that had made Claire spot him. If not for that, he could have followed Fisher to his car and taken the plate number, easy as pie. But he couldn't take the risk that Claire wouldn't mention him sitting there. It was better to act normally and hope she didn't give him away.

"Luke, this is Investigator Ray Harper of the Organized Crime Task Force."

Or not.

"He's the one who arrested Phinehas. Ray, this is Luke Fisher, my new boss."

Ray's mind churned, trying to come up with Plan B: What to Do When Your Cover Gets Blown. He held out a hand, watching Fisher closely. "Nice to meet you." If he expected Fisher to give a guilty start and a few furtive glances out of his beady eyes, he was disappointed. The guy was all sunshine and smiles as he shook hands. Not a care in the world.

Ray turned back to Claire. "I thought you worked at the bank."

"I did. But I got fired, and Luke hired me to do the books at KGHM."

"You work at the station?" *With Fisher? Together, day in and day out?*

"I sure do. At the moment, I'm just getting the place cleaned up and organized, but starting Monday I should be able to get a handle on the accounting software and start contributing."

"You already have," Fisher said with a smile that probably charmed little old ladies and dogs, not sensible women like Claire Montoya.

She lowered her eyes and blushed.

Ray felt like turning away in disgust, but he couldn't. He had a job to do, and do it he would. As soon as he could figure out how, now that he couldn't blend into the scenery anymore.

"So, how is the trial going?" Fisher asked.

None of your business. "It's reported in the papers. They're probably more up to date than I am. I gave my testimony the first day, so I'm done."

"Are you local?" Fisher asked. "Or did they bring you in from your usual beat?" *Are you going to be around to give me competition and/or trouble?* Ray heard as clearly as if the guy had said it out loud.

"I'm with a state agency, so technically we don't have

'beats,'" he said, neatly sidestepping what Fisher wanted to know.

"What did you call it?" The other man turned to Claire. "Organized crime?"

"The Organized Crime Task Force," Claire said. "My best friend is married to Ray's partner."

"Oh." Fisher gave Ray an appraising look. "Combining a little business with pleasure, then?"

He made it sound as though Ray had spirited Claire off to a dark corner somewhere and ravished her. Making him the bad guy. Well, two could play at that game.

"Now that the business part is finished, I was hoping for some downtime here in Hamilton Falls," he said, and added a smile for Claire's benefit. "I have some leave coming, so I figured I'd spend it right here." He glanced at her. "Maybe you could show me some of the sights."

"I'd be—"

"Claire, do you want me to walk you back to the station and help you move the computer into your office?" Fisher asked, taking her elbow in a way that was just too chummy for words.

She shook her head and took two steps in the direction of the station's door. "No, I've already moved it. And I've worked with a couple of systems at the bank, so it shouldn't take long to figure out. Thanks for lunch, Luke. And have a nice vacation, Ray. I'm sure I'll see you around."

Ray smiled and gave her a nod. He was going to make good and sure of that. Especially now that the territorial lines had been drawn between himself and Fisher. One of

Ray's particular talents, as his sergeant was all too fond of pointing out, was crossing lines.

CLAIRE LET HERSELF into the station and walked into the back, where her office was.

Her office.

She may have had ten years of work experience under her belt, but she'd never had her own office before. Even at the bank, the most she'd had to call her own was the new-accounts desk. Now she had four walls on which to put up pictures, a desk to organize the way she wanted it, and . . . a comatose computer.

First things first.

She booted up the computer and scanned the desktop and the program folder. No accounting software. Just Microsoft Excel. She opened up a document called "2006P&L.xls" and found what appeared to be a list of expenses and accounts receivable, but it was spotty and far from complete. Not only that, there was no way to organize it for receipts or invoicing or anything else.

Surely they must have something to use around here.

In the library, stuck in among the CDs and record albums, she found a box of bookkeeping software. It was several revisions old, and when she peered inside, she saw that the CD was missing.

Okay. Think.

She'd have to make a run up to Spokane to the computer store—which was rather like sneaking off to the next town to the liquor store. But for the sake of her job, she had to do it—and she had no doubt that Luke would back her up if someone spotted her and started spreading rumors that she was allowing a computer to act as a window of wickedness in the house of the Lord. Besides, she knew for a fact that Elsie Traynell was running her baby-clothing business over the Internet, and if she could do that, then Claire could buy software.

But until she got the tools she needed, she could still make some sense of the sticky-note system.

While Toby Henzig's gentle voice murmured in the background, Claire found a box in the music library that was stuffed so full of envelopes, invoices, paperwork, and sticky notes that it would hardly close.

"Good grief," she said aloud. "I hope there aren't any bills in here."

She carried it back to her office and began sorting through the layers of paper. Three hours later, a couple of things were very clear.

One, whoever picked up the mail obviously just dumped it in the box, and whoever had a free moment seemed to rescue the odd bill and pay it. Probably Toby.

Two, the station's new programming was probably going to do everything Luke said it would. Claire sat back in her chair and gazed at the biggest of her piles. Envelope after envelope contained money—checks, wrinkled bills, money orders—and letters. They asked for prayer, they asked for songs, they even asked for a moment of Luke's time on the phone to talk over some spiritual problem. There was more money sitting on her desk than she had ever seen in one place outside of the bank.

The contents of this cardboard box alone would take care of the invoices needing to be paid in the second largest pile. Operating costs, it appeared, were not going to be a problem.

"This is amazing," she said aloud over the sound of someone calling in to the open mic. "I think he's going to do it."

"Do what?"

She turned to see Toby Henzig leaning against her door frame, his hands in his pockets. The open-mic program must be able to take care of itself. Whoever was speaking didn't sound as though he was planning to stop for breath anytime soon.

"Luke," she told him. "He told me he was going to turn this station around. From the looks of the donations we're getting, I think he's going to do it."

"How much do you reckon is there?"

She waved her hands at the pile a little helplessly. "Ballpark? I'd say a couple of thousand."

His eyes widened. "You're kidding."

"I'm not. I need some accounting software for that computer in the worst way."

"That's more than we ever took in in a whole quarter," Toby said. "He's only been here a couple of weeks. How is this possible?"

"With God all things are possible." She felt a little odd, using the Lord's name outside of Gathering, but after all, Toby was a "worldly preacher," wasn't he? He would understand a reference like that.

"With Luke all things are possible, it seems." Frown lines

appeared briefly between his brows, then smoothed out. "What kind of software did you say you needed?"

"QuickBooks. FileMaker. Anything. I've got no way to generate receipts for all this money, and no way to record the payables except on a spreadsheet I found in the computer. I assume that's yours."

Toby nodded. "I can do basic arithmetic, but that's it. This place hasn't needed much more than that until now. Oh, and don't worry about the license and the FCC filings. I take care of those."

"That's good." She smiled. "I don't even know what FCC stands for."

"Federal Communications Commission. They approve our programming and license the bandwidth to us. But I've been dealing with the paperwork to them for fifteen years now, so I'll just keep on doing that. We hired you to deal with this." He indicated her piles. "I'll go over to Pitchford tonight and get you some software, all right? The stores will be open late, and I know how your group feels about computers."

Her mouth formed a wry expression. "I'm not sure anyone's feeling the same about that anymore. Phinehas was the greatest proponent against them, and now that he's—" She stopped. What was she saying? How could she speak out against the Elect's leader—well, former leader—to a worldly man, and a preacher to boot? As Derrick said, Phinehas was innocent until proven guilty. Just because she'd convicted him in her own mind didn't mean she needed to do it in front of strangers.

Stricken, she gazed down at her hands, which were scored with paper cuts.

"Now that he's been called into question, perhaps everything he stood for should be examined, too?" Toby's voice was quiet as he finished her ill-advised sentence. Claire looked up.

"Have you been talking to Luke?" she asked. "He said the same thing."

"It's reasonable to question some of his ideas. After all, you've got to admit the strictures against computers and different colored clothing aren't in the Bible."

It was one thing to hear this in Gathering from Owen and Luke, but quite another to hear it from outsiders. Even if what he said were true, Melchizedek had preached many a sermon on what the Devil did when he got the chance— and she'd handed an opportunity to bad-mouth her religion to him on a plate.

"Maybe not," she said with dignity. "But it does tell us to present our bodies as a living sacrifice and to think on things that are pure and lovely." Ha. She probably knew the Scriptures better than he did.

He bit his lip. "Now I've gone and offended you. I didn't mean to."

His humility undercut her flash of pride. How could she be offended by someone who agreed with Luke and Owen? It didn't take away from the fact that the community in which she'd grown up had sheltered her and protected her from the temptations of the world. That was a good thing, a worthy thing.

"That's all right," she mumbled, and Toby went back to

the studio to open the phone line for someone else to rant about taxes or highway maintenance or the dismal price of beef.

But it *wasn't* all right. Between the teachings of the past and the changes in the present, she needed to find her balance. And that was turning out to be harder than she'd expected.

Chapter 5

RAY JUST HAPPENED to be oh-so-coincidentally seated at one of the coffee bar's sidewalk tables drinking a latte when Claire came out of the station at five o'clock. Fortunately—since he'd been nursing it for nearly an hour while he'd been watching the station's door—the place made an excellent latte.

She did a double take when she saw him, hesitated as if deciding whether it would be politically correct to talk to him, and then walked over.

"Hey, Claire." Swinging his boots off the wrought-iron chair opposite him, he waved her into it.

"You look as if you're enjoying your holiday," she observed.

He straightened out of his comfortable surveillance slouch. "I am. This place makes good coffee and lets you hang out and people watch for as long as you want."

"Do you like people watching?"

He did it for a living. Long nights of surveillance, wiretaps, undercover ops—all were concentrated forms of people watching.

"Sure. This town is full of interesting types. Plus I noticed there's been a lot of traffic into the bookstore."

"Luke's going to start a reading club."

"A what? When?"

"Next week. 'Hamilton Falls for Literature' or something like that."

"I hope Quill and Quinn has a lot of copies of the books he's chosen, then. People have been going in and out of there as if she's having a sale."

"Luke probably gave Rebecca a heads-up. She doesn't usually stock that kind of thing, so she had to do a special order."

"What kind of thing?"

"Christian fiction."

He stared at her. Something wasn't computing here. "She's a Christian, isn't she? Why wouldn't she stock Christian fiction?"

Claire bit her lip, and Ray found himself unable to look away. "She—we—um, at one time we believed that other churches were deceived. We're only supposed to read the Bible, not other books."

" 'At one time?' "

Something had become very interesting on the latch of her purse. "I'm not exactly sure about some things now. A lot of what I thought was the truth is changing."

Ross had told him once that the Elect believed their ways were mandated by the Bible and could not be changed. They must really be hurting if one of their own could admit that change might actually happen.

"And that bothers you."

"Yes."

She looked up, as though she were grateful for the fact that he didn't make a big deal about it. Why would he? If they wanted to change their rules, it was nothing to him.

"It would be like the traffic laws changing every time a new politician was elected. You'd hardly know what the right thing was until you were arrested, and by then it would be too late."

Discussions about the ins and outs of religion made Ray's skin twitch. "So, are you going to join the book club and read this book by an obviously deceived person?"

"I guess I am. It's part of my job now, to participate. You can't very well have a book club hosted by your boss and not read the book."

"I suppose not. Gotta be a team player and all that."

"Do you read Christian fiction?" she asked.

A swallow of his latte went down the wrong pipe, and he coughed. "Not hardly," he got out when he could speak. "I believe what I believe and try not to think about religion at all."

"Belief and religion are different."

"Are they?" He put his cup down. The roof of his mouth felt dry from too much caffeine.

"What *do* you believe?" Her gaze was direct, honest, as though she really wanted to know, but the whole subject was making him jumpy.

"Look, Ross and Julia don't talk about that stuff with me.

No offense, but I'd appreciate it if you took a leaf from their book, okay?"

That was all he needed—to get into a long discussion about faith, belief, whatever you wanted to call it, with a pretty woman and find himself being led off to a Gathering by his nose. Not gonna happen.

"All right." She stood up and pushed the chair in. "Well, I'm heading home. It's been a busy day. See you later."

Wait a minute. He hadn't meant to brush her off. On the contrary, he still needed to have a bogus conversation with her about seeing the sights of Hamilton Falls. "Claire—"

But he was too slow on the draw. She was already halfway down the block and couldn't hear him. Once again, Prince Charming had come through in the pinch and alienated the one person he could use to get the drop on Luke Fisher. Ray felt like smacking himself on the forehead. Instead, he lobbed his empty cup into the trash can and stalked down the street to his truck.

He was a total idiot. A smart investigator would buddy up to a source like this—one who was tied both to the station and to the group that Luke Fisher was burrowing into with such success. A smart investigator would develop that relationship while avoiding that fine line where professional investment became emotional involvement. It was true that things had turned out well for Ross when he'd fallen for Julia, but Ray had no intention of getting hooked up with any woman who dropped belief and religion into a conversation and seriously expected an answer. He'd had enough of fanatics to last a lifetime, thank you very much. Even now, his mom only invited him for a visit in order to bend his ear about his salvation—or lack of it. She'd started four churches single-handedly, as though it were her mission in life to devise ways for people to give up their ability to make sound decisions based on rational criteria and instead start basing them on a nebulous afterworld that no one could prove existed.

A breeze off the lake tickled the back of his neck and he shivered. He leaned on the driver's door, watching the inhabitants of Hamilton Falls go about their business. The truth was, he was stuck. He had no contact with anyone else in this group, and getting all chummy with Luke Fisher was going to be difficult after the other man had drawn a clear line on the sidewalk in front of Claire Montoya. He had to pull it together and get back into the lady's good graces.

A glance at his watch told him it was five-thirty. There was a pizza place next to the theater on the next block. It was obvious that the famous Harper charm had conked out where Claire was concerned. Maybe crisp dough and Italian sausage would do a better job.

WHEN THE DOORBELL RANG, Claire dried her hands on the bathroom towel and went to answer it. Usually Rebecca called up when she needed something, but once in a while, she trekked up the steep stairs, measuring cup in hand, to borrow sugar or cornstarch.

She swung the door open. "What are you making this t—oh."

Ray Harper stood there with a Mama Rosa pizza box balanced on the palm of his hand. He filled up the whole doorway—or so it seemed. She couldn't think of a single thing to say. Her whole brain was occupied with trying to imagine what he could be doing there.

"If the way to a man's heart is through his stomach, I figured the way to a woman's would be to keep her out of the kitchen," he quipped.

Her brain snapped back into gear and began to function. "What do you want?" Okay, that sounded pretty ungracious. "I mean, what's going on?" Still not brilliant, but better. And why did he want to know the way to her heart?

He shrugged, and his face took on a sheepish expression. "My best friend and yours are married. I figure we're going to be running into each other at birthdays, graduations, and weddings, so we ought to be on good terms. I don't think I managed that earlier, so I'm here to try again."

She had to give him credit for his initiative. And she couldn't really argue with his reasoning, either. It wasn't his fault that all she could think about when she was around him was how powerful he looked and how dumb she felt. He was just being nice, that was all. He didn't have designs on her—how could he? She was clearly not his type. And he was definitely not hers.

First off, he didn't believe in God, and the only thing worse than getting interested in someone from a worldly church was getting interested in an atheist. Well, they were the same, really. Elect girls only dated Inside. It was safer and saved hours of explanations—not to mention a future spent in misery in a divided household, like her sister, Elaine.

Not that anyone here was thinking about dating or getting married. An interrogation and a pizza did not a relationship make.

"You have a point." She opened the door wider and motioned him in. It wouldn't be shameful to have him here alone; after all, he'd been a guest in Rebecca's home, not to mention here the other night. "Thank you. I've been so preoccupied with work that I walked in and realized I didn't have a thing in the house to eat except an orange and two slices of processed cheese."

"Hey, at my place that would make a gourmet dinner."

She laughed and reached into the cupboard to take out two plates. "So, this is purely social, right? They haven't decided to use me as a witness after all?"

"Right. I felt kind of bad that I cut you off earlier, at the coffee bar," he said. "You were being sincere, and I was just being cranky."

She put salt, pepper, and napkins on the yellow kitchen table and found red chili flakes and Parmesan cheese packets in the pizza box. "Most men wouldn't come bearing food because of that."

He shrugged and held up his plate while she slid a steaming slice onto it. He waited for her to serve herself, and then as she bowed her head to say grace.

Silence fell in the kitchen until she was finished. "Hand me some chili flakes?"

He passed a packet to her without taking his gaze off her face. "Ross and Julia do that, too."

"What, say grace? Does it make you uncomfortable?"

He dug into his pizza. "Nah. I was used to it as a kid. But when I left home I never gave that stuff another thought."

She wasn't sure she wanted to get back into a conversation that obviously bothered him. Last time she'd done that she'd been so disturbed she'd just walked away, and later realized how rude she'd been. The Elect didn't talk about spiritual things in public, so why had she expected him to blurt out his beliefs on the sidewalk at the coffee bar?

Face it, Claire. It's not his beliefs that disturb you; it's the way he looks at you. The way his gaze drops to your mouth every time you speak. You big chicken.

She wasn't being a chicken. She was being prudent. Big difference.

As they ate, she kept the conversation light and told him some of the things he could do while he was vacationing there. But because it was Hamilton Falls and not somewhere like Sun Valley or Puget Sound, it didn't take long to get to the end of the list.

"So, do you enjoy working at the station so far?" he asked.

She embraced the change of topic with both arms. Figuratively speaking. "It's a huge job. Toby Henzig—that's the guy who does the stock reports—is going to get me some software tonight so I can try to make some sense of the debits and credits."

"Nobody was keeping records before?" He helped himself to more pizza.

"In a small way, yes, Toby was. But I have a feeling Luke's plans are going to get really big. I need to get things set up fast to handle it."

"Big in what way?"

He was turning out to be easier to talk to than she'd first thought. "In all ways, I guess. Luke's ministry seems to be bringing people out of the woodwork—for the book club, for call-ins. And you should see the donations I counted today. Whew!"

"Bad or good?"

"Good. To the tune of a little over two thousand dollars."

An apologetic glance over his pizza. "I don't know anything about the radio business. That sounds like a lot to me."

"It *is* a lot. That's just what I mean. From what I could tell of Toby's spreadsheet, that would keep the station operating for a whole quarter, and Luke's only been there a few weeks."

Ray, it appeared, was a crust man. Some people left them, littering their plates like logs on a beach. But Mama Rosa made good dough. It was nice to see a man who didn't waste it.

"Where's it coming from?" Ray sounded so amazed she had to laugh.

"All over. Luke says the station has a five-county range. I don't know if that's true or not, but the envelopes were from everywhere. Prayer requests, offers of support, donations to missions care of him, you name it."

"Sounds like a thriving Christian community."

That stopped her. "I—I don't really know. We—the Elect don't really, um, mix."

"Why not?"

Because all other forms of Christianity except ours are deceived and going to hell.

No, she couldn't say that. That sounded awful, even if it was what the Elect believed. Had believed. She wished the leadership would come to some sort of firm conclusion about opening the borders of their faith so that a person could give a reasonable answer.

"Claire?"

"Well, for the last hundred years or so we've been going by that verse that says 'Come out from among them and be ye separate.' But since Phinehas was arrested, things have been a little . . . up in the air."

The frown she'd noticed before formed between his eyebrows. "What difference would Phinehas make to what you believe? Does he set the policy or something?"

"Well, no, the Bible does that." Phineas might not have set it, but he certainly made sure everyone lived up to it. And because he did, the Shepherds under him did, the Elders under them did, the parents did, and the young people did. One great big trickle-down continuum that had worked for a hundred years. But now there was no Phinehas and no one stepping up to the plate to replace him except themselves. The thing she couldn't figure out was, would those changes be approved by God or inspired by worldly influences? And how would a person know, so that they could have confidence in their salvation?

"It's a little difficult to explain." What a cop-out. Claire hated it when people asked about her beliefs. She ought to be able to impart the Spirit in such a way that people would see the light and come flocking to Gathering. But that never happened. Mostly they were like Ray, giving her a puzzled look while she sifted through the heap of do's and don'ts embedded in her brain and tried to find an answer.

"Julia's told me some of it. Mind if I get a glass of water?"

"Oh, no, I'll do that." She jumped up, glad to have something to do, and filled their glasses at the sink.

After taking a drink, he said, "There's a lot of traditions, right, stemming from Victorian times? Things to do with dress and the black and the hair."

"Yes."

"Okay, so I don't get what that all has to do with worship. But I guess that since I'm not in your religion, I don't have to get it. What does Luke say?"

She seized on actual facts with relief. "He thinks we should modernize things like our appearance, and open ourselves up to new ways of thinking."

"That sounds reasonable."

"Yes, well, the problem is it's never been done. Never even been thought of." Except in private. And people certainly didn't share their seditious thoughts with one another and risk them getting back to a Shepherd. You could be Silenced for that. But if things changed, what would happen to the people who had been Silenced or had gone Outside? Would that mean Julia, Dinah, and Tamara would be welcomed back in Gathering again? Could things be dead wrong in one generation and then switched over to be right in the next? Didn't the Bible say "yesterday, today, and forever"?

Yes, but that was Jesus. He's the Way. And He gave us the way to worship and that way isn't supposed to change.

Maybe the way and Jesus weren't the same thing, as the Shepherds had always told them. If the Elect's way was changing, it couldn't be Jesus, could it? Or was she just looking for excuses to do what she wanted to do, which was cut her hair and never wear black again as long as she lived?

Ray finished the last of his crust, and she was thankful he couldn't hear what was going on in her mind. The guy was the next thing to an atheist, wasn't he? And if he could hear her doubts, that would cast doubt on the Kingdom of God, and there would be no hope for him then. That guilt at the loss of his soul would be on her head forever.

"I guess you're getting to know Luke pretty well." He leaned back in his chair, and it squeaked as if it wasn't used to bearing such a burden. Which it wasn't. There hadn't been any men around the place since Derrick Wilkinson had helped her move in.

Claire pushed that depressing thought away. "There isn't really much time for talking," she replied, "unless you can do it in three-minute increments while the songs are playing."

"So, you don't know where he's from or anything?"

"He mentioned he was an assistant pastor at a church somewhere in L.A. But I can't remember the name of it." Names of worldly churches meant nothing to her. The important part was that he was Elect now. "And, of course, he's pretty well-known in the radio world. He was on one of the national programs."

"Yeah? Which one?"

Luke hadn't been specific, and it was out of her sphere of knowledge, anyway, since up until recently, listening to the radio had been a sin.

She shrugged. "Why do you want to know?"

"Oh, no reason. Just storing up things to tell Ross and Julia. They're sure to have me over as soon as I get back."

Of course, he was. Mentally, she shook her head at herself. Deep down, had she really been thinking he was trying to get the drop on the competition? There was no competition because there was no contest. She couldn't date either of them. Ray because he was an Outsider and Luke because he ... because ... well, why *couldn't* she date Luke?

Because he's not interested, for starters. Hiring you and taking you to lunch during your first week is not dating behavior.

Margot had done that much when she'd started at the bank. Claire needed to remember the first row in Gathering. She didn't have a chance with all the widows lining up. Maggie Bell's husband had been gone for three years and she was only thirty-six. Not to mention blonde.

On the other hand, Claire worked with Luke. Not that he'd ever look at her twice. He was a nationally known evangelist, and who was she? A small-town nobody who disguised it by shopping from big-city catalogs. A lonely woman masquerading behind a career. Someone who didn't have the spine to protest about not being allowed to move to the city because at least here she had some measure of respect and the Shepherds thought she was a fine example to the young people.

She didn't want to think about that. Instead, she glanced at the clock. "Oh my, it's ten after eight!"

Ray looked a little alarmed. "Sorry. I've hung around too long." He stood and brushed pizza crumbs off his jeans. "See you tomorrow?"

"No, no, you don't have to go. It's just that Luke is launching a new program tonight and I promised I'd call in with a prayer request."

She got up and turned on the small radio and CD-player

combination she'd picked up at the drugstore, having justi-fied it to herself because after all, she listened to the radio in the car and all day long at the station. What could be wrong with having such a small thing in her home?

"What do you mean?" Ray wanted to know.

"You ask Luke to pray for you on the air."

"And presumably you then send in money?"

"That's the idea. It's a fundraiser for our various giving campaigns."

The song that had been playing came to an end and Luke's voice replaced it. "That was Sarah Kelly, one of our favorites here at KGHM. And now, folks, I'd like to invite you to join me in a new program for the glory of God. Do you feel the need for someone to pray for you? Do you have a need that you feel called to share with other listeners? If you do, call in here at 555-KGHM and I'll take your requests. We can all pray together over the air and just watch the Spirit do its work! All the lines are open—just dial 555-KGHM."

With Ray still standing uneasily in the kitchen, that wrinkle back between his brows, Claire grabbed the phone and dialed.

Busy.

"Wow," she said over her shoulder. "I know his console has six lines. Every one of them must be jammed. I'm going to keep trying."

She dialed again and again. "Maybe I'd better go down and write him a note and stick it on his window," she joked. But when she looked around to see if Ray shared her humor, the only thing that moved was the kitchen door.

Which was just closing behind him.

RAY FOUND IT necessary to remind himself that his visit to Claire had been an interrogation, not a dinner date. He'd wanted to see if he could get information out of her, and he had. Which didn't really explain why he felt so angry about her attention switching so quickly from him to Luke. He'd gone there with nothing but a pizza and the intent to deceive, so he had no excuse.

Or choice. She obviously thought Luke Fisher walked on water, and until Ray had some hard evidence to prove otherwise, he was just going to have to suck it up and accept that the woman had terrible taste in men.

The guy was just too smooth. And as far as Ray was concerned, it was a pretty handy coincidence that Brandon Boanerges—if that's who he was—had landed in Hamilton Falls just when the Elect's need for a strong leader was so acute. How had he found out about the fall of Phinehas? The papers? Had he just waltzed into town, seen a weakness, and settled in to exploit it?

Because Ray knew in his gut the guy was going to exploit it. He was a sociopathic charmer. He'd preyed on those women who were desperate for love and now he'd moved on to a whole town full of idealistic people desperate for a leader.

Ray headed back to the motel. At least he'd come away with one snippet of useful information. Fisher had been an assistant pastor at a church in L.A. That was something he could check out. Not that he was about to call every church in the L.A. basin. No, he could start right here.

At the motel, he stripped and took a shower, then sat on the bed and turned the radio on.

"—now here's our next caller with a prayer request. Who am I speaking to?"

"This is Claire." Her voice stroked down Ray's spine like a finger on velvet. "I've been trying to get through for fifteen minutes. This is great."

"Thanks for your persistence, Claire. What prayer request would you like to share?"

"Can you pray for forgiveness? I had a—a friend at the house tonight and h—they went away angry. I think."

"I can certainly do that. Folks, pray with me—except for those of you driving right now. You need to keep your eyes open and your passengers safe." He laughed. "Father God, I lift up Claire's friend to you, who may have let Satan in through a crack in the door and that way caused anger in his or her heart. May they be reconciled, Father, and may you protect the heart of our sister so she would not be discour—"

Ray turned the radio off in disgust. So, yeah, he had been a little miffed when he'd let himself out of her apartment. But wouldn't a reasonable woman bring it up the next time she saw him? Did she have to make his behavior public and get everyone all sympathetic about the angry man who'd let Satan in?

What a bunch of horse puckey. He needed to get to work.

He dug his cell phone out of his shirt pocket and pressed auto dial with his thumb as if he were squashing a bug.

"Malcolm," his partner answered crisply after one ring.

"Hey. What's up?"

"Not a thing. I'm sitting in an alley behind a fish market, waiting for an informant to show. What are you doing?"

"I need a favor of the undercover kind."

"Shoot."

Ray gave him the station's call-in number and told him what he needed.

"That's it? That's all you want?"

"Yep. And can we do it on a three-way? That way you don't need to relay it all back to me."

"As long as you don't have any background noise. Wouldn't want your target identifying you."

"Nope, I'm in my motel room and not expecting company." Unfortunately. "And if he asks you if you have a prayer request, say no, okay?"

Ross laughed. "Expect a call in about ten minutes."

Accordingly, about ten minutes later, Ray's cell phone rang and, once he had his partner on the line, Ross called the station.

"KGHM, this is Luke Fisher, rockin' for Jesus!"

"Cool!" Ross said in a voice at least ten years younger than his natural one. Ray, who had known him for nearly five years, could have sworn the guy was leaning on a surfboard, brushing blond hair out of his face. "Great show, man. Totally dig the prayer requests."

"Thanks! Can I do one for you?"

"Thanks, man, but I've got a different gig going here. I'm going to be going to L.A. for, like, the very first time and I want to hook up with my brothers and sisters in the Lord when I'm there. Can you tell me what church you were with?"

"My friend, you can go to any church in L.A. and they'll welcome a brother."

"But dude, if I go to your old church I can tell them you're doing great and their prayers are, like, totally working. You know, and carry any messages you have."

Luke laughed. "How, like, totally considerate of you. Well, you'd have your choice. I was with Lakefield Central in Downey, Good Shepherd in Newport Beach, Holy Spirit in L.A. proper, and Second Congregational in Hollywood Hills."

"Man," Ross's voice was confused, "can you say that a little slower? And let me get a pen?"

"Sorry, dude, ministry calls. But hey, let me play a song for you. How about 'Safe Journey Home'?"

"Yeah, that'd be great, but . . . did you say Congregational Hollywood Strip?"

"Bye, man. Safe trip!"

Luke disconnected and a few seconds later, on Ray's radio in the motel room, some guy began singing about his life's long journey being like walking in the dark until he met Jesus.

Ray thought that was pretty lame. People made their own way in life. He didn't need anyone to pray for him, thanks.

"Sorry about that," Ross's voice said in his ear. "The guy talks like a machine gun. Did you get any of that?"

"Totally, dude." Ray grinned. "That's why I wanted to listen. It's on a tape in my head. Lakefield Central in Downey,

Good Shepherd in Newport Beach, Holy Spirit in L.A., and Second Congregational in Hollywood Hills."

"How do you do that?"

"It's a gift. In college, I had to hire girls to read the textbooks to me. If I read them, I couldn't retain a thing."

"Cheap way to get dates, Harper."

"At least I don't have to arrest them."

"I never arrested Julia. She came willingly."

"Thanks for the help, bud. Give her my love."

"I'll do that. Looks like my guy isn't gonna show and this place stinks of fish guts. I'm heading home."

Ray hung up and wrote the names of the churches in his notebook, then fired up the laptop and began to research each one.

Lakefield Central in Downey. No record of either Luke or Brandon being on the staff, and their archives went back as far as 1998.

Good Shepherd in Newport Beach. Didn't exist, at least on the Web. He pulled the phone book out of the nightstand and called Information, only to find out there was no church of any kind in Newport bearing the name of Good Shepherd.

Okay.

Holy Spirit in L.A., when typed into his search engine, brought up half a dozen churches with that phrase in it, along with a number of New-Age places. Ray searched each one, and when he found no record of Luke or Brandon, he called Information for that area code. That yielded three more. But he wouldn't call them tonight—he'd just get answering machines. No, he'd start again in the morning.

He was beginning to see a pattern, even with limited research, and he had a feeling the calls would net him exactly what he was getting now—a big bunch of nothing.

The next morning, after jogging downtown for a latte and a bagel, he found that Second Congregational in Hollywood Hills not only existed, it was open at eight A.M., even on Saturdays.

"Second Congregational," a woman's voice said. "How can I help you?"

"My name is Ray Harper, ma'am, and I'm an investigator with the Organized Crime Task Force in Seattle, Washington."

"Yes?"

"Let me give you a phone number where you can call and verify my identity." He was taking a breath to dictate the number at the office when the woman interrupted him.

"That won't be necessary," she said. "Do people tend to not believe you?"

"No, it's just procedure. Who am I speaking with?"

"My name is Margaret Paulson. I run a women's group here Saturday mornings and I happened to be walking past the office when the phone rang. How can I help you, Mr. Harper?" she asked again.

"I'm interested in knowing whether a man named Brandon Boanerges or Luke Fisher ever served as assistant pastor at Second Congregational."

"No."

She sounded so positive that Ray found himself letting out a breath, as though he'd been punctured. "Ah. You know the congregation pretty well? Enough to be positive of that?"

"I've been with this congregation for forty years, Mr. Harper. I know everyone in it."

"And neither of those names is familiar." He might have known Fisher's whole history was a puff of smoke. There were still the other numbers to try, but he'd put money on them not panning—

"I didn't say that. Boanerges, of course, is—"

" 'The sons of thunder,' " he finished. "Yes, I know."

"Well, yes, but it's also the name one of our volunteers took for an Internet ministry. You know, what they call a screen name. I'm not sure of the details, but it ended badly and he left the church after that."

"How long ago was this?"

"Oh, three years at least."

His boy Brandon had been playing mind games with defenseless women for two years before Ray had tripped over his trail. Could he have gotten started with an Internet ministry and met them there? Was that the connection that had tied these unrelated women together—the one piece of the puzzle that had eluded him all this time?

"What was this volunteer's name, Mrs. Paulson? Do you remember?"

"Oh, yes. His mother, Mary Lou, is part of our congregation. Ricky Myers."

"Ricky?" Disappointment spiraled into his gut. "Sounds like a teenager. The man I'm looking for is in his late thirties."

"Oh, that would be about right. Everyone called him

Ricky, though, like a nickname. He was such a charmer, you see. Even still, there are those among us who can't quite believe such a nice, good-looking boy could have been so wicked."

Chapter 6

"PREACHER CONVICTED of Rape," the headline of the *Inish County Courier* said in heavy black type on Monday morning. Claire dropped a quarter in the newsstand and pulled a copy of the paper out. She could hardly blame the *Courier* for getting excited about the news; the most exciting things it usually had to report were escaped cattle and the occasional robbery or vandalism. A rape case—particularly when it involved a man like Phinehas, who was supposed to be celibate, holy, and good—was major news.

She tucked the paper under her arm and went into the station, waving at Luke, whose shift started at eight A.M., the same as hers. When she'd asked him why he liked eight to noon and eight to midnight, he'd said he liked to be on the air when people began their day and when they ended it. "I want to help them set a praiseful tone for their day, or a thankful tone for their evening," he said with that endearing grin. "Hey, it's not much, but it's something good to think about."

Those four-hour stretches were also the highest traffic times now as far as calls and listeners went, but who could blame him for wanting to catch the most people when he could? And Toby didn't seem to mind being bumped out of the prime slots. He was just happy the station's business was turning around.

A brightly colored box of software sat on her desk, still in its shrink-wrap. FileMaker Pro. "Thank you, Toby," she said aloud. She stashed her purse and the paper in the bottom drawer of her desk and opened the box. This was better than a birthday.

With a computer as slow and obsolete as hers was, it took half an hour before the application was up and running. The rest of the morning was spent entering the numbers from Toby's spreadsheet and the receivables she already had. The mail had brought another landslide of checks, cash, and money orders, not to mention a number of fan letters for Luke. She set those aside. If there was anything in there she needed to know about, he'd tell her. She wasn't sure she wanted to know what else the owners of the feminine handwriting had to say.

By two in the afternoon, Luke had gone home and she had a semblance of an accounting system in place. Just for fun, she asked it to produce a profit-and-loss report. The computer crunched happily for a couple of seconds and the line items popped up on her screen, laid out just the way she liked them.

"Wow!" Claire goggled at the bottom line. Did that really

say ten grand? Just to be sure, she ran the report again, and it produced exactly the same number. Eight thousand dollars in this morning's mail alone? She sat back in her chair, feeling a little winded. It was a lucky thing Toby had bought the package when he had. Any longer and she wouldn't have been able to stay on top of this burgeoning river of receivables.

At least they weren't going to have any trouble meeting payroll for the three of them, or in giving to the ministries Luke had talked about.

Claire made a to-do list and pinned it to the bulletin board on the wall next to the desk. Then she gathered up all the deposits, slid them into an envelope, and generated an itemized deposit slip. Her first deposit for the station, she thought as she walked down to the next block, where the bank was. What would Margot say to this?

When she walked in, the first thing she saw was that they hadn't filled her position yet. A forlorn little "closed" sign sat on her desk, and the tellers looked just as harassed as they had last week when she'd left. She'd just moved into line with her big, fat envelope when Margot looked up and waved at her through the glass that formed one wall of her office.

"Come in," she mouthed, motioning toward the door.

As the branch manager, Margot could take a deposit as well as anyone else, or approve a loan, or any of a dozen jobs. Claire tried not to feel triumphant, because vengeance belonged to the Lord, but her back was a lot straighter going in this morning than it had been coming out last week.

"Claire, it's good to see you," Margot said. "Have a seat. What brings you here today?"

"Business deposit." She indicated her envelope. "I'm at KGHM now. Accounting manager."

Margot looked impressed. "That was quick."

"It was . . . meant to be, I think." She still wasn't convinced that God had a hand in getting people jobs, but it certainly had been a nice set of coincidences, hadn't it?

"I'm glad for you, but on the other hand, I'm disappointed." Margot paused and took a deep breath. "I'm afraid good front-office people are hard to find at the moment. When I saw you I thought you might . . . well, that's beside the point. Never mind."

"Might what?" Claire asked.

"Be coming back."

Why would I beg for a job when you fired me because of how I look? "No," she said. "I'm here strictly for business. Can you take my deposit?"

"Sure." Margot reached for the envelope. "What's the account number?"

By the time they'd reached the end of the lengthy transaction, Luke's prophecy was on a fair course to coming true. Margot was all smiles and sunshine, seeing Claire to the door as if she were some corporate bigwig, and there was no more mention of anybody coming back begging for a job.

How about that.

She wondered how many other things Luke was right about. And what effect that was going to have on the Elect's way of life. Or, for that matter, on hers.

RAY HELPED HIMSELF to an unused workstation at the Hamilton Falls P.D., grateful for the joint-forces agreements that the OCTF had in place with every law enforcement agency in the state of Washington. With a few keystrokes, he could tap into the most comprehensive criminal databases in the world—and he had every intention of doing just that. He'd run a warrants check on Brandon Boanerges months ago, but now—if Mrs. Margaret Paulson was correct—he had the guy's real name.

Richard Brandon Myers. *Oh, you are so nailed, my friend.*

NCIS, AFIS, and California's CJIC system provided him with a string of charges for Richard Brandon Myers, date of birth April 13, 1974, from West Hollywood, California. A number of misdemeanors, including vandalism, some traffic stuff, all taken care of—presumably by his mother—by paying a fine. Petty theft. Fraud. Fencing stolen property. All drummed down to the lowest penalty or dropped altogether.

Bottom line, either Myers/Boanerges/Fisher had been in the wrong place at the wrong time and proven innocent, or he was a master at flashing that smile at a judge and earnestly promising that he'd learned his lesson and would never do it again.

Under that name, at least.

Luke Fisher, date of birth July 20, 1973, was as clean as a whistle. He owned a car—the almost new Camry parked behind the station eight hours out of twenty-four—but other than that, he'd never even had a parking ticket.

And at the moment, there was nothing but Ray's gut feeling and his knack for remembering voices to connect petty criminal Richard Myers with either Brandon Boanerges or Luke Fisher. But what he had was enough to make him stick around Hamilton Falls for another couple of days.

That and the look in Claire Montoya's eyes when Luke smiled at her.

Ray was no knight in shining armor, and he didn't make a career of saving women from themselves—especially if they weren't willing to press charges. But nobody deserved to be taken in by Luke Fisher, including his best friend's wife's best friend. If Ray had a sister, he'd look out for her. He and Claire were practically family. Not that he thought of her as a sister or anything. Not with the way her voice played in his head just before he went to sleep, or the way he found himself watching her mouth when she spoke. But he did feel a little protective toward her, for Julia's sake. There was nothing wrong with that, was there?

Enough. He was supposed to be thinking about Luke Fisher and how he was going to keep him away from Claire.

No, no. He was supposed to be thinking about Luke Fisher and how he was going to tie all his identities together. Not that he could do anything once he got that confirmation. Unless Fisher committed a crime by Saturday, Ray was just sitting here using up the taxpayers' money on motel bills and a per diem.

He could tie Fisher to Boanerges with the voice. But how to tie Myers to Boanerges with something more than the fact that they had the name Brandon in common?

For what seemed like the hundredth time, Ray pulled the

battered case file out of his backpack and opened it. Once again he went over the reports and interview transcripts it contained. By now he could practically recite them verbatim.

Hmm.

Like a gopher poking its head out of its hole, he half stood and scanned the workstations around him in the bull pen. It was a quiet afternoon. Everyone was out on patrol, leaving only the administrative assistant, who was busy at her computer.

"Excuse me," he said, and the woman looked up.

"Need something, Investigator?"

"Do you have a couple of minutes to do me a favor?"

She shrugged. "As long as I get this report done by the time Lieutenant Bellville gets back from his accident scene, sure."

"It won't take long. It's going to sound weird, but can you read these reports to me?"

She looked through her bangs at him. "Read them to you? What's the matter, need glasses?"

He shook his head. "I'm one of those people who retain what they hear, not what they see. This case is driving me nuts. I figure if I do something different, like listen to these reports instead of staring at them, I might catch something I missed before."

"Okay." She left her desk and rolled a chair over to where he was sitting. "Where do I start?"

"They're chronological. Start at the beginning."

"Should I look for something, too?"

"If you can do two things at once, why not? I need a connection between a guy who ran an Internet ministry in Hollywood named Richard Brandon Myers, a guy named Brandon Boanerges who romanced women until they signed their money over to him, and Luke Fisher, who—"

"Luke Fisher!"

Ray sighed. Great. Of course the woman would be a fan. "You're bound by your confidentiality agreement."

"What, you think I'd blab the stuff I learn around here? I learned from my predecessor's mistakes." Her chin tilted. She didn't look much more than twenty, but she must have passed all the security checks and then the traditional police hazing that not all support staff survived. "Let's get on with it."

"First I need to know why you reacted."

"He's just the closest I've ever been to a celebrity, that's all. Plus he's this great Christian guy. One of the pastors at my church works with him. It surprised me that his name would come up in a file."

"In this business, nothing surprises me. Come on. Start there." He indicated the document at the bottom of the folder.

An hour later, the woman's voice was getting a little hoarse, but she gamely kept reading page after page. She did a good job, too. Maybe she'd had a couple of acting or elocution classes. She put expression into the dry lines, particularly when they got to the transcripts of the women Boanerges had defrauded.

SHONBERG: The last night I saw him, Brandon said he had
    something special for me, and I was to meet him at La

Colombe, a French place that we'd gone to on our first
date. I was convinced he was going to give me a ring.

HARPER: And did he?

SHONBERG: He spent nearly an hour going through the ex
files.

HARPER: The what?

SHONBERG: You know, all his ex-girlfriends. It's part of the
mating ritual.

HARPER: It is? Never mind. What did he say about them?

SHONBERG: Oh, that they each meant a phase in his life. You
know, Michelle Groning was his first love, Teresa White
was the first one he slept with, blah blah blah. But those
phases were over, and he was now with me. The operative word being *now*.

HARPER: To your knowledge, did he treat these women the
way he treated you? Trying to defraud them?

SHONBERG: I have no idea—

"Wait a second." Ray held up a hand to stop the woman's
voice.

She looked up from the transcript on the desk. "What?"

"I never followed up on those two."

"Two what?"

"The girlfriends."

"You think he'd give real names?" She sounded a little
cynical. Maybe there was a recent breakup in the picture.

"Rule number one when coming up with a story is stick
to the truth as much as you can. That way you don't trip
yourself up on the details." He smacked himself on the forehead. "Bad investigator." He took the file from her and

tapped everything into order. "Thanks for helping me with this. I owe you."

"Everybody in here does," she said.

LUKE'S FACE LIT UP with joy and awe when Claire told him about the money that had come in practically overnight thanks to the prayer program. Her heart gave a great big thump and she made an effort to keep her face friendly, calm, and professional.

"This is great!" He grabbed her in a jubilant hug and swung her around her office.

Friendly and calm and professional, oh my! She laughed and tried to get her feet back under her, but her blood was flying around in her veins and she was sure the goofy grin on her face was going to stay pasted there all day.

"God is great!" Luke put her down at last and she got her breath back, self-consciously patting her chignon into place.

"Maybe so," she said, "but we should make some decisions about what to do with it. Charities, what do you call them—ministries. Something. We can't just sit on it."

"Of course not." Luke parked one hip on the corner of her desk and grinned at her. It was just after noon and he should have been on his way out, but the good news had stopped him in his tracks. "This money is earmarked for God's good work. I have a couple of ideas, but first off is a fully equipped van so we can take the show on the road and reach more people."

"The down payment is certainly taken care of," Claire allowed. "What else?"

"There are a couple of worthy ministries I've been supporting for years. A check for a few grand could support a homeless outreach in Idaho run by a friend of mine for months."

He practically glowed, and Claire gave herself a mental slap. He was her boss. She had to remember that. Okay, so most bosses didn't pick you up and waltz you around the office, but then, Luke wasn't like any man she'd ever met, boss or not.

Unlike most of the Elect men, who kept a woman guessing about their feelings in case something better came along, Luke put his right out there. If he was happy, everyone around him knew it. If he was passionate about something, it was so infectious you found yourself caring about what happened to—to homeless people in Idaho. Something, she had to admit, she'd never even thought about before. The Elect usually did their outreach right here at home, by inviting people to Gathering.

"Okay, so earmark money for a van and the homeless outreach." She bent over her desk and made notes on her to-do list. "If you give me the address, I'll send a check. Oh, and Luke, we should meet with a lawyer to make sure our gifts are covered regulation-wise. Toby tells me we're a nonprofit, so we need to make sure the money's distributed correctly."

Luke waved a hand at her. "I'm just the front man," he said. "You're the accounting manager. Do what you think is best. I trust your judgment."

"Careful. I might go on a power trip and give myself a raise."

He shrugged. "Go ahead. Give us all a five-hundred-dollar bonus."

"Luke!" He couldn't be serious. That was theft. Wasn't it?

"We get paid out of that money in any case. God is using us, and I'm sure He won't object to our rejoicing in the fruit of our labor for Him."

First prayer, now giving. *This was normal*, Claire reminded herself. She needed to modernize her thinking.

"For my part, I'll send five hundred to the food bank," she suggested. "How's that for a compromise?"

"Like I said, you decide the how, and I'll come up with the what. And," he said, with a boyish smile that reminded her of someone with a delightful secret, "I have an idea cooking. I'm going to let it simmer and pray on it some more, and then I'll tell you all about it."

"I'll look forward to that." She had no doubt it would be something spectacular—and fun at the same time. "Meantime, will you be at Gathering on Wednesday night? No, wait. Of course not. You're on the air."

"I wouldn't miss it."

She paused. "How can you be in two places at once?"

He strolled to the office doorway. "Thanks to the wonders of technology, I pretaped a program. All I have to do is load it in the player, go to Gathering, and come back and pick up where I hear myself leaving off."

The man thought of everything in order to put God first. She could take a leaf out of his book. "I'll see you there, then."

He twinkled at her. "Save me a seat."

As he went outside and the street door cut off his

whistling, she wondered what he meant. Save him a seat? Was he joking about the fact that since he'd started speaking at Gathering, there was hardly an empty seat in the hall? Or had he meant the unspoken sign of courtship when a woman maneuvered to keep a seat empty next to her so her man could sit there? Of course, everyone knew what the woman was up to and some of the kids made a point of sitting there just to get her steamed. Or worse, the guy you'd been avoiding decided to make his move and took that seat just as the guy you'd been waiting for walked into the Hall.

Oh yes, seating politics were serious stuff when you were young. Thank goodness she was past that kind of thing and could sit wherever and with whomever she pleased. The fact that there were no real prospects in town made it a lot easier.

Or at least, there hadn't been until Luke arrived.

CLAIRE SETTLED INTO the chair second from the end in her customary seventh row on the right. Around her, the mission hall slowly filled, parents hushing their kids and old people tapping down the aisle leaning on canes or each other. In the front row, the No Pride Club wriggled and craned their necks, keeping an eye on the door to see who would spot Luke first.

Having just been embraced by Luke a couple of hours before, Claire felt very virtuous about keeping her eyes on her open Bible.

Which is why she jumped about a foot when a large male body settled itself onto the metal folding chair next to her.

"Hey," Ray Harper said in a whispered greeting.

Her mouth dropped open and she completely forgot how to use the English language.

"Is this all right?" he whispered. "I don't have to be a member, do I?"

The gears in her brain ground and finally engaged. "Yes. I mean, no, you don't have to be a member."

He flipped through the hymnbook someone had given him at the door and she sat back, feeling a little shell-shocked. Ray Harper? At Gathering? He'd told her point-blank that discussing religion made him twitch. What did he think they were going to discuss here? Traffic safety?

It couldn't be possible that Ray wanted to know more about God and the Elect way, could it? No. Impossible. But then, who was she to say what was impossible? Six months ago she would have said it was impossible that the Elect could have embraced a stranger the way they were embracing Luke. Look at her, embracing him herself.

In a strictly businesslike way, of course.

Businesslike or not, she had a leg up on the No Pride Club, at least.

On her right, Ray sighed, and his arm brushed hers, the most tentative and casual of touches. She thought she caught a whiff of his cologne, and she came out of her thoughts of Luke abruptly. She'd never been regarded as petite in her life, but something about Ray Harper made her feel delicate and feminine, especially when she was as close to him as this.

What on earth had brought him to Gathering?

She leaned over and felt his shoulder against hers, rock-solid. Dependable, even. "Why are you here?" she whispered.

"I thought I'd come and see what it was all about." His return whisper puffed against her earlobe, and she broke out in goose bumps all the way down to her elbows.

Thank goodness Luke came in at that moment, or she was sure Ray and the entire row sitting behind them would have seen it. She straightened and watched Luke make his way to the front of the hall to sit next to Owen. At seven-thirty on the dot, Owen rose and announced a hymn. As they sang, Claire discovered Ray had a very passable but hesitant baritone. Certainly nothing like Owen's glorious tenor. There was a reason he always led the singing.

When the hymn was finished and Owen had said a short prayer, he adjusted the microphone and looked out at them all.

"People of God," he said, "no doubt you saw the headlines in the paper this week. A jury has found our Senior Shepherd guilty of terrible crimes, and we have no choice but to accept that, as abhorrent as it is."

Beside her, Ray shifted on his chair.

"This has brought me to many hours of prayer and fasting," Owen went on, "and many conversations with our brother Luke Fisher and my father-in-law, the other Elder of this church. We have concluded that the leadership of Phinehas has been flawed, and God's people have been making sacrifices that perhaps have been too hard to bear.

"For instance, it's not scriptural that His people should wear black alone. We understand the significance of it, but we also understand that a life surrendered to God has its own fragrance and doesn't need to have attention brought to it by clothing. So, starting from this Gathering, the people of God are free to wear black if they wish, or any other color they choose."

Claire drew in a sharp breath, and a sound like the wind blowing over a field whispered through the hall as people shifted in their seats and looked at each other.

Luke rose and leaped up the steps to the microphone, where Owen surrendered it to him.

"Remember, my friends, that our lives speak to others. It's not our clothes or how we do our hair. It's our spirit and our actions. That's how God's love is transmitted one to another. We're so used to sacrificing things like clothes and hairstyles because of Phinehas's ideas that we've lost sight of the truly important things, like reaching out to our brothers and sisters or helping those in need. That's what real sacrifice is, friends. A giving heart is so much more pleasing to God than someone bundled up in black who is so focused on how they look that they forget how they're supposed to relate to those around them."

People looked at one another, and Claire saw every expression, from confusion to guilt to elation—the last being particularly evident in the faces of the teenage girls who had just realized they'd been given permission to wear red or yellow if they felt like it.

"People who love Christ give in His name," Luke went on. "We have a chance to take the focus off ourselves and put it on others, and you know what? That means it will give glory to God and be reflected back on us again. If you feel you need to sacrifice, then send a gift in God's name to the station. Let your sacrifices be the kind that do good in the world, that make a difference and glorify God."

Now Luke yielded the microphone to Owen. "Luke has an idea that I think will be as much a monument to God as the Temple was in Jerusalem of old," he said. "There are hundreds, maybe thousands, of godly people in this area, and they have nowhere to meet in fellowship, to learn, to even have recreation time with their families. Our own Summer Gatherings are transient at best, with tents temporarily set up and a lot of work for people to manage only once a year. Luke has found property here, lakefront property. What if there was a conference facility there, with meeting rooms, a dining room, cabins to sleep in, and hiking paths and other recreation? What if we could host corporate events there that would bring in thousands of dollars? What if we could have our own Summer Gatherings there, and hear God's Word in comfort instead of sweltering in tents and putting up with pit toilets and flies?"

"That's not a conference facility, that's heaven," someone—Linda Bell's husband, Claire thought—quipped from the back.

Luke grabbed the mic, and Owen grinned and stepped back. "Exactly!" he said, his hand open toward the ceiling. "It would be a little piece of heaven right here on earth. Instead of wearing odd clothes and worrying about how our women look, we should be glorifying God in concrete ways. A place like this would be renowned not just all over the state, but all over the country. The land is there. The vision is there. The need is certainly there. All we need to do is act on it."

"How much money are we talking about?" Derrick

Wilkinson stood up on the other side of the hall. "This sounds like a huge investment."

"Not as huge as giving your life to God." Luke smiled at him, but Derrick didn't smile back. "The land is three hundred fifty thousand, and I estimate two and a half million to develop it and build the conference buildings and other facilities. A volunteer workforce will keep construction costs down, and of course our loyal listeners will continue to contribute."

Almost three million dollars! Claire fought back the urge to laugh. No one was going to do this. No one in this room had ever even seen that much money, much less donated it to anything. The Elect didn't do it that way, anyway. If they *did* give to charity, it was in secret. No one kept records, and no one knew where the money went because God was in control of it through His Shepherds, who never spoke about such things.

"I know it seems like a lot," Luke said earnestly, "and it is. But think of it this way. Claire?" Unerringly, he found her in the seventh row. "Claire, how much did the station receive in gifts to God in just seven days?"

Claire looked around a little wildly. Surely he wasn't going to ask her to speak aloud in Gathering? Women just didn't do that. It was unheard of.

Without the help of the microphone, Owen called, "It's all right, Claire. You may speak in support of our brother."

Slowly, she stood. "In—in seven days we received twelve thousand, two hundred and thirteen dollars and sixty-seven cents." Her knees gave out and she sat rather suddenly, her cheeks scarlet.

But no one was looking at her. "You see?" Luke waved an expansive arm. "In seven days we're well on our way to a down payment on the land alone. Seven days. My friends, it's clear that this area is ripe to glorify God. And I believe the Elect are called to lead this effort. Feel free to talk about it. The Elders and I are already talking with the bank and an architectural firm. But in the meantime, just remember that this is not for us. It's for the glory of God, and we are just His instruments. Let's sing and praise Him!"

Owen launched into "Building on the Rock," and people flipped to the right page in their hymnbooks, half of them singing from memory. Next to her, Ray Harper gave up trying to find the right page. Claire had the uncomfortable feeling that he was watching her sing, but it would hardly do to ask him not to do that. Instead, she moved her hymnbook over so he could read the words.

Only people who are about to get engaged share a hymnbook.

Nonsense. He was a Stranger and she was simply being courteous.

She kept the hymnbook low, though, so Luke wouldn't see it from the front of the room. He may have gone Outside at one time, but he wasn't a Stranger now. And she wouldn't want to give him the wrong idea.

Chapter 7

WHEN THE WEIRD SERVICE that hadn't actually been a service was over, everyone shook hands as if they'd just been introduced. Since he knew a grand total of about four people, Ray thought Claire would stick around and help him out.

But no. She was off like a shot to join the hungry female crowd around Luke Fisher, some of whom were already digging out their checkbooks as though it would buy them a ticket straight into his little black book.

Women. It never ceased to amaze him how they were bamboozled by good looks. That and this glorifying-God thing had them totally hosed. The only sensible person he'd heard all evening was the lanky guy on the far side of the room, who had a couple of pens in his pocket and looked like he'd been sucking on a lemon.

"Good evening, Investigator."

Ray turned at the quiet voice behind him and looked

into the direct gaze of Rebecca Quinn. "Hey, Miss Quinn. Nice to see you."

"I'm sure it is. You only know a few of us, am I right?"

"Yeah, and two are missing. Dinah and Tamara."

"It's not likely we'll ever see them at Gathering again." Ray couldn't tell if the lady was sad about this or not. She merely stated the facts and let the listener make up his own mind. "That's why I came to speak to you," she went on. "They're at my place now, planning to leave in the morning now that the trial is finished. Would you like to join us for a cup of coffee?"

"There wouldn't be a conflict of interest now," he allowed. "Thanks. That's nice of you."

"It's purely selfish of me," she said crisply. "I may not get to see you all in one place again, so I have to finagle it and hope you don't see how transparent I am." He had to smile. "I'd like to ask Claire, too." She craned her neck. "Do you see her?"

"She's over there with the radio guy. Fisher."

"She and every other eligible female over fifteen. Dear me. I see I'm not the only transparent one." Ray kept his mouth firmly closed. "Perhaps you'd pass on the invitation for me when the crowd thins, Mr. Harper? I want to get home and put the coffee pot on."

Feeling as though he'd been outmaneuvered, but not sure how it had happened, he replied, "Sure. Be happy to."

"See you in a bit, then."

She turned and made her way to the door, spine straight, silver hair shining under the overhead lights. He smothered a grin. She reminded him of his gram, who could teach trained surveillance specialists a thing or two.

Five minutes of casual sauntering and smiling vaguely at well-meaning people who introduced themselves and shook his hand brought him to the edge of the little crowd around Luke Fisher. He sidled up to Claire.

"Miss Quinn says you're being transparent," he said out of the side of his mouth.

She shot him an indignant glance. "I am not. It's my job to deal with the money he's collected. See?" She moved away from the group, opened her handbag, and showed him the fat wad of envelopes and checks. "I am not a member of the No Pride Club."

Whatever that was, it didn't sound good. "Okay. Miss Quinn also invited us to coffee at her place."

"Us?"

He wasn't so sure he cared for those upraised brows and pickled-looking lips. What was he, a social leper?

"She invited me. And she asked me to invite you. She wants to have a get-together with Dinah and Tamara before they go."

"Oh." The sour expression faded. "That was kind of her. I've hardly seen anything of them because of the trial. Of course, I'll come."

"Come where?" said a musical baritone full of laughter behind him. "Are you two making off with the Lord's cash?"

With an effort, Ray unclenched his right fist. *Bad hand. No decking people after the nice service.*

"No, Ray was just passing on an invitation." Claire adjusted her purse strap on her shoulder and smiled at him.

"Was he? Are his intentions honorable?" Fisher stood a little too close to Claire for Ray's taste. "Should I come along as my employee's chaperone?"

Technically they were both employees of whoever owned the radio station, but Ray didn't see it would gain him any brownie points to mention that.

"I'm sure you'd be welcome." Claire glanced at Ray. "We're just going to have coffee at Rebecca Quinn's. She's my landlady, and she has some friends of ours staying with her."

"I didn't know you and the good investigator had mutual friends. But sure, I'd love to come. Can I give you a ride?"

Ray had opened his mouth to make the same offer. He closed it again when Claire shook her head. "No, I live upstairs, in her rental suite. It would be silly to make you drive me back here afterward to get my car. I'll meet you both there."

With an airy wave, she headed out the door. Ray nodded at Fisher and did the same. So, the guy had invited himself along to a private party. Either he was one of those gregarious types who just loved people, or he was doing it on purpose to get under Ray's skin.

Not that he was paranoid or anything.

But these things balanced out, he told himself, trying to be philosophical. He wasn't going to be alone with Claire, but at least he'd have a chance to observe Luke Fisher up close and personal. And if they were all going to be together in one big happy tea party, he'd just as soon be there to run interference.

Metaphorically speaking.

When he got to the old house on Gates Place, Fisher was just pulling up in his Camry. His 2002 Camry, according to the state motor-vehicles database, purchased in Seattle.

The guy's affability never falters, he thought as he followed him up the path to the door. *But some of the things he says can be a barb if you're looking for one.* Such as "Are your intentions honorable." Ha ha. Big joke. But very successful at putting a little doubt in Claire's mind if she were so inclined. Not that he had any intentions toward her, honorable or not. He was just looking out for the girl until he figured out what the deal was with Fisher-of-the-many-faces.

Claire was already there, lit up like a Christmas tree and hugging Dinah as if they were never going to meet again. Behind her stood the guy with the pens in his pocket whose name Ray didn't know.

"I'm so glad you won," she was saying to Dinah as Ray and Fisher came in. "With all your time in court I've hardly seen you. You wouldn't believe all the things that have happened because of this case."

Dinah, whom Ray had always thought was kind of plain, with hair she wouldn't allow to curl and a haunted look around her eyes and mouth, was a changed creature herself. He actually did a double take. Was this the same girl he'd seen the night he arrested Phinehas—or even the same girl he'd done the wrap-up interview with a few days ago?

She was wearing a thick knitted sweater in a dark gold that did amazing things for her coloring and a black velvet skirt that just grazed her knees instead of falling practically to the ankle like the skirts many of the Elect women wore. Her hair had been cut, allowing curls and waves to float around her shoulders instead of being imprisoned in a shapeless bun on the back of her head.

"You look really great," he said, shaking her hand when Claire had finally let go of her. "Wow."

"Don't sound so surprised, Ray," Tamara said from the depths of the easy chair, where she lounged with both legs slung over one of its overstuffed arms. "My sister has always had the looks in the family."

"Very funny." Dinah looked a little embarrassed. "I told Matthew I wanted to make some changes, so he said I should. I figured I'd surprise him when I got off the plane."

"You'll surprise him, all right." Tamara swung her legs down and approached Luke Fisher with her hand out. "I don't think we've met. Tamara Traynell, vindicated rape victim."

He blinked, but his smile never faltered. "Luke Fisher, prodigal son. I have a radio ministry out of KGHM. Claire's our accounting manager."

"Wow." Tamara's gaze moved between them. "Not just listening to the radio, but actually playing the songs and working there. The times, they really are a-changin'."

"Bob Dylan, 1964," Fisher said promptly. "And change isn't always a bad thing. 'Yesterday, today, forever' doesn't apply to clothes, hair, and music, for instance."

"Says you." The pen guy came forward. "Derrick Wilkinson." He nodded at both Fisher and Ray, but didn't offer to shake hands. Fisher didn't seem to notice. Ray stuck his hand out and after a second, Wilkinson shook it.

"Says Owen and the elders, too, apparently," Rebecca put in. "Coffee and cake, anyone?"

Dinah took the cups from her and, like a good hostess, made sure everyone had something to drink and a fat slice of what looked like carrot cake with thick, creamy frosting. Ray's stomach grumbled and he took the plate gratefully.

" 'Yesterday, today, forever' applies to the way," Derrick went on around his cake. "You can't just walk in and change the way people have been worshiping for a hundred years. I don't get how that can be right."

"Things change or they die," Fisher explained gently. "And with the Shepherds not in control anymore, the sheep have to do as the Holy Spirit prompts them."

"They could just sit tight and wait for another senior Shepherd to be chosen, like they're doing down south in the Tri-Cities area."

"But then you'd have the same difficulty of one man assuming all the power, and possibly being corrupted," Dinah said. "It isn't healthy for things to be set up that way."

"The Elect should look at how other churches do it," Tamara put in. "They have, like, boards and things to make sure their leaders don't get carried away. People should be accountable to each other. That's why things got so bad in the Elect, and why it's falling apart now."

"We're not falling apart, we're just . . . re-establishing our footing." Claire had a bit of frosting clinging to the corner of her lip, and Ray had the sudden urge to wipe it off with his fingertip. In the next second, she dabbed at her mouth with her napkin and he shook his head at himself.

Focus. Learn something. Don't be a dope.

"We're all part of the body of believers," Dinah said. "No church is better than another because of what it teaches. If

I've learned anything in the last few months, it's that the Elect way isn't the only way to heaven."

"It's the way we've been given, though," Fisher put in smoothly. "That's why the elders and I have been talking about ways to make it more welcoming to Outsiders."

"Besides dismantling our example?" Derrick grumped, half audibly.

"Refocusing it." The guy had endless patience, Ray would give him that. "Instead of concentrating on our looks, we should concentrate on our actions. And that means things like charity and praise in the form of the worship center. Let those things be a monument to God instead of how Claire does her hair, for instance."

Claire blushed as everyone glanced at her. "Some monument. More like the leaning tower of Pisa."

"These are new and radical thoughts, Mr. Fisher," Rebecca said. "Don't rush us old-timers. We need to think on these things and pray about them."

"Of course. But the fields are white unto harvest, so we shouldn't wait long. In the time it would take to elect a new senior Shepherd, we could have the land cleared and the foundation poured for the worship center. I've already found an architectural firm and they're putting together some concept designs as we speak. But I want everyone in the flock to see them and give us their input. This will be a hymn of praise in physical form for all of us."

"Or another tower of Babel," Derrick muttered, but it seemed that only Ray heard him.

Claire glanced at the clock over the kitchen door. "Luke, how long is your tape? It's almost nine-thirty."

He grinned at her. "I had two ninety-minute tapes in the deck, so technically I have half an hour to go, but you're right. I should be getting over to the station."

"What do you mean?" Dinah looked from one to the other.

"I'm skipping out on my duties, just for tonight," Luke said.

"Don't listen to him." Claire began stacking the empty dessert plates. "He made a tape to play so his program would stay on the air and he could also go to Gathering. I think it's brilliant. It's not every day you meet a guy who can be in two places at once."

"The downside is I have to listen to myself on the drive in." Ray resisted the impulse to roll his eyes. "Thanks for dessert, Rebecca. Good night, everyone. See you tomorrow, Claire."

"You will," she said.

When the door closed behind him, it seemed to Ray that everyone took a breath and relaxed, as if they'd been "on" in some kind of performance, and now they could go back to normal.

"I'm half tempted to go down to the station tonight, too." Claire picked up her handbag and peered inside, as if the checks and envelopes collected at Gathering might have evaporated. "It makes me nervous, walking around with all of these."

"It's not likely you'll be robbed on your way upstairs," Ray pointed out. "Or is the crime rate in Hamilton Falls worse than I thought?"

"No, of course not." She put the bag back on the sideboard. "It's just strange treating gifts to the church like real receivables, that's all. We're so used to the right hand not knowing what the left is doing."

"What do you mean?" Ray was a literal kind of guy. When people spoke in metaphors, it always made him feel a little slow. He wasn't real keen on that feeling.

"Our gifts have traditionally been made in secret," Rebecca explained. "The Shepherds accept them, and we just have faith that they'll be used where they're needed."

"And they're not required to give any kind of accounting?" Ray had no idea how churches usually worked, but in any corporate body, this kind of behavior sounded like a bad idea.

"Not until now. But Luke, I think, is right." Rebecca glanced at Claire. "It's better to have everything above board and viewable by anyone. Especially when we're talking about gifts from Outsiders."

Dinah stood and gave them all a regretful look. "I hate to break this up, but I have a nine o'clock plane out of Spokane, which means leaving here at four A.M. I'm going to call Matthew and then go to bed."

Ray stood and watched Claire hug both Dinah and Tamara, exchanging a few whispered words with each. Then, before he knew what was happening, Tamara was hugging him fiercely.

"Thanks for everything you've done for us, Ray," she said against his neck. "Our whole world is different because of you."

"It's different because you two had the guts to make it

that way." An obstruction had formed in his throat, getting in the way of his words. "I just helped out."

"You believed us." She pulled away and looked into his face. She was so young. Just a teenager. And look what she'd been through. "You believed us, and that brought us to tonight, with Phinehas in jail and Dinah and me free. And now I need a tissue. Good night, everyone."

Dinah's hug was less fierce, but it still choked him up just as much. "Tamara said it for both of us."

"Have a happy life," he said gruffly. "I know that sounds stupid, but I mean it."

"It doesn't sound stupid at all. And if God and Matthew and Tamsen have anything to do with it, I will."

Her smile was wide and sincere and Ray felt a funny hollow feeling behind his heart, as if he'd just discovered he was missing out on something.

Something he wasn't ready to think about.

Derrick shook hands with Dinah as though he were a traveling shoe salesman rather than the friend Ray had assumed he was, thanked Rebecca for the coffee and cake, and got himself out the door.

"Poor Derrick," Claire murmured. "I don't think he's quite forgiven Julia or Dinah for leaving town and taking away his chance for the Deaconship."

"Perhaps with all the changes happening among the Elect," Rebecca said, "the favored families will find themselves not so favored and having to live like the rest of us mortals."

"I can think of five girls who would jump at him if he'd only look at them," Claire said. "Talk about single-minded."

"I don't know." Rebecca gave her a sidelong glance. "You two have always gotten along pretty well."

Ray's eyebrows climbed. So, he'd been right. Not that he thought Derrick Wilkinson was any match for a woman as smart and beautiful as Claire Montoya. But at least he was honest and had some integrity, if his lousy opinion of Luke Fisher was anything to go by. Ray could appreciate a man who was a decent judge of character, even if he was buried in a backwater town with not much in the way of ambition.

Claire laughed. "Don't even think it, Rebecca. I'm saving myself for—" She stopped suddenly and glanced at Ray, then blushed.

"For whom?" Rebecca turned in the kitchen doorway. "This is news."

Claire mumbled something about God's will, then grabbed her handbag and fled. They heard her steps on the stairs at the side of the house, then the sound of a door closing above.

Ray turned to look at Rebecca, and lifted his brows in inquiry.

Rebecca sniffed, a ladylike sound that transmitted disbelief and maybe even a smidgen of warning. "Don't look at me." Cake plate in both hands, she turned back into the kitchen. "I'm not the one who needs to get a move on."

RAY WAS STILL TRYING to figure out what code Rebecca Quinn had been speaking in as he pulled into the motel parking lot and got out of the truck. Why didn't women just come out and say what they meant? Had she been talking about his investigation? And if so, how did she know about it? Did she mean he'd outstayed his welcome? Or was it, as he suspected, more personal than that?

But it couldn't be. From what he knew of this group, there was no way a respectable elder lady would encourage an attraction between an Elect woman and an Outsider. Because, face it, there was an attraction there and he wasn't sure he should even be encouraging it himself. It was more like a fantasy, something to keep his mind entertained while he hung around in Hamilton Falls waiting for Luke Fisher to show his hand.

It wasn't like Claire was thinking that way about him. Far from it. If she was thinking about anyone, it was Fisher, and if Ray managed to put the kibosh on that, then he'd consider it a job well done and move on.

With that settled, he unlocked the door of his room and tossed his jacket on the chair. His cell phone rang, the shrill sound like a protest in the silence, and he fished it out of his jacket's pocket.

The 310 area code showed in the display. "OCTF, Harper."

"Mr. Harper, this is Teresa White. Sorry to be so long returning your call, but I've been on location and just got back tonight."

"Thanks for calling back." Richard Brandon Myers's ex-girlfriend. He hadn't been able to track down the other one, but Teresa White still lived in West Hollywood and drove a registered vehicle. After discovering that, getting a phone number from the DMV database had been easy. "Are you in the movie industry?"

"Yes. I do makeup. We've been filming in Thailand, and my body clock is so messed up I have no idea if it's Tuesday, Wednesday, or Thursday."

"It's Wednesday night here in Washington, but in L.A. it could be anything."

She laughed. "That's the truth. So, what can I do for you?"

"Well, you can tell me about a guy you used to date. Richard Myers." A few beats of silence hissed along the satellite beam. "Ms. White? Still there?"

"Yes, I'm here. Man, talk about a blast from the past. I haven't thought about Ricky in years. Is he in trouble?"

"Why do you ask?"

"That used to be my stock question when we were going out. Phone calls in the middle of the night, people stopping me on the street, his mother calling at work. It was always something to do with Ricky and trouble, even for months after we broke up."

"What kind of trouble?"

"Little stuff. The mosquitoes at the picnic of life, you know? Parking tickets, stuff missing, insurance claims. Nothing big, no master crimes or anything, but just enough to upset me. Especially when I was trying to establish a career and money was tight. The last time he called asking me to bail him out I told him I couldn't and just left him in the clink. I never heard from him again. He never even came back to the apartment for his stuff."

"And you haven't heard from him since?"

"Nope. Thank goodness. I'd rather hear from the IRS."

Ray chuckled. "Did he ever mention the name Brandon Boanerges?"

"That sounds as weird as the name of this space creature I had to do makeup for last week." She thought for a moment. "But it's ringing a bell. Hang on. The Rolodex in my head is flipping." He waited, imagining cards on a wheel flipping, flipping . . . "Right. I knew I'd heard it before. Boanerges was Ricky's screen name. You know, for chat rooms and stuff."

"He spent a lot of time on the Internet?"

"Oh, sure. Another reason I was glad to see him go. I had dialup then, and my phone bills were off the charts. Ricky was always between jobs so guess who got stuck paying them." She paused. "No offense, Investigator, but do you have any more questions? I haven't had a shower in about thirty-six hours and I'm dying here."

"Just one more. Do you have any pictures of Richard Myers?"

She laughed. "Are you kidding? That's, like, a majorly closed chapter in my life."

Ray closed his eyes and rubbed his forehead. He couldn't tie Richard Myers to Brandon Boanerges on the basis of a screen name.

"But I'll tell you what," Teresa went on. "My mom is a scrapbooker. I probably sent her a photo in the first flush of romance—argh, we are just so lame when we're in love—and if I did, she'll have it. She keeps everything. She'll be one of those little old ladies with forty cats and hallways filled with scrapbook clippings, I swear."

"If she has a picture, I'd be grateful." He gave her his e-mail address. "If you can scan it and send it to me, it would really help my investigation."

"No problem. I'll call her when I get out of the shower and send you something if she has it."

Ray said good-bye and snapped the cell phone shut. A picture would tie it all together. Despite what Teresa had said, Ray pulled his laptop out and fired it up anyway. It wouldn't hurt to check his e-mail and see what was cooking on some of his other cases. Ross could handle a lot of their caseload, but he had a wife and family to think about now. Double shifts and voluntary overtime, while still a reality of the job, would be something he'd have to negotiate now on both sides of the commute.

Ray cleaned up a bunch of e-mail, calendared some court dates that had come in, and wrote a report for Harmon that with any luck would pacify him for a day or two more. And lo, when he refreshed his mail screen, there was a message from one *teresa.white@carmelassoc.com* with a honking big two-megabyte attachment. With a sigh of regret that he wasn't at the sheriff's office with its handy T1 connection, Ray told his system to start downloading and went and took a shower. When he got out, it was ready, and he opened the file with a twist in his gut. It wouldn't be this easy. It never was. The file would show some other loser, some guy with a biker ponytail and a bunch of tattoos.

But it didn't.

An ordinary-looking girl with an extraordinary smile sat on a couch, behind which was an overdressed Christmas tree. And sitting with his arm around the girl was Luke Fisher.

Back then he'd been blond and suffering from a held-over case of acne and glasses he'd obviously ditched for contact lenses. But that confident smile couldn't be altered, and neither could the cocky attitude.

Not unless Ray could find a way to alter it for him.

Permanently.

Chapter 8

BETWEEN THE MORNING'S MAIL and the contributions from the night before, Claire put nearly fourteen thousand dollars on the books on Thursday morning. This was nothing short of a miracle. She had no idea there was that much spare money floating around in this part of Washington State, much less people who were willing to give it to support the work of God. They couldn't all be misguided, as the Shepherds had always told them. The methods of giving and receiving might be different, but any community of believers needed money to do things for each other. If success was the measure of blessing, then they were being blessed like nobody's business.

"How are we doing?" Luke stuck his head in her office door.

"Almost fourteen thousand, between last night and this morning. If I hadn't seen it myself, I'd say it was impossible."

"God's work is never impossible. Sometimes improbable and often unbelievable, but not impossible."

She laughed. "You're right."

"If we apply for access to the repeater tower on Mount Ayres, we can broadcast to an even wider audience. I've got Toby working on that now. In the meantime, it's time for the mobile unit."

She saluted. "You're the boss."

He leaned on her doorjamb, looking casual in khakis and a button-down shirt. His chestnut hair curled around his ears and Claire fought a sudden urge to walk over and smooth it back.

"God's the boss, otherwise our ministry wouldn't have this much power." Which confirmed what she'd just been thinking. "I've got our unit all picked out; it's just a matter of handing over a down payment and then getting it outfitted with broadcasting equipment."

"Do you want me to cut you a check?"

He grinned at her. "You read my mind. When my show's over I'll drive up to Spokane and buy it. No point in waiting. God's time is now."

"But won't you need someone to drive it back for you? How are you going to get both vehicles back down here?" Not that she was fishing for an invitation, but she hadn't been to Spokane in ages. Maybe they'd have a late lunch together before they went to the dealership. She couldn't think of anything she'd like better than a long conversation with someone as interesting as Luke. They were practically on the same wavelength. And then maybe he'd see that—

"I may as well have it outfitted while I'm there. And we'll need to get the station's logo painted on it, too. All that will probably take the rest of the week."

"If you tell me where and what, I'll get it set up for you."

"Thanks for the offer, but I know what we need. I'll take care of it. What I need you to do is handle the back end when the bills come in."

"Will it be expensive?" She was used to handling large amounts of money at the bank, but that was in a corporate environment. Here at the station, the money almost seemed bigger because the environment was so small and intimate.

"I won't lie to you. The broadcasting equipment will probably cost as much as the van, even if I get some of it on the used market. But look at it this way—God will provide for our needs as long as we use it to glorify Him. Right?"

"Right. Oh, by the way, a guy from Amato and Son called. A first pass at the worship center's design is ready, and he wants to get on your calendar to go over it."

"No kidding? Wow, they must be hard up for business if they got that through so fast. Maybe we're their only client."

Claire thought that was highly unlikely. Amato was the only design firm in the valley, and with the discount store going in and all the people who had come into the bank wanting custom homes, he had to be busy. "Should I set him up for tomorrow?"

"Sure, right after the morning show. Then I can bring the drawings to Gathering on Sunday and get people behind the plan. Somehow seeing something on paper makes it more real than just my running off at the mouth about it."

She'd hardly call his style "running off at the mouth," but his self-deprecating humor was endearing.

"Okay, so." He held up a hand and began counting down on his fingers. "Ten thousand to Cascade Chevrolet for the van, and ten thousand to the Good Shepherd Church for the homeless program—those are the ones we talked about last week. I'll get you their addresses. A thousand to Amato and Son for a deposit on the drawings, and . . . are we missing anybody?"

"Five hundred to the food bank in lieu of my bonus," Claire reminded him.

"Right. If you get those cut today, I can drop off the Amato one and mail the others." He glanced at his watch. "Thirty seconds left. Thanks, Claire."

He spun out of her doorway, and moments later she heard his smooth voice back-calling the previous couple of songs. By now she was used to the rhythm of the station, where conversations happened in multiples of three minutes, and silences fell when Luke was talking, even though the DJ's booth itself was soundproof. It would be just her luck to be yakking on the phone with someone the day Luke forgot to shut the door, and everyone within five counties would hear her in the background.

He came back after launching another song and gave her the addresses of the ministries on his omnipresent yellow sticky notes. If anyone took them away from him, he probably wouldn't be able to function, she thought with a smile as she stuck them to the sides of her monitor and began to prepare the checks.

Okay, one to Pastor Richard Myers, care of Good Shepherd at a P.O. box in some little town across the state line in Idaho, one to Amato, one to the food bank, and one to the Chevy dealership. When the checks printed, she signed her name carefully on each one, not without a sense of happiness.

This was ministry. Not fighting with your hair every morning in the hopes that someone would be impressed with your so-called example and ask a question about what you believed. No, real ministry was supporting the work of God, buying food for people who had none. This was service. This was what God wanted.

Thank heaven for Luke, who had opened their eyes at last.

THE SERGEANT'S PHONE rolled over to his cell and rang twice before he picked it up. "OCTF, Harmon."

"It's Harper."

"You still out there, running up motel bills?"

"Yes, but I've got a good reason. I've tied Brandon Boanerges to Luke Fisher and a character called Richard Brandon Myers, formerly of Hollyweird, California."

"Tied them together as in they're all the same guy?"

"Yes, sir. And I'm seeing a pattern of increasingly serious fraud. First petty crime, then an Internet ministry that led to this lonely hearts thing in our files, and now . . ." Ray's voice trailed off as he tried to think of what Luke Fisher might be up to next.

"Now?" Harmon prompted.

"He's spinning records at a gospel radio station, and I haven't figured out what he's up to." Ray's voice was a little flat. Harmon wasn't going to go for this.

"Christian radio. Harper, did it ever occur to you that maybe the guy saw the light and decided to go straight?"

Ray pinched the bridge of his nose while the plain beige

carpet on his motel room's floor blurred as he closed his eyes. "Yeah, it occurred to me. I just don't think it's likely."

"And why is that?"

Harmon wasn't going to buy it. He wasn't going to let him stay here on the state's dime until he figured out what Fisher was up to.

"Because it's my opinion that this guy Myers, Boanerges, Fisher, whatever you want to call him, is exhibiting the behavior of a sociopath. He doesn't feel emotion, so he can perpetrate these scams on people and just walk away. A sociopath doesn't get a revelation about God and turn over a new leaf, because to him God is just an abstract, like anger or love, which he can't feel. He can't have a relationship with God because he can't feel it. And therefore God won't change his behavior."

"Since when are you a psychologist?" Harmon wanted to know.

"I listen to textbooks on tape, sir. I have the depositions from these women who say that Boanerges was just going through the motions of courtship behavior, that they never really felt that he loved them. That makes a certain personality type try harder to get his attention, which is why he was so successful."

"So, how does this relate to him now? This guy playing Christian music at this station?"

"If his behavior is escalating, I'm thinking he's got something bigger than lonely hearts up his sleeve. I just don't know what it is, yet. Everything he's doing seems to be legit, and he's got the community squarely behind him."

"So, other than sitting around drinking coffee and waiting for him to rob a bank, what's your plan?"

"He's gotten himself involved in this church Ross Malcolm and I have both investigated. You know, the Elect of God."

"Malcolm did the case where the Elder's wife had Munchausen's by Proxy, yeah, and you arrested their head guy, who's a rapist. Nice bunch of people you hang around with."

"They are a nice bunch of people, in the main. So nice that I don't think a guy like Fisher can resist setting them up for something."

"Another week."

"What if that's not enough time? Whatever he's got cooking could take months."

"You're not staying out there for months unless it's on an unpaid leave of absence. Do what you can in another week. Then you're coming back."

"Yes, sir."

"And Harper?"

"Yes, sir?"

"Do your best to nail this guy. I really hate lowlifes masquerading as Christians. It gives us all a bad name."

His boss hung up with his customary abruptness, and Ray blinked in surprise. Five years of working under him and he'd never suspected the good sergeant swung that way.

WHATEVER CLAIRE HAD been expecting when she walked into Gathering at the hall on Sunday, it wasn't the rainbow of color she saw. Mixed in with the holdouts who were not convinced you could just decide that wearing black was no longer a standard of godly behavior were those who embraced this brave new approach wholeheartedly. Linda Bell wore—ouch—orange. All the singles edged toward the new standard in brown, beige, blue, and green. The teenagers had gone all out and sported flowered skirts in hot pink and lime. People who were undecided chose a black skirt with a muted blouse in white or gray.

Clearly the stores in Hamilton Falls, Pitchford, and even Spokane had been raking in the sales this past week as Elect women came out of their closets in droves. Even Rebecca, Claire saw with amazement, wore a pretty silvery gray outfit that complemented her hair perfectly.

"You look lovely," she whispered to Rebecca as she sat next to her.

"Black never did anything for me," Rebecca whispered back. "But there was no point in getting a bad spirit about it, was there, since there were lots of other women in worse shape than I. Poor Julia with her red hair, for instance. That green is very nice on you. It matches your eyes."

Claire had wondered if she would stick out like a sore thumb as the only person wearing color in the entire congregation. But as she'd put on the stylish little mail-order skirt and jacket this morning, she'd told herself that she was supporting Luke and Owen. If they said it was time for a change, then that was good enough for her. It was liberating, in a way, to see her sisters in Christ smiling at each other and passing around compliments like candy. But just in case anyone went overboard, there was always Alma Woods and her little flock of cronies, dressed in black as usual, as though it were a badge of righteousness, and staring daggers at Rebecca.

"I don't think Alma cares for gray," she pointed out, leaning close to Rebecca's ear.

"I don't think Alma cares for anything," Rebecca answered tartly. "She probably thinks eating liver and parsnips is counted unto her for righteousness, too."

Claire stifled a giggle, and the service began. Halfway through the first hymn, the street door opened, and a ripple went through the room as Ray Harper made his way up the aisle, stepped over the knees of four people, including Rebecca, and settled on Claire's other side.

"Hello again," he said.

Claire stopped herself from looking around to see who was staring. "Hello. Hymn 156." She was going to have to have a little talk with him about seating etiquette. Ray couldn't know that by sitting with her in more than one Gathering, he had just declared to everyone present that he was interested in her. Now she would have to fend off the concern of people like Rebecca and Linda Bell, who would feel it necessary to caution her about the dangers of looking Outside.

After testimony time and the closing prayer, Owen announced another hymn. "We're going to sing number 284, 'The Faithful Carpenter,' " he said. "I think it's very appropriate given what Luke is going to talk to us about after the service."

Melanie Bell, who was playing the piano, launched into the opening chords and Owen led them in song.

The carpenter is standing
On a barren plot of ground
But in his mind the house is complete and new.
He uses all his years of skill
To make the foundation sound
Look up, carpenter, the walls must be straight and true.

Her foundations were sound. Even if he decided to become Elect, Ray Harper just wasn't her kind of guy. He was a cop, for one thing, and didn't cops carry guns in order to shoot people? She'd never seen a gun on him, but still. At least he wasn't as intimidating as he used to be. When he'd hugged Dinah the other night, she'd seen he was capable of softness—tenderness, even, for a friend. And now it was somewhat endearing to see the battered leather cover of the hymnbook held so awkwardly in his hands. He had nice hands, she had to give him that, whether they actually held a gun or not.

He's labored all his life
To build a temple unseen
Its walls are strong, its rooms are filled with love.
He invites his Lord to dwell there
Whatever cost it means
Look up, carpenter, and peace will come from above.

Peace was in short supply in her life lately, between the excitement of working for Luke and the unsettled feelings she was having about Ray—not to mention what he was doing to her reputation. But hadn't she been moaning not so

long ago that she needed some stirring up? Did that count
as an answered prayer, too?

Now he stands in that great doorway
That leads to heaven and home
He sees the roofs of those heavenly mansions fair
His journey now is ended
No more on earth to roam
Look up, carpenter, the Savior awaits you there.

As the last notes died away, Luke Fisher walked to the
front with a long roll of paper in one hand. Claire straightened and marshaled her straying thoughts into order. It had
to be the plans for the worship center. What would people
say? Would they get behind the vision, or would they murmur politely and fade away, which was the usual Elect way
of indicating disapproval without actually being accused of
judging their neighbor by saying so.

Luke adjusted the microphone and smiled at the crowd
the way the angel must have smiled at Mary when he told
her the good news about her pregnancy. "God is good," he
said. "Thanks to people who have responded to His prompt-
ings in their hearts, we've been able to make a down payment on a mobile station, give to worthy ministries, donate
to our own food bank, and . . ." He shook out the drawings
and Owen began taping them to the wall behind him.
". . . begin designing the Hamilton Falls Worship Center."
He motioned to the crowd. "Come on up and look. I had
them make multiple copies so everyone could see."

Claire was one of the first to the front, followed closely by

Ray. The drawing showed a huge central hall (*Seating capacity 1,000* said the caption), with a kitchen in one wing and several breakout conference rooms in the other. Down a path were cabins and a smaller building that held gatherings of as many as fifty. There was an administration building with offices and a couple of dormitories (*Capacity 50 beds*). The gathering rooms had fireplaces and large windows that looked out on the lake, and each cabin had its own view.

"This is beautiful," Claire breathed, almost to herself. "No one has ever thought of something like this before. It's amazing."

"He's amazing," Maggie Bell, Linda's widowed sister-in-law, sighed. "You're so lucky to work with him, Claire. I don't know how you get anything done."

Did she think Claire spent her days with her chin in her hand, gazing dreamily through the studio window? "I take my job seriously, that's how," she replied. "To everyone else it may just be accounting, but to Luke it's the Lord's work."

"And you get to help him with it." Maggie shot her a sidelong glance. "So . . . is anything going on between the two of you?"

For half a second, Claire debated. If she said yes, Maggie would back off. But you could guarantee Luke would hear about it, and that would be embarrassing if he didn't feel the same way. If she said no, the field would be wide open. But the field was wide open now. Better to stick to the truth.

"He's very focused on God's work," she said. "So far there hasn't been time for anything else."

"Oh," Maggie said with a rising and falling inflection that told Claire the black-and-white flag had just fallen at the racetrack. Well, the widow was welcome to make a fool of herself if she wanted. Claire still had the inside lane.

"And are *you* just as focused on God's work?"

She practically jumped out of her skin at the low voice behind her. She'd thought Ray had moved on through the crowd after looking at the drawings.

"Of course," she answered. Well, what else could she say?

"No distractions, huh." Though he spoke from just behind her shoulder, he kept his gaze on the drawings hanging in front of them as if they were the most interesting things in the world. They were practically alone in the crowd; Maggie had already drifted purposefully in Luke's direction.

"And what does it matter to you?" she murmured. Her distractions or lack thereof were none of his business.

"It matters," he said.

Oh. Oh, dear. Maybe he did know how seating worked at Gathering. Maybe he'd sat next to her for a reason.

"It does?" *Great, Claire, that was so intelligent.*

Behind her, she felt him shrug. "I just wouldn't want you to get hurt, that's all."

"I don't think there's any danger of that." There was nothing quite as insulting as a guy who just assumed you'd be the one to get dumped and consequently hurt.

He moved beside her and looked at her as though he'd just figured out she was not amused. "I was just letting you know what I thought. As a friend."

Sure, he was. "Good night, Investigator." Head high, in her new bottle-green suit that matched her eyes, definitely not the sort of woman who was in the habit of getting dumped, she walked out of the hall.

"Claire, wait. Please."

She stopped halfway across the parking lot, where scattered groups of people stood talking about the worship center. Some could see how far-reaching Luke's vision could be and what a great thing it would be for the community. Some were stuck in the Elect rut that automatically treated something new as suspicious and even sinful if it wasn't first proposed by a Shepherd.

She turned as Ray caught up with her.

"Look, I didn't mean to offend you." She couldn't see his eyes very well—the streetlights behind him and his shaggy hair combined to hide them—but his tone was contrite. "I'm better at setting up drug deals than talking to pretty women, to tell you the truth."

It had been so long since she'd received an honest-to-goodness compliment from anyone in pants—Luke excepted—that it took the edge off her chilly exit by quite a bit. "Drug deals?"

He fell into step beside her as she walked to her car. "Yeah. With cokeheads the procedure is pretty straightforward. Introduction, buy, takedown. With women, there is no procedure. A guy just takes shots in the dark."

She had to laugh, he was so ingenuous about it. "Women are easy to understand, Ray. No matter what, just give them their own way."

"Yeah, but first you have to find out what that is without looking dumb by asking."

"There's nothing wrong with asking."

"Okay, then, let me ask you this. Do you want to go somewhere and get a piece of pie and some coffee?"

Zing! She hadn't even seen that coming. Or maybe she had. He'd sat with her twice. That was usually a pretty good indicator that a request for a date was forthcoming. The question was, how was she going to answer him? The Elect seemed to have resolved the clothing and hair issues, but no one had brought up the deeper issues of how they might relate to the people for whom they were broadening their horizons.

Put simply, was it now okay to date Outside or not? And for that matter, what about her sister, Elaine? She had married Outside and was struggling to hang on to her salvation. Might things change for her now, too?

But wondering about that wasn't giving Ray an answer. She stopped at her car and unlocked it. "I don't usually go out with Outsiders, Ray."

"It's just coffee. I'm starving and I want some company, that's all."

"But you sat with me. Twice."

He gave her a puzzled look. "Sure. You and Rebecca are the only people I know."

You and Rebecca. Of course. Rebecca had been on her other side both times. Maybe it wasn't a courtship maneuver. Maybe it was just what he said it was.

"What's the big deal?" he asked.

She was going to have to tell him. "Well, this may sound a little weird to you, but in the Elect, if a man sits with a woman on purpose, it's an indication that he's interested in her."

He didn't respond. In fact, he looked a little flummoxed.

"You've sat with me twice now. People are going to start

to talk." She smiled at him cheerfully. "But, of course, you're right—Rebecca and I are the only people you know. If they start teasing me about you, I'll just tell them that."

"Oh, sure." He sounded a little muffled. "We're just friends."

"Exactly."

"So, as just a friend, will you have a piece of pie with me before I starve to death?"

It sounded so harmless. A piece of pie with a friend. An hour in a restaurant with an interesting guy who—face it—would be leaving when his holiday was over. And she hadn't had a date in a year.

Just an hour. Couldn't she have just an hour?

No, she couldn't. Melchizedek's voice sounded in her memory, giving her the reasons why she couldn't move to Seattle. Chief among them was the fact that she was the only example of a single-but-godly woman that the younger girls had. Deep inside she might resent it, like having to do a job she didn't want, but there it was.

"I really can't, Ray. It would set a bad example."

"Come on, it's not like I'm a criminal."

"Of course not. But we're not encouraged to look Outside. If some of the younger girls saw me doing it, they'd be tempted to look Outside, too, and that could lead to bad decisions."

He bowed his head and chewed on the corner of his lip, looking for all the world as if he were coming to some kind of decision.

Or maybe she'd just hurt his feelings. "I'm sorry, Ray. I didn't mean to—"

He lifted his head. "What if I wasn't an Outsider?"

She stopped in mid-sentence. "What?"

"What if I wanted to join your group? Would you have coffee with me then?"

Her mouth opened and closed a couple of times as fragments of sentences blew through her brain.

Ray a convert?

You don't even believe—

I thought you were an atheist—

"I need to talk to someone," he said, even as she tried to wrap her mind around it. "I was hoping it could be you."

Chapter 9

THE WAITRESS put a succulent wedge of black-
berry pie in front of him and Ray thanked his lucky
stars that, if nothing else, the people in Hamilton
Falls knew how to eat. He dug into it with gusto and
watched Claire pick the walnuts off the top of her muffin.

He'd spouted off about joining the Elect as a last-gasp effort to get her attention, and now he was going to have to
keep up the act. He knew from his partner Ross's accounts
of his time investigating the Elect that converts were treated
like gold. An Elect person would do anything if you indicated interest—up to and including having coffee with an
infidel like him.

Ah, well, desperate times meant desperate measures, and if
he had to join this group to get a closer look at what Luke
Fisher was up to, then that's what he'd do. It wasn't like he
was out to hurt anyone with such a cover story. On the contrary, he was out to prevent a whole bunch of people from
getting hurt.

Or maybe just one.

Claire lifted those gorgeous green eyes from their con-
templation of the walnuts. "So, tell me," she said quietly.
"What makes you think the Elect is the path for you?"

Think fast. "I, um, I want to get to know God better. And
you and Rebecca and the others seem to have a handle on
that, so I figure it's the way to go."

"There's a lot of sacrifice involved, Ray." She tore the
muffin in half and buttered it. "We give up our own wills to
serve God."

"Do I have to wear black?" His wardrobe was pretty limited, especially when he was on the road.

She smiled at him, and he watched a tiny dimple dent her
cheek, down at the left corner of her mouth. How had he
not seen that before? "Not anymore, it seems. Did you see
Owen's blue tie with the green stripe?"

He hadn't. "At least he didn't dye his hair purple. And
speaking of green, that suit's a nice color for you." *You silver-
tongued devil, you.*

"Thanks. But it's more than our appearance, Ray. Gathering is three times a week, and that comes first before what
we want to do. Then there's all the places God's people don't
go, such as movies, clubs, theaters."

"I don't get out much anyway."

"You might have to reconsider your choice of career."

Whoa. "What do you mean?"

"I mean, you carry a gun, don't you?"

"Yes. Well, not now. It's in my truck. But in the city I do."

She spread her hands. "You're in law enforcement, and the
possibility exists that you could kill someone."

"I do everything possible to avoid that possibility. Any good cop does."

"But still. You're in a career where it could happen. Not like accounting or teaching or—"

"Radio work."

"Right."

"Okay, I'll take that under advisement. How do I become a member?"

She sighed, and finished the last of the muffin. "That's a problem right now. Normally you'd come to a number of Mission Gatherings, and then the Shepherd would offer you an opportunity to make your choice public. But at the moment we don't have any Shepherds."

"Wait a minute." Cognitive dissonance set up a buzzing in his brain. "Ross told me that a person is born again, begins a relationship with God, and then they go to a church they choose."

"Well, that's the easy way that worldly churches do it, I suppose. In the Elect, the Shepherd would make sure you have the proper understanding of our ways before he gave you the invitation."

"Your ways? But Ross says you just begin a relationship with God. Learn His ways."

"Well, sure. His ways are the ways of the Elect."

"What about other churches' ways?"

"There's only one way, Ray. Jesus laid it down for us, and that's the path we walk in."

" 'Jesus is the Way.' "

"Right. His way is the way the Elect live."

"You're saying two different things."

She sat back, distress shadowing those eyes. "Now, see, this is why you need to come to Gathering. I'm terrible at explaining. The Shepherds give their whole lives to do it, so they know the words to use."

"So, you're saying that because there isn't a Shepherd around, I can't come to Jesus?"

Her face crumpled, and she lost that salesman-like look of animation she'd been trying to hold up. "I don't know, Ray. It sounds terrible when you say it like that, but I suppose that's the way it is."

"Claire, don't you think that's a little wonky? I mean, I don't know a whole lot about it, but I would think it's more of a heart thing. Like the difference between falling in love and going through the marriage ceremony. One's a heart thing, and one's a legal thing."

She propped her elbows on either side of her plate and ran her fingers up into her hair, gripping her head as though there were a buzzing in her brain, too.

"I don't know. Things are changing, and change is good. I totally support Luke and Owen. But I still don't know how the Shepherds can stand in the gateway, saying who gets to be saved or not. Even though we say we're broadening our horizons, I still don't see how people can be saved if things aren't the way they were. And that's a little scary because nobody's talking about it."

He didn't have any answers, either. It was enough of a struggle to get through a day without adding this extra layer of religion on top of everything. Though Ross seemed pretty convinced that a relationship with God made things easier, not more complicated.

One thing was for sure: He was out of his depth, and when you got too deep, there was only one thing to do. Paddle back to shore.

He tossed ten bucks on the table. "Come on. I'll walk you back to your car, okay?"

"I'm sorry," she said miserably as they ambled back down the block. The evening air was cool, giving a not-so-subtle hint that fall was on its way.

He shrugged out of his jacket and draped it around her shoulders. "Don't be. There's a good reason people don't talk about politics and religion over their food."

"But I *should* be able to talk about it. It's all I've ever known . . . and yet, I know so little about it."

"That depends what *it* is, I guess. God's way or the Elect's way."

"Maybe that's the trouble. Maybe I've been taught that they're the same, and now I'm beginning to think they're not. Maybe I want all the rules about clothes and hair and—and where a person lives to just go away so I can do what I want. But how is that doing God's will?" She glanced up at him as they crossed the parking lot to where her car sat all alone. "And if you tell anyone I said that, I'll hunt you down personally and hurt you."

He tried to look harmless and innocent. "I don't know anyone to tell. Besides, my lips are sealed. I never pass on what my friends say to me."

Her gaze dropped to his mouth, as if she were looking to see if his lips really were sealed. Something sizzled through him and he froze in place, gazing into her eyes as if they were enclosed in a bubble and the parking lot, the few cars, the trees planted along the sidewalk had all disappeared into the night.

She swallowed, as though she felt it, too.

No, some part of his brain said incredulously. *Not this girl. Not now.*

"Ray?" His name was a whisper on the charged air.

"Yes?" The word was practically soundless, a question less of her than of the universe or God or whatever combination of events had led him here to this place, this woman, this sudden halt in the carefree cartwheel of his life.

She shook her head. Did she mean she'd forgotten what she'd been going to say? Or was that voice in her head telling her the same thing? *No. Not this man. Not now.*

There was only one thing to do.

In a single smooth movement, he leaned down, tilted her chin up with the tips of his fingers, and captured that sweet mouth with his.

CLAIRE WASN'T THE most experienced girl on the block, but she'd had a boyfriend or two in the past and she knew what she was doing in the kissing department.

Or so she'd thought.

Single women outnumbered Elect men by such a wide margin that every guy knew he could move on and have another girlfriend by the next Sunday Gathering. Steady dating often involved a careful strategy of mind games, wrestling skills, and the political savvy of a gubernatorial candidate.

But now none of that seemed relevant. Ray's kiss was simply *Hello*.

Hers was *I don't know you.*

His became *Let me show you.*

And oh, hers was *Yes*—

"Hey, hey, hey! We're in the right place for the love of God, but this is going too far."

The laughing baritone popped them apart as though they were spring-loaded, and if Claire hadn't caught herself against the rear fender of her car, she might have staggered backward and fallen over. Ray reached for her arm to steady her, and dropped it once he saw she was going to stay upright.

"PDAs, Claire." Owen Blanchard followed Luke, carrying a box of hymnbooks. His kids, Hannah and Ryan, trailed behind him carrying the roll of designs between them. They were giggling at her. "Public Displays of Affection aren't the best way to show your example." His words held a rebuke, but he was smiling as if he, too, could remember kissing in public. Sometime back before dinosaurs became extinct.

"What are you guys still doing here?" Her face felt the same flaming red as a traffic light. Could they see it in the darkness?

"Just talking." Luke eyed Ray up and down, and the latter stepped between her boss and herself.

"So were we."

"That wasn't how it looked from our perspective." Luke grinned and Claire could see Ray's hand clench.

"No matter how it looked, it's none of your business. Stop teasing her. Can't you see she's embarrassed?"

Luke's smile didn't falter. "Well, now, one of the first things we learn as God's children is that if you keep right with Him, you don't embarrass yourself by your actions."

Claire opened her mouth to say something—anything—but Ray beat her to it.

"She hasn't done anything to be ashamed of. You're laying shame on her, pal, and I'd appreciate it if you'd keep it to yourself."

"It's all right, Ray." She laid a hand on his arm and found the muscles under his shirt were rigid. She swung his jacket off her shoulders and held it out, and he was forced to break eye contact with Luke in order to take it from her. "Thanks for this."

"You're welcome. And it's not all right with me. I don't get why you're not telling him off."

"Luke and Owen are just looking out for me."

"By using shame tactics?"

"Ray, please."

"Okay." His mouth closed on a grim line.

Owen unlocked his car a few spaces away and popped the trunk. The box of hymnbooks made a heavy *thunk* as they landed. He opened the car doors and the kids scrambled inside, Ryan buckling his little sister into her car seat.

"I'll meet you and Mark at the bank in the morning, then," Owen said, handing the roll of drawings to Luke. "With the collateral we put up and the contributions from your listeners, the sale should be pretty straightforward."

"Sale?" Ray asked.

"Please keep this confidential." Owen looked from Ray to Claire. "Claire, you'll be involved because of your position.

Mark and I have decided to offer our homes as collateral for the loan."

"We'll own the land and construction can start right away." Luke's voice held barely contained excitement. "The Lord has been moving in strong and unmistakable ways, calling both Mark and Owen to this task."

"My goodness." Claire fished in her purse for her keys. "I hadn't realized we were so close to getting started. That's wonderful. Well, good night, all."

Luke moved a few steps closer. "See you bright and early tomorrow?"

She looked up from the pit of darkness that was her handbag. "Of course." Didn't he always?

"I was thinking we should get together before my show and go over a few things. Say, over breakfast?"

"Um . . ." Her mind went blank. Aside from the "welcome to the station" lunch, he wasn't in the habit of asking her out for meals. After the show he was always wired and buzzing with energy. He usually took off, drumming up advertising for the station or taking informal polls on the street or going to the big music warehouse in Pitchford to troll for new music—doing the zillions of tasks that went into the seamless production that was his show. Meals with the accounting manager didn't usually fit in with that level of activity.

"We need to talk." Luke's voice was always filled with music and humor, but there in the parking lot, she detected something new. A hint of intimacy. A note that told her he maybe didn't want to talk about fundraising strategies or music.

Oh my.

Ray said something under his breath and then cleared his throat. "See you around, Claire." He turned and strode up the street, his long legs making short work of the blocks that lay between here and wherever he was staying. Maybe he had better things to do than stand around in parking lots talking to her and her friends. Cop things. Even vacation things. Things that mattered. Not whether or not she was going to have breakfast with her boss.

"Claire? What do you think? Is seven A.M. at the diner too early?"

She brought her mind back with an effort. "No, it's fine. See you then." Her fingers finally closed around her car keys, and she unlocked the door.

"I'm looking forward to it," he said.

She had the distinct feeling he meant it a little more than your average boss should.

An hour later, showered, moisturized, and blow dried, Claire lay in bed and watched the branches of the tree outside the window make patterns on the wall.

You kissed a worldly man.

Her brain was taking this a lot harder than her body. The latter had given in with hardly a murmur, falling into Ray's kiss with the ease of water leaping over a waterfall. Her brain, meanwhile, kept hearing Luke and Owen's smiling admonishments. They were right. What would the kids think? What would other people think when they found out, as they surely would? How could she have been so careless as to kiss a worldly man right out there in public—and in the mission hall parking lot, no less? She was lucky Alma Woods hadn't been behind a tree watching. She would have had to kiss her reputation good-bye.

But it had been wonderful, sighed her body.

A lot of help you are. Go to sleep.

Because if he really meant it about joining the Elect, then everything was different, wasn't it? If Ray wanted to come to God, there would be nothing standing in the way of a relationship.

Nothing but Luke and probably half a dozen members of the No Pride Club, who would trample her in the stampede for the attention of another eligible man.

Not that Ray would have anything to do with them. He was too honest. He would know when a woman just wanted him for arm candy, wouldn't he? Besides, he had his career to think about. In Seattle. Where she wasn't allowed to go unless she wanted to disobey a Shepherd and by extension, God.

On that disturbing thought she finally fell asleep, but in her dreams Ray and Luke were paddling kayaks on the Hamilton River, trying to get to her as she was swept along by the current. She soon saw it was more important to them that one beat the other to where she flailed along on the surface, as though it were a race and she was the finish line.

Neither of them was actually thinking about rescuing her.

THE EARLY BIRD might not get the worm, but he certainly got the coffee, the menus, and a hefty dish of sliced fruit. Judging from the goofy smile on the waitress's face, Claire figured that last item wouldn't be showing up on the bill. She slid into a chair opposite Luke, and the waitress came back to pour her a fresh cup of java.

"Nice outfit," Luke said as she put her purse on the floor beside her chair.

"Thanks." The soft periwinkle-blue jacket and the matching flowered skirt were the farthest from black she'd been able to come. So far. Experiments with color were turning into a community event—on the female side, anyway. Some were disastrous, such as Linda Bell's orange wraparound dress, and some were great, such as this little number. But when you'd never worn anything but black, how were you to know what looked good with your personal skin tone and hair color unless you tried?

She ordered an omelet with everything—even at this hour, breakfast was her favorite meal. Then she realized that Luke's gaze lay on her, as warm as a comforting hand.

Except that she didn't feel very comfortable.

She sipped coffee and wondered what was on his mind. "So." *Just dive right in.* "To what do I owe this honor?"

Luke forked up a couple of banana slices and a purple grape from the fruit dish. "After last night, I think you know."

"If I knew, I wouldn't be asking."

He smiled. "Okay. I'll spell it out for you. The Elders approved the design for the worship center unanimously, with a few little tweaks that I'll take back to Anton Amato today. After the sale goes through, thanks to Mark and Owen, we'll come to the fun part—the actual clearing of the land and building. That's where you come in. I'm going to need you to—what?"

Claire set her cup down carefully enough so that it only rattled a little. "The worship center?"

"Yes. What else?"

Would she ever learn? Had she really dressed in her very best to hear about the worship center? Not that that wasn't a worthy cause, and one she was probably about to devote most of her working hours to, but she'd expected . . .

Come on, Claire, admit it.

Okay. She'd expected him to read her a little lecture on the dangers of kissing in parking lots, and then tell her that the reason he cared so much was because he was interested in her himself.

You are so lame.

Who did she think she was? Did she seriously believe that every eligible man in town—and some who were the farthest thing from eligible—was going to fall at her feet just because she was feeling alone and achingly available?

"Claire?"

Could she just hide in the diner's restroom for the rest of her life, please? "Nothing, Luke." The waitress brought their plates and she dug into the steaming omelet. "Go on about the plans. I'm dying to hear."

"The Elders and I are meeting with the Realtor to finalize the sale. Whatever money we bring in this week is dedicated to the down payment. I'm going to change the prayer program so that for a gift of a hundred bucks, the listener can not only call, but can send in a written prayer and have it read on the air. It'll be more than what we were doing before—every quarter hour around the clock. Toby's going to cover his shift and we might even ask you to take a shift, too, until God gives us what we need."

Four hundred dollars an hour times eighteen hours a day times seven days a week equaled—well, glory to God is what it equaled.

Wait a minute.

"Me? Take a shift? Are you crazy? I don't know anything about doing a show." She put her fork down and stared at him.

He waved off her objections with one hand. "It's a snap. One session and you'll have it down. All you'll have to do is play the CDs, back-call them, then read the prayers on the quarter hour. Simple."

"Luke, I've never played a CD in my life. I'm still getting used to having the radio on in the car and my kitchen."

"I have every confidence in your brains." He speared a sausage with gusto and pointed it at her. "Anyone who can crunch numbers can work the CD decks."

"What if something goes wrong and all I do is produce dead air?"

Dead air, she'd learned, was the disconcerting silence on the airwaves that indicated someone in the studio had forgotten to slide up the lever on the mixing board that modulated the power to the microphone. Toby sometimes got distracted and forgot to do it, but so far Luke had not. He was too much of a pro. Which was another reason this was crazy.

As if he'd heard her doubts, he leaned toward her. "Claire, we need to work together on this. Toby and I can't put in twelve-hour shifts, and with the amount of money that I suspect will be coming in, we can't hire someone temporary. We need people onsite that we can trust."

"What about a premade tape?" Oh, good thinking. Surely technology would get her out of this predicament.

"We'll be doing those, too, for when we all have to be off-site or doing other things. But tapes have time limits. Come on, Claire. You'll be fabulous. Your voice is made for radio. In fact—" He sat back, looking as inspired as if a light had gone on in his mind. "—why don't you guest with me this morning? After you've counted the gifts, of course," he added hastily. "I don't want to hinder you from doing your part of God's work."

"Why don't we wait and see how that goes," she suggested. Even if only five dollars came in, she'd make sure she was so absorbed in entering it in the database that there wouldn't be time for him to teach her how to operate the microphone.

She glanced at her watch. "Luke, look at the time! It's nearly eight."

If she'd expected him to leap to his feet and dash off to work, she was mistaken. He shrugged. "Toby will stay on duty until I show up."

"But people expect your show to start at eight. You said yourself you like people to start their day with praise."

"Relax, Claire. Don't be so anal." His grin flashed. "Besides, this is all work-related. Technically, your day started at seven. Charge the station for the overtime."

"I can't do that. And I'm not anal."

"Okay. You're conscientious."

"You make it sound like a bad thing. In the bank, a per-

son would lose her job if she wasn't." Maybe it was the coffee. Maybe it was coming this close to totally embarrassing
herself. Or maybe she was just a tiny bit confused about his
attitude. "Besides, people are depending on you."

"It's radio, Claire, not life support."

"But you said—"

"I hope you don't memorize everything I say. I'd hate to
think what might come back to haunt me later. Here, have
some more coffee and let's talk."

She didn't want to talk. His lighthearted attitude stung.
She had walked in here with anticipation, feeling fairly
cheerful despite her lack of sleep. Now she just felt confused
and a little annoyed and, yes, a bit let down and defensive.

"No, thanks. I'm going by the post office and then to
work." She found her purse and pulled her wallet out.

"Don't even think about it." He stood and pulled his own
wallet out of his back pocket. "The station is picking it up.
Here, I'll walk out with you."

But by the time he'd taken care of the bill, she'd already
escaped out the door.

At the post office the clerk had to bring the station's mail
in a plastic bin instead of just handing it to her. "What are
you guys selling, lottery tickets?" she asked as she pushed it
across the counter.

"Listen to KGHM sometime and find out." Claire
dredged up a public-relations smile, tossed her purse in the
bin, and lugged everything across the street to the station.
Luckily, Toby met her at the door and held it open.

"Looks like the junk mail people finally found us," he
said, peering into the bin as she squeezed past him.

"It's not junk mail. It's money."

He took the bin from her and carried it into her office. "What, all this?" Together they sorted the contents into piles. He took the FCC and radio-geek stuff, which hardly made a dent, and Claire stared at the rest, hands on hips.

"I guess I'll just start at the top and work my way through it. At least I won't be guesting on Luke's show." She glanced at Toby as he stood in her doorway, thumbing through his little pile of envelopes. "I assume he's talked to you about the changes to the prayer program?"

"The every-quarter-hour thing? Yes. People have seemed pretty receptive to it so far."

"He wants me to do a show." She still felt a little incredulous. "I don't even know how to turn the mic on."

"If things keep up like this, you won't have time to do a show." He looked up from his mail. "Just take one thing at a time. We don't have to fall in with every single thing Luke suggests, you know. This isn't a dictatorship."

"But he's the reason the station came back to life." Then she realized how that must have sounded to Toby, who had been manning the mic for years before anyone had even heard of Luke. "I'm sorry, Toby, I didn't mean to imply—"

"It's okay, I know what you mean. He has revitalized it. He's tapped into a need I didn't even know was there."

"Has he come to speak to your church?" she asked. "Attendance has gone up at our Gatherings. Of course, that might be because things have loosened up a bit."

Toby turned toward the door. "No, he hasn't."

His voice sounded muffled, but Claire couldn't figure out

why he looked so uncomfortable. "Why not? He's a great speaker."

He hesitated, then came back in and closed her door. "How close are you to Luke?"

Close? Did he mean as in working relationship or as in . . . something more personal? "Um . . ."

"You seem pretty loyal."

"Well, I am. But I'm just as loyal to you. We're all in this together, aren't we? The station doesn't succeed without all of us."

"I wonder."

She reached under her desk to turn the computer on, and when it hummed into life, she turned back to him. "Toby, what's the matter? Don't worry about me saying anything. I used to work for the bank, remember? There, even going to the restroom is confidential."

His smile was a brief stretch of the lips. "My wife says I'm crazy, and maybe I am. What do you think of Luke? As a person. As a godly man."

Claire gazed at him while she tried to come up with an answer. What did she think? Or was she too busy being dazzled by his talent and leadership to think?

"He's very good at what he does," she said at last.

"I won't argue with you there. And it looks as though changes are afoot in your church, though I don't know if that has anything to do with Luke."

"It has a lot to do with him. We're allowed to wear color now. And listen to music. And Luke is always talking about widening our horizons to include other believers."

"Like me?" He smiled at her.

"I hope so." What would it be like if Toby were invited to speak at Mission? The Elect were capable of change, but that would probably stretch them so far they'd snap.

"But what about him, personally?" Toby pressed. "What's your opinion there?"

If she answered him, maybe she'd get to the bottom of whatever was bothering him. Of course, that meant she actually had to have an answer. "I don't really know. I like him. He's entertaining and never boring. He's good-looking, of course. But other than that he was raised Elect, I don't actually know all that much about him."

"Exactly." Toby brought a gentle fist down on the corner of her desk for emphasis. "We don't know a thing about him. Not his religious history, not his radio shows, not his hometown, family, nothing. All we know is what we've seen, starting on the day he arrived."

"He must have given you a résumé when you hired him," she pointed out.

"Yes, and when I called his references, they checked out. But he says he's been on national radio shows. When I researched them, I couldn't find anything."

"But if you were looking on the Internet, stuff goes out of date and gets archived all the time."

He twinkled at her. "I thought using the Internet was discouraged among the Elect."

She lifted her chin. "The bank is online. It was part of my job."

Laughter lurked in his eyes, but as always with Toby, it was never directed *at* you, but *with* you. *Unlike Luke*, she thought suddenly. That was what had been wrong this morning. He hadn't said anything mean or unkind, but it was the way he said it. As though he couldn't be bothered to think about whether it would hurt her feelings or not.

"What's on your mind?" Toby must have seen her thoughts turn inward.

"I'm just being oversensitive." Which was another word for *self-centered*, which was a sin.

"I doubt that. Tell me."

She shrugged. "It's nothing." It was almost as if he had been off duty, and didn't have to be . . . as Toby had said . . . a "man of God." But it didn't work that way. Either you were godly, or you weren't. It wasn't a part-time job.

"I'd better get back to work." Claire glanced at her computer screen and with the mouse brought up her receipts database.

Toby opened her door, and Claire gathered their meeting was over. "Me, too," he said. "But I'm going to take the advice of Jesus, and watch and pray."

Praying she could understand. Claire reached over and scooped up the first batch of envelopes. But watching? What for? And whom?

Chapter 10

A T O N E T I M E , Ray had liked his truck. It was sleek, unobtrusive, and had the horsepower to get him where he was going in a hurry. But now that he was spending inordinate amounts of time sitting in it, staring at the radio station's windows from various vantage points up and down Main Street, he was discovering its faults.

Its legroom was shrinking by the day, for one. He shifted around and hung his left arm out the open window. Part of the problem this morning was probably due to the four point five hours of sleep he'd managed to get when he wasn't staring into the dark, thinking about Claire Montoya.

He was thirty-two years old and that kiss in the parking lot two nights ago had transported him back to the age of seventeen, when a kiss had been a mind-bending event. And what made it worse was that he had no business kissing her if he was going to make an arrest and ride off into the sunset, the way he'd meant to when he arrived in Hamilton Falls. What was it about this place that sucked a man in and glued him here? What was it about these women—Julia, Dinah, and Claire—who got to a guy and made him want to love, honor, and protect when common sense urged him to save himself and run?

Ray sighed and resumed his glassy stare at the station's largest window while on the radio the late, great Johnny Cash asked whether the circle would be unbroken. One of the few good things about this town—besides the pie at the diner and Claire Montoya's green eyes—was that Luke Fisher had better taste in music than he'd expected. Even the Christian stuff was starting to grow on him.

Some of the lyrics reflected things he'd thought about off and on. Just this morning, Five Wise, who put out pretty decent swing, had sung,

I'm just living my life, Lord,
Trying to do what's right.
Tell me why that's not good enough
To make me clean in Your sight.

He could relate to that. He wasn't so sure about the next verse, though, which had something to do with the love of God pulling a person close and washing them clean. But the one verse pretty much described him. Just trying to do the right thing. That should be enough, shouldn't it?

A look at his watch told him Claire would be coming out any minute to carry the daily take over to the bank. But today the minutes dragged on and she didn't appear. At ten past noon, Fisher came bounding down the steps, and jogged down the block to the parking lot as if he had somewhere important to go. Finally, at five past one, just about when he was going to storm the door to find out what was going on, she came out with a fat envelope under her arm.

He watched her cross the street to the bank, where a dark-haired woman met her at the door with a big smile and escorted her in. Exactly how much was in that envelope? Was that why Fisher had looked so happy?

He pushed open the door, locked the truck behind him, and strolled in the direction of the bank. But instead of the usual fifteen-minute transaction, it took forty-five. Ray had memorized the titles of every book in Quill and Quinn's window display by the time Claire came out again.

For a guy who would rather listen than read, that was saying something.

"Ray." Claire stopped beside him, sounding as if she were glad to see him. "Looking for a book?"

Everything in the window had a title that related to birds somehow. *A Nest of Sparrows. SisterChicks on the Loose. Boo Who.* Dinah's chickens must be going to Rebecca's head.

"No," he said. "I was waiting for you. Do you have time for lunch?"

She glanced over her shoulder at the station's window. "We're pretty busy today."

At least she wasn't thinking about Fisher, whose dust had long since settled. "Come on. You have to eat, and the diner is fast. A sandwich on me?"

A smile broke over her face and the tension inside him that had been winding tight relaxed. "That sounds great."

RAY APPRECIATED a woman who could eat. As she demolished her Reuben in between dunking her home-style fries in a little pot of ketchup, he ate his Philly cheese steak and watched her.

"What are you smiling at?" she wanted to know around a bite of corned beef. "I'm starving. Give me a break, here."

"Must have been a busy day."

She rolled her eyes. "You're not kidding. Guess how much the deposit was just now?"

"I'm almost afraid to."

She leaned toward him, lowering her sandwich and her voice. "Twenty-five thousand, six hundred and forty-eight dollars," she whispered. "And fifty-five cents."

"People send cents?" he whispered back.

She sat back and said in a normal tone, "You'd be surprised what they send. And that's just the money. Tons of them send gifts to Luke—four potholders and a tea cozy today. Thank goodness I figured out how to do mail merge and generate thank-you letters. We have to acknowledge people's kindness somehow when we send the receipt."

"I have a suggestion on a related but different subject." Something had been cooking in his brain since Luke had shown the worship center's design to the congregation and broached his mind-boggling plan. It had been overshadowed by kissing Claire, but it was part of the reason for the four point five hours of sleep.

"What?" She dunked another fry and ate it with satisfaction.

"Why don't we go out to the site of the worship center this afternoon and have a look around? That probably qualifies as one of the sights of Hamilton Falls."

She stopped chewing and stared at him.

"It's up at the end of the lake," he went on, "so it can't be more than an hour away. Less, if I give my engine a workout."

She swallowed her fry. "Ray, I can't leave work in the middle of the day to go gallivanting across the country. I have responsibilities."

"I know. But this is work-related. Bring along a camera and take some pictures for the before-and-after display."

"What display?"

"You know, the ones they always have in the foyer so people can see what their money—their gifts, I mean—have accomplished. You need something to tell people about in your thank-you notes, too."

Thoughtfully, she dunked another fry. "Hmm. I don't even know where the site is."

"I do. The lot numbers were on the design, so I looked it up at the county recorder."

"I'll tell you what. I'll slip out a little early, say around four. Meet you at my place then?"

He'd have to be satisfied with that. "Deal."

BY FOUR-FIFTEEN, they were speeding down the highway (well, "speeding" was relative; he *always* drove ten miles over the legal limit) with the lake on their right.

"Dinah used to live down there." Claire pointed at one of the exits after they'd crossed the river on a metal bridge that made the tires sing.

"I know—I went out there to arrest Phinehas, remember?"

"Oh, right. Dinah kept one of the river lots, but Elsie sold the rest. Made a fortune, according to Linda Bell—her brother-in-law is a Realtor. A bunch of execs from the new discount store are building houses out there now."

"Far from the madding crowd, eh? Can't say I blame them. If I worked in that place, I'd be hitting the door at a dead run every day at five o'clock."

She grinned and rolled the window down so that the breeze blew in. The day was a little cloudy and felt close, as though there'd be rain by late afternoon. Probably not the best day for a hike by the lake, but at least he was alone with Claire, with no possibility of Luke popping up like a jack-in-the-box to dish out the Elect's particular brand of shame.

About which he was still burned on her behalf.

Or maybe he just couldn't stand the guy. Luke could give her a compliment and Ray would probably get just as burned.

"Crazy Jack Road." Claire pointed at a sign up ahead. "Turn left there."

She didn't seem to mind the silence. In fact, she seemed to be enjoying the ride, with her face tipped into the wind and a little smile curving her lips. As if she'd heard him thinking, she glanced over.

"Sorry, I'm not much of a conversationalist. Look there. Turn here. Would it help if I told you Crazy Jack Road was named for a miner who staked a claim up there?"

"Would it help if I told you I didn't mind a bit? One of the things I like about you is that I don't feel 'on' all the time. Like a performing monkey or something."

She giggled, an enchanting sound that made him decide he needed to hear it again.

"No one would ever confuse you with a monkey."

"Tell that to my boss sometime."

Another sideways glance, longer this time. "Do you like police work?"

Spinning the wheel to make the left turn on the crazy miner's road, he nodded. "Yeah, I do. The OCTF is a state agency, so we have a lot of jurisdictional freedom. Which is why I can come here to testify on one case and stick around to investigate anoth—" He cut himself off, resisting the urge to smack himself on the forehead. What had he almost said?

"Oops, watch the pothole." Thanks to the road, his slip had gone right past her. He dodged the gaping hole in the road and straightened the truck out. Pines and long grasses, burned to a lifeless gold by the heat of summer, whipped past the windows.

"We should see the lake again over that hill." She pointed. "This bit of land kind of sticks out into it. Have you ever shot anyone?"

Yow. Talk about dodging conversational potholes.

"Not with the OCTF, no. But when I was on traffic detail years ago, I made the mistake of stopping a carload of crackheads for having no working taillights on their '86 Toyota. They pulled a gun and took off, and I discharged my firearm trying to stop the car. Unfortunately the bullet hit the gas tank."

"Oh, no."

"Oh, they all survived. It's not like in the movies where there's a big explosion and everyone gets blown to bits. They all piled out of the car. The driver fired at me, though, and I returned fire. He died in the OR."

"I'm sorry, Ray." Her voice was quiet. Really quiet. He'd probably shocked her stockings off.

"Yeah, me, too. I spent nine months with the in-house shrink. It wasn't fun."

" 'Thou shalt not kill,' " she said to the window.

"I believe that. But I also believe in 'Thou shalt not be killed.' I did what I had to do to save my life."

They crested the hill, and the lake spread out in front of them, a changing kaleidoscope of blue and gray as clouds scudded across the sky and the breeze kicked up a chop on the water. Twenty minutes brought them to a dirt track with a For Sale sign tacked on the fence. He coasted to a stop.

"This is it. Can you see if the gate will open?"

She hopped out and pulled off the loop of chain, swung open the gate until he drove through, then closed it again. When she got back in, it was clear the subject of shooting people was closed. "I wonder what the architects have in mind for the gate? Can't you just see something welcoming in stone and wood?"

It was hard to see anything but the long stretch of grass,

bush, and pine trees as the land sloped away to the lake. His truck handled the dirt road easily, taking the turns in low gear and blowing a plume of dust behind them on the straightaways. "They'll have to do a lot of work on the access," he said. "I can't see the family motor home negotiating some of these potholes."

Another sign at a fence told them they were on private property. Ray shoved the truck into park and got out. Claire joined him, looking over the barbed wire.

"Are you game for a little trespassing?"

"Technically, we own it, don't we?" She pulled a little camera out of her jacket pocket and snapped a long shot that took in most of the view. "Or we will as soon as the deal goes through. I'm not sure about the financial details. That's the Elders' business. Is the station buying it? A couple of private partners? It won't be the Elect, that's for sure."

"What do you mean?" He separated two lethal-looking strands of barbed wire and indicated she should slip between them.

"We're not a registered religious body," she explained from the other side, holding the wire for him. "Just a group of people who believe in God. So, we can't make purchases in the group's name."

Okay. Whatever. "They could buy it as a partnership. That happens all the time. A group of guys gets together and buys a fishing cabin, then they split up the time each one gets to vacation there."

"Maybe." She stood with her hands on her hips, scanning the landscape. "Where do you suppose the worship center is going to go?"

"It looked to me as if they were going to incorporate the creek somehow. The cabins were planted alongside it, and then the auditorium part was between the creek and the lake."

"So, over there." She aimed the camera at a swampy area where the pine trees left off and cattails and willows began, and took another shot. "I hope they plan to drain a lot of this."

He did, too. "I hope they plan to raise a lot of money. It's going to take more than twenty-five grand just to dry things out."

The last part of the hike consisted of leaps from hillock to hillock of ground solid enough to support grass, and ducking under willow branches. By the time they got to the spot where the auditorium was supposed to be, Ray was sweating, scratched, and sporting a nice collection of mosquito bites. Claire hadn't fared much better. Worse, probably, because the willows had pulled her neat hairdo to shreds, and because she was wearing a denim skirt that gave the mosquitoes more real estate on which to land.

"I swear, I'm going to get my hair cut off," she grumbled, pulling out pins, raking her fingers through it and pinning it up again. He couldn't exactly see the improvement, but what did he know? "If I'm wearing color now, how much worse can a new hairstyle be?"

Ray wisely kept his mouth shut.

"This must be it." She gave up on her hair, moved to the side about ten inches, shook the water out of her shoe, and looked at him. "Right? We're standing where the auditorium will be?"

"As far as I can tell." They looked over the marsh together. "Maybe it's not what we think. I could have the scale wrong. After all, a quarter inch to a foot is standard, but maybe it was an inch or something. That would put the auditorium up there, on that slope." He pointed.

"Yes, but then the cabins wouldn't be near the creek, they'd be in the trees. You're sure they were along the creek?"

"Yup. So, we are right. I'm no builder, though. What do I know about drainage? The contractor probably looks at this and thinks it's a piece of cake."

"More like stew." Claire shook her wet sneaker again. "Yuck. Come on, let's go poke around in the trees. I'd rather swat flies than mosquitoes any day."

A brisk hike up the slope brought them to a granite outcrop that had broken down over time to produce a tumble of boulders. Ray scrambled up on one and reached down to pull Claire up beside him. They sat on its flat top, legs swinging, and surveyed the site.

"This is my last shot." She took the picture and the camera buzzed as it rewound. "The view of the lake is beautiful."

"It is from up here. The mosquitoes down there kind of spoil it for me."

She nodded. "You've got to believe the Elders know what they're doing. It must be workable or they wouldn't have approved something that's never been done in the Elect before. We don't believe in church buildings, you know. The Mission Hall is just a room with a roof. Nothing fancy."

No organization, no building, no written rules . . . How did these people function? Not that it mattered to him. If he were going to approach God, he'd do it out in the woods and look up into the sky through the trees. Or maybe he'd cruise Ross's church one evening and see what the big attraction was.

"Didn't Luke say they'd be renting out the space for corporate retreats and whatnot? So, it's not as though it's a building strictly for worship. But still . . ." He gazed at the view. At the marsh and the water. At the absence of surveyors' stakes or septic lines. "It's going to be a huge job. So is paying for it."

"That's what the prayer pledges are for. The down payment."

"Yeah, I heard. Prayer every quarter hour with your donation." He glanced at her. "Doesn't that strike you as mercenary?"

"It's all God's work," she said. "Though I do think we need to be good stewards and focus our efforts. I don't see how we can give to homeless shelters and have a mobile station and build a worship center, too. At least, not to start. Maybe later."

"You're giving to homeless shelters?"

She nodded. "That ten thousand would probably have bought the gate and a few feet of driveway. Not that I have any idea what those things cost. But I suppose I will when the estimates start coming in. We have to hire a building contractor. I'm going to need to set up accounts." She clutched her head in mock dismay. "So much work, and here I sit on a rock, doing nothing!"

"But Claire, why do you have to deal with this? You work for KGHM, not whatever corporation will be formed to run the business."

She nodded and her makeshift chignon began to unravel again. "I don't know. Since Luke is spearheading it and I work for Luke, I just assumed I'd handle it."

"Well, money to support the station is one thing. Money to support the Elect's community efforts is another. I'd be careful to keep them separate."

"Toby looks after the funds for running the station."

"Will his church be getting a cut of some of it?"

She frowned and relocated some hairpins. "If he asked, I suppose it would. We're supposed to broaden our horizons, but it's hard to change people's minds when a hundred years of preaching has said that other churches are worldly and deceived. Personally, I don't see someone like Toby that way."

"So you figure what the Elect collect, the Elect can disburse?"

"No, of course not. The homeless outreach in Idaho wasn't affiliated with the Elect at all. God brought the need to Luke's attention, and we sent off a check, no questions asked."

"How?"

A sidelong glance. "By mail, of course."

"Very funny. How did God bring it to his attention?"

"I have no idea. His job is to reach the people. My job is to cut the check."

"No auditing? No approval? Just like that?"

"I sent a letter with it requesting a receipt. My goodness, Ray, you are such a cynic. Don't you trust anything?"

I trust you. I trust your faith in people. But that's about it. "I'm not in a job that promotes trust except in my team. Sometimes that can mean the difference between life and death."

"Trust in God is like that, too."

"I'd rather trust in something I can see, thanks. Like a partner."

"I see God all the time. In people."

"In the Elect. Yeah, I gathered that."

"No, not just them. In Toby. In Ross, and the way he loves Julia and Kailey. God is alive and breathing all around me. That's why prayer is such a great thing. I can see Him and talk to Him, too."

Maybe it was the location. Maybe it was the company. But in a flash of self-analysis, Ray looked at his obstinate refusal to have anything to do with God and saw it for what it was: loss. He didn't have this. What he had was an emptiness he was trying to soothe with work and socializing and friends, covering it over with a cynical outlook on life so people wouldn't see it. He was doing what his dad had done after his mom had left—covering up his real feelings so people wouldn't think he was weak.

"Does a person have to be Elect to have a direct line to God?" he asked.

Claire opened her mouth to reply, then seemed to change her mind about what she'd been about to say. "I don't think so. And I don't even think it's a sin to say that. If I say I can see God in Toby, it's obvious he's a praying person, too. How can the Elect say other people's prayers don't even reach the ceiling?"

"They say that? Even mine, if I were to give it a try?"

"Don't let what the Elect say stop you, Ray. Don't wind up like me."

Which, when it came down to it, was about as honest an answer as he could hope to get.

Chapter 11

S HE SHOULD NEVER have said that. All the way home, sitting in Ray's truck and listening to Toby read the six o'clock news, Claire kicked herself. No matter what she did, she only managed to give an unfavorable view of the Elect's way of life, thus pushing Ray farther and farther away.

Which, of course, was what she was supposed to do from a personal standpoint. Despite all the changes, the fact remained that he was an Outsider who was going to leave town one of these mornings, while she was stuck here until she was as shriveled as an unwanted apple. She'd never see him again except maybe twenty years from now at the weddings of Ross and Julia's kids. They'd look at each other and remember a kiss in a dark parking lot and think, *Look what I was saved from.*

"Lord, what wilt Thou have me to do?" Saul's prayer on the road to Damascus came into her mind as she gazed out the window. The promise of the clouds and wind had turned

into the reality of rain, and the wipers slapped back and forth.

She should just cut bait and stop torturing herself. Ray, funny and appealing and completely wrong about everything that was important to her, had to go. Now, if she could just find the guts to tell him so and get on with her life.

Such as it was.

If Luke's ministry took off the way it promised, she would get great exposure. People in radio would know her name. Maybe she could convince Owen that her place was in Seattle or Spokane, enlarging the boundaries of the kingdom, and then maybe the narrow little puddle that was her life would turn into a bigger lake of possibility.

They passed the enormous construction site where the apple processing plant had been and where now the steel and concrete structure of the discount store was going up. Maybe in a few weeks the worship center's site would look like that.

A few minutes later, Ray slowed the truck to take the turn into Gates Place. "Well, I can't say this has been the best day ever." He spun the wheel and came to a gentle stop in Rebecca's driveway. Claire deflated even further. Two of Dinah's chickens, wet but determined to get the last of the bugs under the rose bushes, ran from the truck and took shelter under a shrub near the door.

"Between the mosquitoes and the swamp and the rain, I really know how to show a girl a good time." He leaned on the steering wheel and faced her. "Sorry about that."

She had to stop taking things so personally. "Don't be

sorry. This was a business meeting, remember? A girl expects a little adversity."

He laughed and something in his eyes made her scramble for the words to the "I-can't-see-you-anymore" speech. She opened her mouth to say the words—*Ray, this was fun, but I can't go out with you*—and instead heard herself say, "Do you want to come in for a hot drink?"

"Sure."

And by the time he'd jumped out and come around to open her door her opportunity had passed.

She'd find a way to work up to it again. She had to. Because she couldn't go on like this, feeling the blood jump in her veins every time she saw him on the street, feeling her face heat when he looked at her. Next thing you knew, she'd be dreaming about him and doodling his name on yellow sticky notes. And that just wouldn't do.

She herded the two stray chickens around the side of the house and into Rebecca's enclosed backyard, where they had a cozy coop, then led Ray up the outside stairs and into her suite. He toed off his boots just inside the door.

"It might not be holy ground, but I don't think you need any of the worship center's mud in here."

She smiled and pulled off her own shoes. Did he have to be so considerate? And did he have to look quite so tousled and damp and appealing?

Argh.

She put the kettle on and found a box of Dutch Almond hot chocolate mix in the back of the cupboard. It had been there since she'd received it for a white-elephant present at the bank the previous December. Company holiday parties always made her feel awkward, not just because she looked so plain in her black suit when everyone else was glittering in their festive dresses and earrings that lit up like Rudolph's nose, but it had literally not occurred to her that she needed to go out and buy a present. Consequently she'd been grateful to get somebody's standby present of hot chocolate mixes instead of something expensive, like the silver salt-and-pepper set Margot had oohed and ahhed over.

When the kettle boiled, she stirred up the mugs of hot chocolate and carried them over to the couch. "You're probably used to something stronger after a cold day in the swamp," she said a little diffidently. An Elect boy wouldn't think twice about hot chocolate, but it occurred to her moments too late that Ray might want something like a brandy. Isn't that what people drank when they came in from skiing?

"This is great." Ray took the mug and sipped from it cautiously, steam rising past his nose. "I'm not much of a drinker. Cops tend to polarize—either they drink every chance they get or they abstain. But alcoholism killed my dad about thirty years too soon, so it doesn't appeal that much to me."

To Claire's knowledge, her dad had never touched a drop. Could any two people have less in common?

"I'm sorry," she said awkwardly. There wasn't much comfort a person could offer. Even if Ray believed in God, she couldn't very well say she was sorry his dad had gone to a lost eternity, now, could she?

"Thanks, but it happened a long time ago, when I was in high school. He was a cop, too."

"Is that what made you go into law enforcement?"

Ray shrugged. "Maybe. One of the things he instilled in me was a strong sense of fairness. Maybe I wanted to be a cop to even things out a bit. Make sure ordinary folks got a fair shake."

"You could have been a lawyer."

"Nah." He grinned at her. "They don't get to sit in dark alleys late at night or kick drug dealers' doors in. Or walk through swamps, for that matter."

"A real thrill seeker, you are." She smiled behind her mug.

"Yeah, surveillance is a thrill a minute." He snorted and took another sip of chocolate.

"This sure doesn't seem like much of a vacation for you."

Slowly, he lowered the mug and gave her a long look, as though he were making up his mind about something. "To be honest, it's not. I've been working. Doing surveillance," he said.

She sat up in surprise. "Surveillance on what?" Her chocolate lurched in her mug before she settled back down. "Or on whom?"

"A guy named Richard Brandon Myers. I've been chasing him for awhile now, and I finally tracked him down."

"Why are you chasing him?"

He shrugged. "He's a ripoff artist. Preys on vulnerable people, and I hate that. So, I've just been doing the usual— surveillance, license-plate checks, and background work. All I'm waiting for now is for him to make a move."

"Like, commit a crime? Rip somebody off?"

He nodded. "But I'm running out of time. If something

doesn't break by Saturday, I'm going to have to pull out. My lieutenant wants me back in Seattle Monday morning."

"Monday?"

She didn't even have to make the speech. All she had to do was wait until the weekend and he'd be gone. Easy.

Then why this sense of panic rising under her ribcage like a flock of frightened starlings?

"Do you have a problem with that?" His voice was soft. He put his mug on the brass-bound trunk she used as a coffee table and took hers out of her hand.

"A—a problem? You have to do what you have to do."

"So, I can hitch up my pony and ride off into the sunset and it won't bother you?"

"I—"

"Because it's really going to bother me."

Oh dear. Here was the moment for the speech. Here was her opportunity to say, *Ray, it's good you're going home because there is no way we could ever have anything together. Have a safe trip.*

Say it.

"Ray, it's—" *It's good you're going home. Come on.*

"It's not really this case keeping me here," he went on when she choked on the rest of her sentence. "I could have handed the details over to the Hamilton Falls PD and skated on home a couple of days ago. But I didn't. Ask me why."

"Why?" she whispered. *There is no way we could have anything togeth—*

Somehow, instead of sitting in opposite corners of the couch, they were now practically sharing a single cushion. He touched her chin with one finger.

"I think you know." His voice was a caress of sound.

Say it, quick—

Her lips parted, but she would never know whether or not she would have actually said the words, because Ray's mouth met hers. His arms went around her, and instead of feeling engulfed or intimidated, as she might have before, she felt cradled in safety. Her hands slid around his neck and up into his hair. He changed the angle of the kiss, and she began to lose track of where she was. Her whole being fell into his as he wooed her mouth, and the faint scent of his cologne—something that combined wood chips with ocean spray—intensified as their temperatures rose.

When at last the kiss ended, Claire was breathing as if she'd just run up the stairs and Ray's gaze was a little unfocused.

"See what I mean?" he breathed. "How is a guy supposed to just get in the truck and drive away from you?"

Others have. Elect guys, who got together with her, had a few dates, and then moved on simply because they could. The grass was always greener in somebody else's Gathering. But here was Ray, who didn't want to leave. The question was, what was she going to do with him?

"This is crazy," she murmured at last, and turned slightly to lean into the crook of his arm.

"What? Us?"

"That's just it." *Say it.* "There can't be any us."

"Why not?" Just like that, he responded calmly, as if she'd said she couldn't go swamp stomping again tomorrow. But then, he was a cop. They were probably used to keeping their emotions and reactions under wraps. Coward that she was, she felt a little relieved. Maybe this wouldn't be as hard as she thought.

"I told you before. Well, maybe your being an Outsider isn't so much the point now, but you still don't believe in God."

"Are you so sure of that?"

"I know you don't think the Elect is the right path for you. And I—"

"I get the feeling you don't, either."

"I still believe."

"So, we're doomed from the outset because of religion?" he asked. "Our sense of humor, the way we talk about things, those don't count?"

"They can't." How could she explain this? "Belief in God has to be the foundation for a relationship. If that's missing, if two people don't have the same views on what's important, the relationship will never work."

His hazel eyes were disconcertingly direct. "What's important to you, Claire?"

"God, of course. But I have my salvation in the Elect. I can't give that up."

"No one's asking you to. I just think we have something worth fighting for, that's all."

"It'll be something to fight *about*, trust me. My sister married Outside, and she's miserable. Andrew doesn't understand her in so many fundamental ways and it's just not . . . right. I don't want that for myself."

"We're different people, different personalities. I don't care if you take off and go to Gathering three times a week."

"It's not only that. Once they come back, the Shepherds

won't stay in a divided home, so you lose that privilege. And what about Summer Gathering and supper invites? I'd have to go to everything alone. It's just not worth it, Ray."

"So, you're saying you'd rather have a social life than the possibility of something with me."

The hurt ambushed her with a punch to the stomach. "You don't understand."

"I have to say I don't. I ask you what's important and you give me a social calendar."

"It's not the social calendar, it's what's under it. Fellowship."

"That's the price, huh?" He pasted on a smile. "It's pretty high. And no guarantees."

"No," she said miserably. She had hurt him deeply and it was too late to take it back.

He pulled his arm from under her shoulders and stood up. She felt very small and alone on the couch by herself. "If it makes you feel any better, I do think about God once in a while. But all the rules and regulations you believe in—it's worse than boot camp, Claire. I can't believe that's what God wants me to spend my life on. God gets me the way I am or not at all."

He pulled on his boots. "Thanks for the cocoa. I'll go down to the PD in the morning and hand off this job to them. Maybe I can get back to Seattle and take a weekend off for once."

"Ray—"

"Good-bye, Claire. I hope that someday you find the guy you deserve."

He meant it kindly, she thought as the door closed behind him. But at that moment it sounded like a curse.

AT LEAST LUKE still thought she was wonderful. To Claire's bruised feelings, his welcoming grin through the studio window was like a healing salve. It didn't do much for the circles under her eyes, and it didn't fill the empty hollow under her ribs that was one part defensiveness, one part loneliness, and two parts regret, but it helped.

When she finished entering the day's receipts, she took a moment when the next song began to knock on the window and wait for Luke to beckon her in. The surfer beat of Jars of Clay singing "It Is Well with My Soul" surrounded her until Luke turned the studio feed down.

"Sorry," he said. "I like this one."

"I do, too." She gave him a big smile. "Thirty thousand so far this week. Thirty-one thousand, to be specific, not counting last weekend."

He held up a hand for a high five and she slapped his palm.

"The prayer times are working. I knew they would. Who can resist hearing themselves on the air?"

"And those are only the brave ones who call in. You get far more prayer letters to read out loud. And I don't think it's that people want to hear themselves. They want to give. It's all the work of God."

"Of course, it is." His warm gaze melted over her. "So, today I have an assignment for you."

"Sure."

"The general contractor dropped off an invoice this morning, and we need to get it paid." He scooped an envelope off the top of the CD player and handed it to her.

She scanned it. "Okay. Twenty-seven thousand for heavy equipment for drainage and foundation trenches. Five thousand for subcontractors to clear the land and level it. They want all this up front?"

With a shrug, he turned to the console and cued up another CD. "They've already started. They have to pay the little guys. You know, their subcontractors."

"That will clean out the receipts we were saving for the down payment."

"There'll be more," Luke replied with the supreme confidence of faith.

"I hope they get something going. We were out there yesterday taking pictures for the before-and-after display and it doesn't look as though any kind of work has started."

"Didn't you see surveyors' stakes and tape and trenches?"

"No."

"I did when I was there the other day. Did you go to the right place?"

"Ray said it was." But had it been? Clearly not, if heavy equipment was already working. No wonder it had looked as if no one had been there since Crazy Jack had staked his claim. Mentally, she rolled her eyes at herself. All those mosquito bites for nothing.

"Ray?" One of Luke's eyebrows rose in inquiry. "What's Ray Harper doing poking his nose into Elect business?"

"Oh, he wasn't. It was just something to do. He must have got his directions mixed up."

"Something to do? As in, on a date?"

This was what the media referred to as *damage control*. Since there was no hope for Ray—in more ways than one—she needed to clear up Luke's mistaken ideas.

"No, not a date. We're not going out. He doesn't know many people around here so I was showing him the sights."

"Be careful, Claire. Elect women can be very attractive to a lone-wolf type like him."

"You don't need to worry about me, Luke. I'd never get involved with an Outsider."

"I haven't seen you involved with anyone, have I?"

Jars of Clay faded out and the Nashville Bluegrass Band came on. Indicator lights changed from red to green on the second CD player.

"No. There isn't anyone in Hamilton Falls to get involved with, except Derrick Wilkinson, and I've known him since we were in diapers."

"There's someone," Luke said softly. "Someone who thinks you're the most beautiful thing he's ever seen."

A draft blew in through the open studio door and ran soft fingers up the back of her neck. Claire shivered. "Who?"

Luke turned back to the microphone and cued up the tape player for the 10:15 prayer request. "If you don't know, you'll have to wait until he's ready to tell you. Let me know when that check's ready, okay? I want to give the contractor a heads-up when it goes in the mail."

Puzzled, Claire closed the door behind her and went into her office to enter their first payable into the database. She'd generate the check and post it after she made her daily trip to the bank.

Who on earth had Luke been talking about? It couldn't be the Kowalczyk twins—they were five years younger than she. It wasn't Derrick. So, who was left?

Luke himself.

No, that couldn't be. They worked together, that was all. He'd never given any indication he wanted more than to be workmates or even a big-brother figure, as evidenced by his joking lecture over the kiss in the parking lot.

He'd never given any indication—until now, that is. He'd said he wasn't ready, hadn't he? What was he waiting for? For the worship center to get off the ground? For Ray to leave town? For the station to reach a certain number of pledges and be financially secure enough for him to back off on the fundraising and actually have a life?

Or maybe he was waiting for her to wake up and act like something other than his sister in the Lord. But was she even interested in that? When Luke walked into a room, did her blood jump and her breath come short the way it did when she saw Ray? Or did she fall into his arms whenever she got within five feet of him?

Her reaction to Ray was a bad standard to hold Luke to. She had to think about their spiritual compatibility before anybody fell into anyone's arms. Ray was an unbeliever, so there was no future with him. Luke was an enthusiastic advocate for God—you couldn't find a more committed believer. But did that mean there was a future for her there?

With a sigh, Claire reached for the stack of mail that hadn't contained prayer pledges or donations. Bills, circulars, newsletters from various radio-geek associations that Toby belonged to—why couldn't they all join up and form one group, anyway?—and an envelope with a church logo in the corner. She pulled out the letter inside and saw that it was a thank-you note from the Good Shepherd Church in Idaho.

> *Our outreach appreciates your contribution to our work so very much. You can be assured that your generosity will mean that your name will be lifted up in prayer and thanksgiving each morning as the homeless here partake of the food you have helped to provide.*
> *Sincerely,*
> *Richard Myers, Pastor*
> *Good Shepherd Congregational Church*

Claire set it aside to show Luke when his show was over. Then she picked it up again and looked at the signature a second time.

Richard Myers.

How funny that a pastor in Idaho would have the same name as some criminal Ray was tracking in Hamilton Falls. But then, both names were pretty common. And it wasn't very likely that a pastor was going to be ripping people off, was it?

At eleven, she took the receipts over to the bank, dropped off the general contractor's check at the post office, and at noon was back at her desk, eating a sandwich she'd grabbed at the coffee bar. With FileMaker it was easy to generate a report of everyone who had contributed to that day's deposit, load the addresses into a Word file, and generate thank-you letters and receipts.

"I love technology," she murmured around her chicken

and avocado. Just imagine the time it would have taken to hand-write thank-you letters for thirty thousand dollars. Luke, of course, was the guy who had to sign them all, but he did it cheerfully in between song announcements.

Her thoughts must have conjured him up. Luke leaned in her doorway.

"Hey, Claire, I'm on my way up to Spokane. The outfitter called earlier to say the mobile station is ready to roll." He caught sight of the neat pile of letters and envelopes on her credenza. "Uh-oh. Are those all for me?"

" 'Fraid so. The price of success is writer's cramp."

He grinned at her. "A small price compared to what we're able to do. Hey, did you mail the check to the contractor yet?"

"Yes, I did, when I went to the bank. Sorry—did you want to hand carry it?"

He waved a negligent hand. "It was just a thought. If the project manager was around, I had some ideas for the sanctuary I wanted to run past him, but I can do that another day. Need anything from Spokane?"

"Don't tempt me. Now that we don't have to wear black any more, I have a whole wardrobe to replace."

"You're welcome to come with me." His gaze on her became warm, intimate. "It's not often we get to be alone together."

Claire tilted her head and gave him a wry look. "We're alone right now. And I have a ton of things to do this afternoon."

"Do them tomorrow."

Smiling, she shook her head. "It's almost the end of Sep-

tember, in case you missed it. Who's going to do the month-
end reports for Willetts?" The station's owner hardly ever
showed his face, but apparently Toby had been doing his best
to provide the man with a report on how his investment—
such as it had been—was doing.

"Willetts has gone without reports for twenty years. He's
not going to miss them."

"I don't know about that. Toby's been giving him a
spreadsheet every month. I wanted to really jazz him with
my nifty P&L that the database generates."

He laughed. "You're just as geeky as Toby."

She straightened a little. "Competence isn't the same as
geekiness. I like to do a good job, that's all."

"Oh, get off your high horse. I was only kidding. Okay,
I'm out of here."

Part of her wished she could go with him as she watched
him lope down the short hallway and out the door. This was
the second time he'd asked her to go to Spokane with him.
Why had she turned him down?

Is this why she was alone so much? Here two men in the
last twenty-four hours had let her know they were interested, and she'd said no both times. Was she crazy?

"What am I thinking?" she said aloud. After hitting a key
to lock her computer and grabbing her purse, she ran down
the hall and out of the building. She looked up and down
Main Street, but Luke was already out of sight, and by the
time she walked around to the parking lot where he usually
left his car, the silver Camry was already gone.

Chapter 12

LIEUTENANT BELLVILLE of the Hamilton Falls PD steepled his fingers and leveled a long gaze at Ray.

"So, what you're telling me, Investigator, is that the star citizen of our fair town has a years-long record of fraud and petty crime?" He glanced at Ray's file on his desk, the topmost item of which was the digital photo Teresa White had sent him.

"Yes, sir." Ray hoped the good lieutenant wasn't a Christian, too, or convincing him to take the case was going to be difficult.

"But you've got no proof he's involved in anything now."

"No, sir. It's possible he's turned over a new leaf and gone straight, but to be honest, I doubt it."

"You know this is going to be a hard sell, don't you." It wasn't a question.

"Yes, sir, I figured that."

"He's all anyone talks about these days. Even my wife listens to KGHM, and with the new youth music program over at the community church, my kids are bugging me to join so they can be part of it."

"There's nothing wrong with that, sir."

"Yeah, but if they find out I'm investigating the closest thing they've ever seen to a celebrity, my name will be mud."

"It happens all the time, sir."

"What, that my name's mud? Don't remind me."

"No, that celebrities get investigated. I'm not saying this should go any farther than this room. I'm just telling you that he has a record in a couple of states and you should keep an eye on him. I'm being called back to Seattle, so I need to leave it in your hands."

Bellville closed the folder and handed it across the desk to Ray, who stuffed it in his backpack. "Understood. Thanks for the information, Investigator. And thanks for your work on that rapist preacher, too. Ugly case. I'm glad it's done and we got a conviction."

"I am, too. I wonder what these folks—the Elect—will do for a leader now?"

Bellville shook his head. "They've always been a funny bunch. Great folks to talk to. Sincere, well-meaning. But keep to themselves so much it isn't healthy. I'd like to see them join forces with the community church, but that's a long way out of my bailiwick. One of my golfing buddies is assistant pastor there at the church. You've probably heard him on the radio, too. Toby Henzig. Decent guy. They'd do themselves a favor if they'd get a leader like him."

"That's outside my bailiwick, too. The whole church thing is foreign to me." How had he gotten into this conversation with the lieutenant, anyway? What was he doing blabbing about personal stuff on company time?

Bellville gave him another look, only a twinkle lurked in the back of it. Ray began to understand why this station ran like a well-oiled clock and why the crime rate in this town was so low.

"It's too bad people think about faith as only a church thing," the lieutenant said. "That's one of the problems the Elect have—they look at the structure itself instead of what it represents. Get all hung up on the appearance of things and forget about the reality. But faith, now, that's different."

"I wouldn't know anything about that, either, sir."

"Well, this isn't the time or place to talk about it, probably, since I have to brief the next watch in ten minutes. But you keep your heart open, Investigator. You might be surprised."

That, Ray reflected as he shook the lieutenant's hand and left the station, was probably the strangest conversation he'd ever had with a fellow law-enforcement officer.

But then, he'd been having a lot of strange conversations since he'd arrived in Hamilton Falls. And a lot of them seemed to revolve around God and belief and a bunch of other stuff that had never bothered him in Seattle. In fact, getting back home and *not* talking about God for a change would be a relief.

Why he was dragging his feet was a mystery. He'd checked out of his motel this morning, briefed Bellville, and now there was nothing left to do but put gas in the truck, grab a sandwich, and head west like a rational person.

Right.

That must be why he was now standing in front of the radio station, the need to see Claire and say good-bye—again—an ache in his gut.

Go on, you dope. Get out of here. There's no point.

On the outside speaker, the open-mic program was in full force and some guy was haranguing the county at large about the price of gas. Toby Henzig pushed open the station's door and stopped on the step.

"Sorry." Ray moved out of the way.

"Coming in?" Toby held the door. "I was just on my way to indulge my secret weakness for a double latte, extra whip, until this caller runs out of steam. Don't tell my wife."

Ray had to laugh. "She trying to keep you alive on a low-fat diet or what?"

"No, she's on the diet and I'm in sympathy mode. She craves the whipped cream, and I'm the one who sneaks off and gets it. Are you stopping in to see Claire?"

"Busted." Ray gave Toby a halfhearted grin. "I'm going back to Seattle and thought I'd say good-bye."

"Back to Seattle?"

Ray now leaned on the open door, his back to the hallway, while Toby gazed at him from the sidewalk. "My vacation's over, and the bad guys didn't take time off while I was gone."

"Vacation, huh? Somehow I thought you were here for . . . other business."

"The Leslie case? Yeah, that, too."

"No, that wasn't what I meant." He gazed past Ray in the general direction of Claire's office. "Have a safe trip."

He turned and made his way through the sidewalk tables

outside the coffee bar, leaving Ray with nothing left to do but shut the station's door behind him.

He found Claire at her desk, with some mystifying maze of numbers arrayed on the monitor in front of her. She was studying them intently, giving him a few quiet seconds to appreciate the way her hair waved over her ears and into the elegant coil at the nape of her neck. She had a beautiful neck, long and smooth. She wore a crocheted sweater over a blue T-shirt that matched her skirt. Gone was the old-lady Victorian look and in its place was a modern woman any sane guy would snap up in a second.

Why did she have to believe so stubbornly that without her kind of religion, they had no chance? What a waste of a future.

"Hey," he said from her doorway when it became obvious she didn't know he was there.

She turned in surprise. "Hey. What's up?"

Levering himself off the doorjamb, he said, "Not much. I just came by to say adios." Her office wasn't very big. It didn't take long for him to look it over while he waited for her to burst into tears and beg him to stay. Or maybe say she was sorry for chasing him away.

Or something.

"Oh," she said. "Already?"

"I handed my case off to the HFPD just now. I'm on my way out."

His tour around the office had brought him to the side of her desk. Behind her on the credenza was a plastic bin with "Property of the U.S. Post Office" stenciled on the side. A stack of letters and envelopes sat next to her computer, and a row of cards was arranged on the sill of the interior window that looked into the hallway. Through it he could see another window into the record library and the studio. How nice. She and Luke could wave at each other while they worked.

To fill the silence, he picked up a card. " 'Your program has brought meaning to our day,' " he read slowly. " 'Thank you from the Wyslicki family.' "

He picked up another. Same sentiment. These people clearly needed to get a life. "Are all these to Luke?" he said aloud.

She nodded, and he picked up another one. This was dumb. She wasn't interested in whether he was there or not. Why didn't he just take a hint and leave?

"Ray?" Her voice sounded uncertain, with none of its usual warmth and confidence.

"Yeah?" He fingered a letter that had been taped to the window, over the cards on the sill.

"Before you go, I want to say I'm sorry. I hope you're not angry with me."

"Angry?" His gaze tracked the lines of the letter without really seeing them. "I'm not angry. Disappointed, maybe. Hurt, a little. And my nose is probably out of joint over this whole religion thing. But I'm not angry."

Behind him he heard a soft sound that might have been a laugh. "Somehow that doesn't make me feel better."

He gave up on the letter and turned. "What do you want from me, Claire? I tell you I'm interested, your kiss tells me you are, too, but your words say I don't measure up. Now you want me to make you feel better about it?"

"I knew you were angry," she whispered.

"I can't stand that you're letting religion get in the way of what could be a good thing."

"You don't understand."

"Yeah, you told me that before." Frustrated, he swung toward the door. "I came to say good-bye, not get into an argument. You have every right to do what you want with your life."

He had a strange feeling in his gut, as though he were on a ship that was pulling inexorably away from a dock. He didn't want to be on this ship. He didn't want to leave, but that was what he had to do. Anything else was pointless.

"Good-bye, Claire. Maybe I'll see you at Ross and Julia's sometime."

He thought he heard her say his name, but he couldn't be sure. Instead, he recognized the voice of Derrick, the unhappy guy he'd met at Rebecca's, as he came on the phone line to give the world his opinions about praying over the air.

Ray let the door swing shut behind him.

"MIND IF I JOIN YOU?"

Claire looked up from *Daughters of the King*, the personal style guide she'd just picked up from Quill and Quinn that was the following month's pick for "Hamilton Falls for Books." Derrick Wilkinson stood there, looking rumpled and hot, though the air was cool. The sandwich wrapped in wax paper that he held looked a bit squashed, as if he'd made a fist while he'd forgotten he was holding it. She moved the remains of her smoothie and the bagel she'd had with it to one side of the round glass table she occupied outside the coffee bar.

"Have a seat, Derrick. How are you?"

"I'm confused, I'm angry, and I just said a bunch of stuff I shouldn't have over the radio."

Claire had a vague memory of a familiar voice coming from the studio, but she'd been too miserable to care. "Well, other than that."

Ray had left town and she was sitting here at a table for one again. The trees in their planters along Main Street had begun to turn yellow. The ducks and geese were leaving in long, straggling V's, their wild calls in the cold blue vault of the sky a haunting sound. Summer was over, and she hated the fall—it always meant that rain and cold were just around the corner. Some people became excited because it meant the beginning of the school year and hockey season, but she only saw fallen leaves, dead plants, and birds who got to fly away.

Why had she let him leave? What was the matter with her head? Or, to be more specific, her heart?

"Fine." Derrick bit into his sandwich savagely and she roused herself out of her funk.

"What's up, Derrick? I don't usually see you like this."

"You don't usually see me at all. Nobody sees me, nobody listens to me. It's like everyone's asleep with their eyes open around here."

She blinked at him. She'd never seen the guy say anything but the right thing, or do anything but help old ladies in and out of his car, or go to work every day punctually at nine o'clock. Something was seriously wrong if Derrick Wilkinson was upset and showing it.

"What do you mean? Tell me what's going on."

He swallowed the last of his homemade sandwich and she wondered if he'd tasted even one bite. "The Elders were in to see us. They just left."

"You mean our Elders? In to see the attorneys you work with?"

"What other Elders are there? Owen, Mark McNeill, and your boss came in to draw up articles of incorporation." From his tone, you'd have thought they'd come in to sell illegal drugs. She thought Luke had gone to Spokane. He'd obviously made a stop along the way.

"Incorporating what?"

"The Elect. As a legal entity."

She sat back and stared at him. "That's impossible. We can't be incorporated. We're a spiritual body, not an earthly one. Not to mention we have no official name."

"We do now. We're officially known as the Elect of God of Inish County, and you know what else?"

"I can't imagine." She couldn't. The fact that they were a spiritual church with no earthly ties and no guidance but the will of God as spoken through his Shepherds had been a foundation of doctrine since . . . well, forever. Their founder was Jesus Himself, in the tradition of the prophets, and this set them apart from worldly churches who were of the earth, who had buildings and boards that kept them accountable to themselves. The Elect's prophets were accountable only to God. If the Elect had incorporated, that made them the same as anyone else. Why, she might as well go worship at the church Toby went to.

"The reason they've incorporated is so they can buy the land for the worship center. So now, not only are we a registered legal body, we're going to hold land, too."

"We own the hall," she pointed out.

"No, we don't. It's leased on a twenty-year agreement with John Willetts. He owns stuff all over town. The Elect have never owned land—except for people owning their own houses, of course. It's just wrong. The Elders could have gone in as a partnership or something."

"No, they couldn't," said Claire the former bank employee. "With a corporation you get a bunch of tax breaks in this county. They're trying to encourage new construction."

"Well, they're going to get it. Owen told me that he and Mark have put mortgages on their houses, but the bank won't give them a loan until they run through their own money. With the corporation it's easier to track it." The more he talked, the more agitated he became.

"Times are changing, Derrick." She tried to sound calm and soothing. "If Luke and the elders think this is the right thing to do, then obviously God has led them to believe that."

"*Luke* has led them to think that way. Things have been changing entirely too fast since he first stood up in Mission."

"No, it started before that. With Dinah and Tamara. Maybe even with Julia."

She'd obviously hit a nerve that was still raw. Derrick stood abruptly. "I've got to get back to work. I just know they're going to ask me to prepare those papers, after I worked a bunch of overtime doing the research last night."

Have a good day seemed a little lame. "Thanks for sharing your lunch with me," she said finally. At least it had taken her mind off her own problems for twenty minutes.

He stood looking at her for a moment. "You don't think there's anything wrong with this, either, do you?"

"I think that change is sometimes painful," she said carefully. "But I support what the Elders are doing the same way I support the Shepherds."

His mouth thinned. "I just hope it's not going to cause more pain than we can stand," he said, and turned and left her.

She didn't want to think about the fact that he was the third man to do so that day.

A FEW MINUTES before eight the next morning, Luke bounded into Claire's office as she was putting her purse in the bottom drawer of her desk. She hadn't slept more than a couple of hours the night before, and her eyes felt gritty and her muscles too loose. Coffee, and lots of it, was the answer, not Luke, who positively buzzed with animation and energy. Instead of charging her up, he just made her feel even more tired.

"Claire! I've been waiting for you."

She glanced at the clock over the door. "I'm not late, am I?"

"Who cares? Come on, I've got something to show you."

"Luke, your show starts in three minutes."

"And you're holding me up. Come on."

She didn't protest or respond. Or care very much for his tone. She followed him out the door and around to the parking lot, where he made a "ta-da!" gesture with both arms.

"What do you think?"

There was nothing there but a bunch of cars, a van, and a pickup truck. The same vehicles that were parked there every day. "About what?"

"About the van! I went and got it yesterday, remember?"

She'd been so consumed with Ray's departure, Derrick's news, and her own stupidity that the fact Luke had gone to get the new mobile station had completely fallen off her radar.

He grabbed her wrist and dragged her over to the new white van, one of the biggest she'd ever seen. "It's got a V-8 engine in it and a state-of-the-art GPS system."

Claire looked over the passenger compartment and tried to catch his enthusiasm. She'd have had more success if he'd had a cold.

"And look at this." He whipped back the sliding door so that it jounced on its track. "Here's where our equipment will be."

The rear compartment of the van was pristine and carpeted, and smelled of brand-new upholstery, but that was about all you could say for it. "Luke, I thought it had been at the outfitter all this time. Where's the equipment?" Leaning back, she checked the door, which had shivered into stillness. "And where's our logo?"

"We haven't designed a new one yet, so it isn't there."

"But the equipment? Aren't they going to install it?"

"It didn't all arrive in time, so I told them to call me when they had everything. No point driving up there more than once. Meantime, I brought it back with me to show you. Isn't it great?"

It's a van, not life support, she could have said a little waspishly. But instead, she said, "Yes. Totally great. How long until they get everything?"

Luke shrugged and slid the door closed. "I don't know. A few days. A week."

"Where's your car? Did someone drive it home for you?"

"No, I left it at the outfitters. They said they'd just lock it in their yard until I came back. I didn't want to mess around with ferrying two vehicles all over the state."

"But—"

"Come on, Claire, don't get so bogged down in the details. We're halfway to having a mobile station. Halfway to being able to reach a bigger audience than ever before. Doesn't that make you want to sing God's praises?"

"Sure." She summoned up a smile and put it on. "But Toby won't be singing your praises unless you get in there and start your show. Meantime, I'm going to the post office."

She had just retrieved her purse when she heard Luke go on the air: "Good morning, Washington! This is Luke Fisher, rocking for the Lord at 98.5 KGHM!" She walked over to the coffee bar and got herself a venti latte with a shot of chocolate. By the time she'd poured a third of it down her throat and walked to the post office, the world was looking like a happier place. When she finished it, maybe she'd even be able to get excited about the van.

The pile of envelopes today was a little lower than it had been recently, but she still had to use the plastic bin to carry it all to the station. It took most of the morning to get it all entered in the database, generate the deposit slip, and get the printer started on the task of spitting out thank-you letters.

Another invoice had come in for the general contractor, this time for an astonishing number of yards of concrete and what seemed like enough pipe to plumb a small city. Well, she'd seen towns in Washington that were probably the same size as the worship center complex was going to be, so she supposed that was reasonable. Still, fifty thousand dollars was a lot for just pipe and concrete.

It also wasn't due for—how many days? She glanced again at the invoice. "On receipt"? That was odd. Usually companies ran on a thirty or forty-five day cycle. Maybe things were different in the construction business. Or maybe it was an oversight. A negotiable oversight.

She picked up the phone and called the Spokane exchange printed on the letterhead. It rang at least six times before a sleepy female voice said, "Hello?"

"I'm sorry. I must have the wrong number. The invoice I have says this is the number for Brandon Brothers, General Contractors."

"Yup, this is them."

Clearly someone was having as bad a day as she was herself. "Oh. Well, good. I just wanted to check that your receivables really are due on receipt of the invoice."

"Huh? Oh yeah. Sure, they are."

"Oh." Claire felt a little silly. "Most companies run on a thirty-day cycle, that's all. Yours just seems a little short. I'm wondering if, since this is such a big job and it will be on-going for a number of months, we could negotiate a bet-ter—"

"If it says it's due on receipt, then it's on receipt."

Yikes. Maybe someone should be sent on a customer-relations course. "Right. Well, thanks very much."

The woman hung up without even a good-bye. Claire made a face at the phone and tossed the invoice in the to-do pile. Just for that, the woman could wait the standard net thirty.

She slipped the deposit into its bag and walked down to the bank. Margot spotted her as she was pushing open the glass door, and waved her into her office.

"It seems as though every day is deposit day at KGHM," she said with a bright smile. Margot could teach the slob at Brandon Brothers a thing or two about customer relations, even though Claire had a feeling that 20 percent of that smile was chagrin at having to cater to someone she'd fired.

"God is good," was all she said, however, and smiled a completely sincere smile back.

While Margot made the entries, she said, "I guess you folks are happy about going ahead with the worship center, aren't you? It's going to be quite the project."

As well as managing the tellers, Margot was the bank's loan officer. Of course she would know the Elect's business. "Have you seen the drawings? It's going to be beautiful. Not to mention good for construction jobs—and service jobs when it's done."

"Yes, I have seen the drawings." Margot's polished nails clicked busily on the computer's keys. "The gentlemen representing the corporation—Mr. McNeill, Mr. Blanchard, and Mr. Fisher—were required to give us a cost breakdown, from initial permits to final signoff, as part of the loan process. It's . . . very ambitious, I must say."

"But it's doable. With the donations pouring in, plus the mortgages on their homes, the down payment won't be a problem."

"They're required to come up with 50 percent, actually, but you're right, for the cost of the land it shouldn't be a problem. Which brings me to something else."

She finished up the entries and a receipt began chattering in the old-fashioned printer.

"What's that?"

"I have to go out to the site this afternoon to do the loan inspection. Would you be free to come with me?"

"Me?" The receipt finished printing and Margot handed it to her. "But I don't really have anything to do with that part of it. The Elders have been managing it."

"Yes, but it's the middle of a working day and I don't have time to wait until one of them is free. This afternoon is good for me. How is your schedule?"

She didn't really have anything pressing except to pay a couple of utility bills, and that could wait until tomorrow. And frankly, the thought of getting away from the station— okay, and Luke—for a little while was appealing.

"The only problem is, I don't know where the site is," she said to Margot. "A friend and I went to where I thought it was, but there was nothing there."

"Don't worry about that," Margot said briskly, ushering her out. "I have all the lot numbers, of course."

"Of course." And knowing Margot, she had them in triplicate and notarized. The lady left nothing to chance. "I'll run home and get changed, and meet you back here in, say, an hour?"

"Perfect. See you then."

When Claire got back to her office, it was to see Luke sitting in her chair, hunting through her stacks of thank-you letters.

"Can't wait to sign those, hey?" She kept her tone light and teasing to make up for her grumpiness earlier.

But, as though they were on an emotional seesaw, where he went down when she went up, his ebullient mood seemed to have evaporated. "No. I'm looking for the check."

"What check?" Had he asked her to cut one and she'd forgotten? Oh, dear. Maybe she'd better take a refresher on customer relations herself. "I'm sorry, Luke, did you ask me to cut a check for someone?"

"No, no. Not for me. For the contractor."

"Who, Brandon Brothers? Their invoice is in there." She indicated the tray containing the to-do pile. Or, in the case of the contractor's invoice, her to-do-later pile. "But it just came this morning. I wasn't going to pay it until—"

He turned. "What do you mean?"

She slid her purse into her drawer and nudged him out of her chair. "What do I mean about what?"

Big mistake. He towered over her, a hand on each arm of her chair, and leaned in as though he were going to kiss her. Which he wasn't going to do—since his mouth was narrowed and his eyes were flat and angry. "What do you mean, you aren't going to pay it?"

She frowned, trying not to be intimated and not quite succeeding. "Luke, give me some space, please."

He blinked and seemed to realize how threatening he was being over nothing. His push with both hands off the chair sent her rolling backward a couple of inches. Claire realized with a sense of shock that her breathing was fast and her heart was beating practically out of her chest. She'd felt this way when Ray had kissed her—sort of. But that had been pleasure. This was something else. Fear?

No. Couldn't be. Luke was just being conscientious, that was all.

"I didn't say I wasn't going to pay it. Just that I didn't need to do it this minute. I have to go out to the—"

"I want you to pay it today."

"Luke, this isn't your job. I won't let us get in arrears, I promise."

"What's the big deal? The invoice says to pay on receipt, doesn't it? You received it today, you pay it today."

"Well, technically we have a certain number of days before we have to—"

"I don't care about *technically*. I care about our Christian example to our possibly unbelieving contractor. What's he going to think if our check comes straggling in weeks late and he has to front his own money to the subcontractors? Is that going to make him care about our job? Is that going to make him an ally? Or for that matter, is that going to make him think positively about Christians? Do we want to be responsible for turning someone away from God because of sloppy business practices?"

Claire gaped at him, wondering which question he really

meant her to answer. Not that he'd let her get a complete sentence out even if she tried. And where did he get off, taking that tone with her, as if she were a misbehaving child?

He slapped the wall in emphasis and swung back to the studio, where an alarming silence proclaimed to five counties that someone had not cued up a CD in the second deck. "Cut that check, Claire," he called while he smacked a CD into the tray. "Now."

In a pig's eye I will. How dare you? Claire's mouth was mutinous as she glared from him to the offending invoice. She put it in the queue with the other check requests and, just in case anybody got any bright ideas about printing a check while she was out with Margot, she changed her computer password so that it wouldn't open up once it hibernated. Then she snatched up her purse and jacket and marched out of the station.

Nobody told Claire Montoya, a seasoned banking professional, how to do her job.

Chapter 18

CLAIRE LOST HER TEMPER maybe once a year, and always found it again fairly quickly. She just wasn't a temperamental person, which was good if you worked in the field of accounting. There, being detail-oriented, careful, and willing to ask questions when they needed to be asked were good qualities, not something to be laughed at or called into question. Luke may have hired her, but he wasn't the one who signed her paycheck every other week. He wasn't the one who gave her job assignments, though she had let him think so because, up until this morning, she had thought they were part of a team.

She had thought a lot of things that probably weren't true. That Luke was attracted to her, for one.

Ha. Even if he was, she most emphatically did not return the feeling. The kind of man she could care about didn't loom and threaten and yell when he didn't get what he wanted. Her ideal man made her feel safe. A little delirious with desire sometimes. Tongue-tied, maybe. Excitingly unsettled. But safe.

The way Ray had made her feel.

Right, and you managed that so well that he left town.

Margot stopped the car at the same cattle gate that Claire had opened for Ray and looked over at Claire in the passenger seat. "Would you mind hopping out and getting that gate for us?"

Claire double-checked the landscape. Crazy Jack Road. Same long, potholed approach. Same pines and golden grass waving in the breeze. The only thing that had changed between now and the day she and Ray had been here was the deep blue in the sky that proclaimed October was nearly here.

She got out and did the gate routine, and when she got back in the car, she said, "I don't think this is the place, Margot. I was here once before and there's nothing down there."

"There isn't supposed to be anything. We haven't approved the loan yet."

"But then, why—" Claire stopped herself. Some wires had gotten crossed somewhere. Maybe work had started in advance of the loan, in the form of getting materials and equipment ready to go. A little imprudent, maybe, but she was no expert on the construction business. She should be proactive and do some research on it. Maybe call up Brandon Brothers and ask to speak to someone other than that girl who—

"Ow!" The car, a sedan definitely not built for potholes the way Ray's truck was, jounced into and out of a hole in the road. Claire grabbed the armrest, and Margot gripped the steering wheel a little more firmly.

"Sorry."

"We parked here." Claire pointed out a flat spot in the grass where the track degraded into something only dirt bikes could navigate.

"Lucky thing we changed." In khaki pants and a practical windbreaker, Margot got out of the car with the roll of plans for the worship center. She locked the doors, even though there was nothing but cows for a mile in every direction. "I knew it was undeveloped, but I was at least expecting reasonable access."

"The tractors and trucks must have found a different way in," Claire said as they set off down the hill. "Luke says the trenches have been dug and there are surveyors' tapes and stakes everywhere."

"That can't be right. Surveyors' marks I can believe. But no actual work, including drainage and trenches, can start until we've funded the purchase of the land."

Claire lifted her hands in an "I-don't-know" gesture. "I'm already paying invoices out of the listener contributions."

"Well, hopefully we'll see in a moment." Margot's tone was noncommittal.

But when they emerged from the belt of pines, all there was to see was the broad blue expanse of the lake and the acres of cattails, willows, and water-bird habitat that lay between the lines of barbed-wire fencing. Margot unrolled the plans and oriented herself so that the lake lay on her left, as it did in the drawing. Claire looked over her shoulder at the blue lines of the elevations and then at where they should be.

"That's where the creek empties into the lake." She pointed. "The cabins should be over there, where that big clump of willows is, and the worship center itself beyond them."

Margot looked from drawing to swamp and back again. "Hm. Let's have a closer look."

Her mosquito bites from last time were barely healed. Claire bit back a groan and followed her former boss into the swamp. They jumped from tussock to tussock of thick grass and took turns holding back the long, whiplike willow branches for each other. Finally Margot stopped when the ground got too wet and a bank of cattails, fluffy with unreleased seed, reached above their heads and blocked the way.

"If I'm reading these plans correctly, we should be standing about where the worship center's sanctuary would be. And if your information is correct, we should be seeing orange tape and stakes." She lowered the plans and rolled them up again. The edges on one side were wet where she'd slipped and instinctively used the thick roll as a walking stick to hold herself upright. It hadn't worked, which hadn't improved her temper much. "But I don't see any such thing here—including a buildable site."

"There must be a mistake." Claire shivered in the wind off the lake. "Are you sure we're—" She stopped. Of course Margot was sure. It was her job to be sure they were standing where the county assessor said they should be. "I'm positive Luke said work had been done. Let's look around a bit, okay?"

But looking around netted them nothing but more insect bites, some scrapes, and a lost shoe that had to be rescued by Margot, sticking her arm elbow deep in the brackish water.

"This is ridiculous." Margot wiped mud and decomposing leaves from her forearm and shook her fingers in distaste. "This is no building site. I don't know why anyone would imagine they could put a commercial enterprise on such a property. Any fool could tell it was unbuildable. Look at the asking price. It's 70 percent below the going rate in this valley, for heaven's sake."

"Does—does that mean—" Claire couldn't form the words.

"Yes, it does. I'm sorry, Claire. I'm going to have to deny your church the loan. You might be able to put up a duck blind here, but it's no place to build a worship center." She pushed at a thicket of willow in irritation. "Not only that, I'd be interested to know just who you're paying for all this so-called construction."

WHAT WAS IT about the Elect that would make a woman like Claire Montoya put it first before—well, him? Or anything?

Ray Harper dug into Julia Malcolm's excellent beef stroganoff and wondered whether he'd survive asking that question aloud. Ross would capitalize on it and rib him for months. Julia would probably get on the phone and tell Claire in excruciating detail just what she'd done to his reputation as the local commitment-phobe.

The problem was, he really needed to know.

So he asked.

Julia's eyes widened and she glanced at Ross in a way that clearly said "I told you so." Then she sat back with both hands cradling her heavily pregnant belly and said, "Because we're taught to put the Elect ahead of everything, Ray. Family, friends, jobs—everything. But I learned that's a mistake. The Elect have the system and God all confused and mixed up together. It's God we're to put first, not the system of worship."

"That still isn't going to help me figure this out," Ray said. "My mom got four churches off the ground, and to this day I don't know if it's God she loves, or starting churches."

"The thing is, what's important to you?" Ross asked.

"You guys," Ray said simply. "Claire. The OCTF. My sisters. Probably not in that order, though."

"Have you ever thought about where God fits in to those priorities?" his partner asked quietly. Which felt a little weird. He and Ross could talk about everything from the consistency of pure cocaine to the best life insurance to take out when the baby came, but when it came to talking about God, they were treading in uncharted territory.

"Up until recently I've avoided thinking about God," he said. "He just complicates things."

"He simplifies things for me." Julia heaved herself out of her chair and began to clear their plates. "Kailey, can you help me, please?" The eight-year-old hopped down and carefully carried a single dish over to the sink. Then she returned for another, treating each plate with solemn reverence.

"How's that?" Ray asked Julia.

Julia and Claire had more in common than their experiences with the Elect. They had the same kind of smile, the kind that warmed a man and made him want to fall into that warmth forever. The ache under his ribs that had been there since he'd gunned his truck down the freeway away from Hamilton Falls throbbed as if to remind him of what he'd lost.

"It starts with joy, I think," she said. "And gratitude, and love. You find yourself permeated with it, and it makes you want to just give whatever you can to God in return for what He gives you." She glanced at him. "It's a bit like a marriage."

"Yeah, Ross always did have a God-complex," he cracked.

"You know how it is, Ray," Ross said, his grin fading. "It's like love, right? It simplifies everything—all you want is to be with that person. And yet it complicates everything—you have to change things to make it happen."

Now, that was something he could relate to. Something he could understand. "It's all about love, isn't it?" he said, almost to himself. "It's not about what group you belong to. Or clothes or buildings or practices or any of that. It's about the love."

"Going and coming," Julia said softly. "God loves us, and we love Him. When you get right down to it, it's really not that complicated, is it?"

When you got right down to it, he supposed it wasn't. The thing was, he couldn't just leave it hanging, as he'd done for as many years as he'd been fighting his mother's wacky ideas. He was a man of action. Make the plan, implement the plan. That had served him well in law enforcement and in life. So just what was he going to do about God? And once he'd figured that out, what was he going to do about Claire Montoya?

RAY WAS STILL pondering this several hours later, back in his apartment. He'd never paid much attention to his space. It was in a modest building in a middle-income neighborhood, with nothing much to recommend it but great freeway access and a low probability of running into the OCTF's targets in the local restaurants. He was thinking about it now. About how quiet it was. About how it had no feminine touches. Claire's little apartment had photographs and odd bits of brightly colored pottery, and even though her furniture was secondhand, it was comfortable.

He didn't even own a couch. He watched TV from his dad's recliner, which was probably as old as he was but still smelled like the old man. It comforted him, like a big hug from a guy who'd died too soon, before Ray had had a chance to tell him he loved him. Or that he'd forgiven him.

If Claire had been here, he could have told her stories about his dad. There would have been laughter instead of silence, and the sight of her eyes and smile instead of bare, empty walls. There would be companionship and possibility, not this sense that big chunks were missing out of his life that could be filled if he would just give in and let them happen.

Like this God business, for instance. Maybe there was something to it if you just kept it simple and focused on the love, as Ross and Julia did. Maybe it wasn't all about a bunch of brainwashed people acting out of character. Maybe they acted the way they did because they *weren't* in it for themselves, like 99.9 percent of the people he knew. Ross and Julia hadn't had to offer Tamara Traynell a home when she'd arrived in Seattle, desperate and grim and soaking wet because she'd walked from the bus station in the rain. Matthew Nicholas didn't have to be a father to the child of rape that didn't even belong to his fiancée. They did it for love. He had a feeling if he asked her, Claire would say, "and because Jesus would have done it."

Oh, he knew plenty about Jesus. No one who had grown up with his mom could help it. But the Jesus he saw reflected in these lives—so different, and yet knit so tightly together—wasn't the one his mom seemed to know. Or, for that matter, the one the Elect seemed to think they knew. If he had a choice, he'd take this one.

And he *did* have a choice. It was just up to him to make it.

It was after eleven, and he was still sitting in the recliner, pondering what the will of God really meant and missing Claire and generally—okay, he admitted it—moping, when his cell phone rang.

At this time of night, it probably wasn't good news.

"OCTF, Harper."

"Investigator, this is Bellville from Hamilton Falls PD."

Uh-oh. He knew he'd left too soon. Swinging his feet to the floor, he said, "Working swing shift, sir? Don't tell me Luke Fisher slipped up, and you slapped a charge on him."

"No, it's not Fisher at all. It's the other one."

Lightning fast, Ray ran through all the names in his case file and came up blank. "What other one? There is no other one."

"Yeah, turns out there is. This individual has been siphoning off the funds Fisher's been raising since the beginning. Taking advantage of the position of trust."

"Who?" It had to be someone new. Some accomplice Ray hadn't run into yet, who had been operating in the shadows to pull off the crime Ray had known in his gut was going to happen.

"What really gripes me is the whole holier-than-thou angle," Bellville went on. The objective viewpoint of the career law enforcement officer was obviously a struggle, judging from the anger in his tone. "If you're going to be a crook, fine. Be a crook. But don't masquerade as a person of faith and all the time laugh at everyone else who's really trying to do the right thing while you do your dirty work."

At last Ray understood. "Lieutenant, what are you telling me? Surely not Toby Henzig. I would have bet two weeks' salary that guy was solid."

"Well, you'd win your bet. Not him. The other one."

"*What* other one?" Ray repeated.

"The girl. The accountant or whoever she is. Montoya. I've got her in my holding tank until I can figure out which I'd rather charge her with—grand larceny or dragging the God I love through the mud."

CLAIRE HAD ONCE thought that the worst thing that could happen to a person was to be Silenced. In that ceremony, which was called when a person had committed a serious spiritual crime, he or she was barred from fellowship with the Elect, and no one could talk to them for a period of seven years. People generally didn't survive the pain of being Silenced; the majority went Outside and were lost to their loved ones forever.

But she knew now that there were worse things than being Silenced. Being denounced as a thief and an embezzler was at the top of the list. Hearing her mom's frantic voice as she tried to get in but not being able to see her was another. And knowing Luke Fisher had engineered it for reasons she couldn't understand was worst of all.

That was what had kept her awake most of the night on the clean but spartan mattress in the Hamilton Falls PD lockup. The jail was empty of criminals other than herself, so it wasn't noise or light that kept her from sleep. It wasn't the pervasive smell of disinfectant and cold sweat. No, it was the knowledge that someone she'd worked with, laughed with, partnered with—and, face it, had romantic dreams about— could turn on her in the space of a moment.

He'd called the police in at the tail end of her work day, making good and sure she'd made the deposit of the day's donations to the bank and generated yet another stack of thank-you letters. Then when the policeman had arrived, she'd ignored the two of them while they talked in the CD library, out of her hearing, blissfully making mailing labels while he stuck the figurative knife in her back.

"She's in there, Officer," he'd said, ushering the policeman in. "That's Claire Montoya."

She'd looked up, thinking it was an odd way to make an introduction, and had given the policeman a professional smile.

"Claire Montoya?" he asked.

"Yes. What can I do for you?"

"I need to inform you you're under arrest, ma'am."

She gaped at him. The words made no sense. Was Luke playing a prank on her? "What?"

"The charges are criminal impersonation in the first degree, wrongfully obtaining funds by means of deception, larceny, and embezzlement, ma'am," he said politely. "We have a statement from Mr. Fisher, here, laying out the events since you've come to work for the station. According to his information, you've embezzled more than one hundred thousand dollars from this station, and by extension from the listeners of KGHM in several counties. Would you come with me, please?"

None of it had made any sense. Not the booking process, not the panicked call to her parents, not the fact that the soonest they could get one of Derrick Wilkinson's coworkers at the legal firm down here was ten o'clock in the morning.

This morning.

Claire cocked a bleary eye at the window, where the color of the sky told her it was just after dawn. Three more hours until someone would come to help her. Three more hours of lying in yesterday's clothes, the scent of her own fear heavy in her nostrils.

Three more hours to pray.

She'd done little else during the endless night—it was the best use she could make of her time. Not one person outside of her parents had communicated with her in more than twelve hours. It wasn't that she expected a mob of people to storm the police station's door, demanding her release. But surely more than two people in a town the size of Hamilton Falls would stand up for her?

Look how they turned on Phinehas, a voice whispered in her mind.

Phinehas really was a criminal. She was not. And as soon as Derrick's lawyer friend turned up, she was going to tell them so, at great length and in excruciating detail. Somebody had to believe her. Luke had made it all up. She had no idea what she'd done to make him do this to her, but somehow it had to be made right.

If only Ray hadn't left town. If only she hadn't been so rigid and blind. If only she could have another chance to talk to him. In fact, as soon as she got out of here, she was going to get his number from Julia and call him up and apologize. Grovel. Beg. Do what it took to make him believe that she wanted to see if something could work between them, too.

O Lord, please help me. Help me not to panic. Help me to trust that You're in control and will show people that I'm innocent. Soften Ray's heart toward me. Help me to—

"Claire!"

For a moment, she wondered if she'd heard his voice outside in the hall because of the strength of her prayer. In the next second, she'd convinced herself it couldn't be. This whole experience was a nightmare, a dream, and she'd teleported him into it just because she wanted him so badly—

"Claire, are you all right? Sergeant, let her out, please."

She rolled off the mattress and ran to the tiny window that separated her from the normal world where people walked around free.

"Ray?" she croaked. There was water in the little sink, but

she'd been too disgusted with what might have been in there before her to drink out of the faucet. She was unshowered and dehydrated and hungry—and she'd never been so glad to see anyone in her entire life.

The sergeant ran a card key through a slot on the wall and something inside the door chunked open. Before she could even grab the handle, Ray had whipped it back and dragged her into his arms. She burst into tears against the rough wool of his jacket. A fiery mix of joy and confusion and relief flooded her as she dragged the scent of clean fabric and his cologne into lungs starved for a single breath that wasn't tainted with fear.

"I can't believe they've got you in here," he said incredulously. "I came as soon as the lieutenant called. I put the bubble on the roof and drove all night."

She had no idea what the bubble was or what it was for, but if it got him here faster, then she was grateful.

"The emergency light is for police business only," the sergeant said, her mouth pruned up as though someone had pulled strings on either side of it.

Ray's response to that was short and pithy. "If getting an innocent person out of jail isn't police business, I don't know what is. Come on, Claire."

"What—how—" She gave up on trying to speak. Just looking at him was manna to her soul as he practically dragged her up the stairs to the offices of the police department.

"Bellville is letting you out on my recognizance for twenty-four hours," he explained as they went. "In other words, I'm guaranteeing to him you won't skip town and make a run for Mexico."

"I've never wanted to go to Mexico," she said breathlessly, her hand clutched in his as he passed the various offices and bull pens and no one jumped out to stop them and send her back to that eight-by-ten room.

He pulled her into an office where a laptop computer sat, fired up and ready to go, next to the beat-up leather backpack she'd seen in the jump seat of his truck. "I need you to make a statement for me. Use the laptop."

"Saying what?"

"I want you to tell me everything Luke Fisher has assigned to you, asked you to do, told you, or hinted at in any conversation you've ever had with him."

"That could take most of our twenty-four hours." She'd much rather go somewhere quiet with a good lock on it and spend those hours alone with Ray.

"That's okay. Sit right here." He pulled out a chair and planted her in it. "Take as much time as you need to give me as much detail as you can."

She sat, but she didn't turn to the laptop. Not yet. "You believe me."

His hazel gaze felt like the summer sun after a cold plunge in the lake. "Of course, I believe you. He set you up. He's the guy I've been doing surveillance on all this time. He's Richard Brandon Myers."

Claire stared at him. "The rip-off artist? Luke? What?"

"They're one and the same. I knew he had to be up to something, but I didn't expect he'd drag you into it. Now our job is to prove he did all the things they've charged you with."

Her mind reeled. "In twenty-four hours."

"Right. Get to work."

So, she did. It took forever. It took all the way through the breakfast muffin and massive mocha latte he brought her from the coffee bar on Main Street. It took, in fact, the entire three hours before her counsel, Spencer Rodriguez, arrived and was brought into the office for a strategy session. They printed out the statement—all eleven single-spaced pages of it—and gave it to him to read. When he finished, he took off his gold-rimmed spectacles and gazed at the two of them. Light glinted on a head as bald as a bowling ball. He was the guy who would help clear her. Claire thought he was beautiful.

"Fisher is slick, I'll say that for him. Do you have his statement, too?"

Ray pulled it out of his backpack and handed it to him. "I made copies."

Rodriguez glanced at the first few sheets and shook his head. "Point for point, he takes what he told Claire and twists it tighter than a screw so that she looks like the culpable one. He's had some practice at this, I can tell."

"I have some background information you'll find interesting, then." Ray pulled a manila folder out and handed it to him. "That's a snapshot of his last three years, as complete as I can make it. Hamilton Falls PD already has this material. We just don't have any hard evidence to make it stick."

"Without it, it's her word against his."

"We'll get it." Ray's voice was grim, and Claire remembered again how intimidated he'd once made her feel. How she'd once told Dinah Traynell she wouldn't want him coming after her. Now that force of justice, that sense of confidence, was working on her side.

For which she thanked God for about the tenth time this morning.

"We should reconvene at the end of the day and see what we've got," Rodriguez said. "The terms of Claire's release are that she stays in Hamilton Falls in your presence at all times. That shouldn't be a problem, should it?"

"No," Ray said.

"If it turns out to be one, call me." Rodriguez handed him a card. "That cell number is active 24/7." Ray pocketed the card. "What's first on the agenda?" Rodriguez slipped the manila folder into his briefcase.

"The radio station. I have a few questions for Mr. Fisher."

"I heard him on the air as I was driving over."

"Good." Ray offered Claire his hand and she slid hers into it as she rose. "Come on. We have work to do if we're going to get you cleared by tomorrow."

Chapter 14

H ARPER'S LAW: If you assume something, it'll come back to bite you in the butt.

Both Ray and Claire assumed that it would be business as usual at the radio station, but the first thing they found when they got to the building was that it was locked. Southern gospel music flowed happily from the exterior speakers, but the booth drapes were pulled and no one answered the door.

"I have keys." Claire fished them out of the purse they'd retrieved from the sergeant, who had been none too happy about giving them up. They'd spent fifteen minutes at Claire's place so she could shower and change, and now they were ready to take on Luke Fisher. Ray would have preferred to have done it alone, but when Claire unlocked the door and led the way inside, it was clear she wasn't about to be left behind and probably had a few salient questions for Fisher herself.

She pushed open the door to the CD library and then

stopped short at the glass window that looked into the DJ's booth itself.

No one was there.

"He must be in the men's room," Ray said. "Back in a sec."

But he wasn't. Nor was he anywhere on the premises, and when they looked in the parking lot, neither the white van nor his Camry were there. Just then they heard his voice come across the speakers: "That was Ricky Skaggs and an old favorite of mine. Now, for a change of pace, coming up for Melanie and Tracy we have ZOEgirl. This is Luke Fisher, fisher of men, coming to you live from 98.5 KGHM in Hamilton Falls!"

"He must have gone out to grab a cup of coffee." They dashed inside, but when they went into the studio it was just as empty as before.

"Now here's a word from Hamilton Feed and Seed, where all the chicks I know do their shopping." Luke's voice sounded loudly throughout the studio, and then the commercial began.

"Ray, he's put a tape in," Claire said, horrified. Pointing at the deck, where one light flashed green and the other red, she went on, "He probably came in to relieve Toby this morning at eight, stuck tapes in both decks, and took off in the van. And Ray—" She put a hand on his sleeve. "The van doesn't have plates yet. It's brand new."

"So, tracing it is going to be more difficult. Like Rodriguez says, the guy is slick. The question of the hour is, where did he go?"

"With the head start he got, he could be anywhere."

"Maybe there's something around here." He began to go through everything sitting on the console. "A piece of paper. A letter. A statement. Anything."

"Maybe. The only paper he ever used is sticky notes."

A search of the studio and the CD library turned up a whole lot of nothing—if you didn't count the massive dust bunny under the broadcasting console. That left the coffee room, which didn't take long, and Claire's office.

"It would be just like that guy to plant something in here that would incriminate you some more," Ray said grimly, surveying the room.

"Then it's a good thing we got here first, and not that grumpy sergeant at the jail." She pointed at a plastic bin sitting on the floor. "Toby brought in the mail. I'll go through it while you do my office," she suggested. "It's too familiar to me. I'm liable to look right over something important just because I've seen it twenty times."

Ray went through her desk and credenza, then glanced up at the row of cards on the window sill. They were just as innocuous as they had been the first time. Just to be thorough, though, he read through them and the thank-you letter taped to the glass, slowly, until he got to the signature.

Richard Myers.

Surely Fisher wouldn't have been that stupid. Or that arrogant. "Claire, where did this letter come from?"

"One of the ministries we donated to." She was halfway through the bin of mail, sorting it into piles. "It's funny, isn't it? The pastor has the same name as—" She stopped in horror. "Oh, no."

Ray looked more closely at the letter. A little graphic of a church at the top, the address in cutesy Old English script below it. He ran his thumb over it. No engraving. It had come out of a laser printer. There was no reason for a casual observer to think anything of it. Coincidences happened all the time.

Except he didn't believe in luck or coincidence.

"Luke said he'd been donating to them for some time," Claire told him. "I cut them a check for ten thousand the first week I was here."

"You sent ten thousand to a P.O. box on Luke's say-so?"

"I had no reason not to. Then."

His brain was moving at lightning speed. A church in Idaho. Right across the state line. Nice and safe, if you were on the run. But crossing a state line turned a little fraud into a nice big federal felony. "Let me use your phone, just in case it's real. But I bet it's not."

She rolled her chair back and waved a hand at it. "Go ahead."

He dialed Information for the Idaho exchange, and to his amazement, the church on the letterhead actually existed. For a split second, doubt flickered. *No. Never assume.*

"Good Shepherd Community, this is Dineen Strachan speaking."

"Hi, Ms. Strachan. I'm calling for Pastor Myers, please."

"You mean Pastor Torvig."

"There's no Richard Myers associated with your church?"

"No indeed. To whom am I speaking?"

"This is Investigator Ray Harper of the Washington Organized Crime Task Force. I had information that I could find Pastor Myers there. Maybe I have the wrong church. Is there another Good Shepherd in—" He glanced at the letterhead. "—Miller's Ferry?"

"Investigator, there's only one Good Shepherd anywhere." She laughed comfortably, as if she'd made a joke. "But no, as far as churches, we're the only one with that name."

"Okay, let me ask you this. Did you receive a check recently for ten thousand dollars?"

The laugh this time wasn't comfortable, it was incredulous. "Ten thousand! Not likely. The most we'd see around here is a couple of hundred. Should I be on the lookout for it?"

"If it does show up, would you mind calling me?" He gave her his cell phone number. "It was sent to your P.O. box."

"We don't have a P.O. box. The church has a street address and we get our mail right here."

"Ah." Of course, they did. "Well, keep an eye open anyway, Ms. Strachan. I appreciate your help."

"Any time you want to send ten thousand our way, Investigator, you just feel free."

"I'll keep that in mind."

He hung up and glanced at Claire, who was pacing the length of her office between the desk and the credenza. "They didn't get the money," she said flatly.

"No. They don't have a post-office box and there is no pastor named Richard Myers."

"Oh dear. Oh dear." Gripping her elbows in agitation, she made a fast turn. "I'll put a stop payment on the check." She reached for the phone and Ray put his hand on hers. Her fingers were cold under his. He gathered them in his palm and pulled her closer.

"Too bad I didn't figure out a little sooner what he was really doing while he was spinning records for KGHM."

"I knew he was too good to be true," she said. "He's been such a jerk to me lately. I can't believe I didn't figure out something was wrong long before this." Claire pulled away a little, as though it would help her think. "How long did you say you've been chasing him?"

"At least a year. When I came to Hamilton Falls to testify, I heard him on the radio and recognized his voice." He gave her a rueful glance. "So, yeah, I haven't been completely up front with you about why I was hanging around. His last gig was romancing older women to get their money, and one of them had the foresight to tape him one day. At that time he was using the name Brandon Boanerges."

"Brandon." She sat on the edge of her desk and frowned. "Brandon. Why is that name familiar?"

"Have you seen it lately?"

"I've seen hundreds of names lately." She gestured at the stack of new mail. "And I'm a little fried from being arrested and getting no sleep. But I'll remember. I always do."

"Meantime, this check for ten grand was shipped off to Idaho. If you had just pulled off the scam of the century and had a brand-new van paid for courtesy of your fine, church-going listeners, where would you be headed?"

"I'd be going to that post-office box in Idaho to cash my check," she said.

He nodded. "That's my girl, thinking like a criminal. Let's hit the road."

"Ray, I can't."

He stopped in the doorway and slapped the jamb. "Right. You're on my recognizance. You can't leave town."

"Technically, neither can you, right?"

"I don't have much choice. We have a joint-forces order in place, but there isn't time to call in the cavalry. I could notify the FBI, but by the time I got them mobilized, I could be in Miller's Ferry. It's not that far away."

"He's also got a head start."

"Well, let's hope he plans to stop and enjoy the fruit of his labor. I can't see a guy like that saving his pennies. He'll probably blow the lot on radio equipment or something while he looks for another town to rip off."

"He can't."

"Oh, I bet he can."

"No, I mean he can't cash the check and get the actual money right away. There'll be a fifteen-day hold on it, especially if it's a new account. Not only that, the bank might invoke the ten-thousand-dollar rule and notify the Treasury Department."

"No kidding." Sometimes the Feds, in their war on drugs, actually got their red tape in the right place. "I'm glad I have you for backup on this one. So, best case, he's not going to have any money."

"Right. And that will probably make him cranky."

"He hasn't shown any signs of violence, but you never know."

"Ray, be careful." She slid off the desk and stopped in front of him. "Please." Her eyes were huge and frightened, and a little red around the edges from tears. Her skin had that transparent look some women got with lack of sleep, and she was pale.

She'd never seemed more beautiful to him.

"Last time we talked I wasn't sure you'd care if I never came back," he said with a trace of his old attitude. "Something change?"

Her head tipped forward, hiding her eyes. "If we ever get out of this, can we talk about that?"

He wasn't going to let her off the hook that easily. "Only if I have something to look forward to."

When she lifted her head, the beginnings of a smile flickered at the corners of her lips. "You do," she said. "Now go and get Luke Fisher."

THERE WAS STANDING on the edge of the precipice, and there was doing a championship swan dive right off it.

Claire figured that with those words, she'd committed herself. Nothing that she had thought to be good and right seemed to be so in reality, so maybe some of the things she'd thought were wrong weren't so bad after all. Luke Fisher, nationally known radio evangelist and unanointed leader of the Elect, was a con artist. The police, guardians and protectors of the community, had arrested her for—what? Opening the mail, cutting checks, and sending thank-you letters?

So, if Ray wanted to come back to something more than a handshake and a vote of thanks, she was more than willing to give it to him, because he was the only thing in her life that seemed to make any sense at all. That sense of safety she'd felt with him hadn't led her astray—on the contrary, it had been the one thing she could count on through this whole awful experience.

Well, the second thing. God, it was clear, was listening to the incoherent, panicked gabble her prayers had become. She was going to pin what was left of her ability to believe in things on those two, and hope they would bring her through.

Meantime, here she was, breaking the law again by being in the station without Ray to vouch for her. Well, what the cops couldn't see they wouldn't get upset about. She had things to do. Pulling the stack of unopened mail toward her, she picked up the phone, tucked it between her chin and shoulder, and dialed Rebecca's number.

"Quill and Quinn."

"Rebecca, it's Claire."

"My goodness! Is this the single phone call they allow you from jail?"

"No, you've been reading too many detective novels."

"Are you all right, dear? Your poor mother is prostrated."

"That's what I was calling about. Can you let her know I'm okay? Ray Harper came back and sprang me—"

"Did he? How very romantic. I knew there was something going on between you and that boy."

"—and I'm at KGHM, hiding out."

"Goodness. You mean it was a real jail break?"

"No, I have a twenty-four hour pass. Rebecca, something terrible has happened."

"What could be worse than your getting arrested?"

"Luke Fisher setting it up, that's what. He's a con artist. All the money we've been sending to his charities has actually been going straight to him under other names." Rebecca made a choked sound. "You have to call Derrick Wilkinson and get him to stop the land deal. When Margot and I went out to the site, she declared it unbuildable. The bank isn't going to grant the loan, and Mark McNeill and Owen have already mortgaged their houses. Derrick has to get to them and tell them to pull out of escrow before they're stuck buying a swamp."

"Good heavens," Rebecca said in the hushed tones of shock. "Wait, I'm writing all of this down. Mark—Owen—escrow. All right. What else?"

It felt so good to have someone believe her that Claire was close to weeping with relief. But she bit back the urge and plowed on.

"One more thing. When you're talking to Derrick, tell him to break this to Owen gently. Owen's going to feel responsible for this whole thing because Luke hooked him in first. Tell Derrick that the two of them should talk to Toby Henzig. We all need to stand together on this, and I think Toby and Owen can find some common ground."

"You're saying that the Elect and the community church can, you mean," Rebecca translated quietly.

"Yes. As much money came from those folks as from the Elect. We've lost money and trust over this, and the only way we'll get it back is to work together. I don't care how radical or sinful that sounds, it's the truth."

"Oh, I agree with you. And from what I understand, Derrick has actually had a word or two with Mr. Henzig already. He is a very angry young man, our Derrick. Spearheading a recovery effort might just be the thing he needs."

Claire rocked back in her chair with a huff of laughter. "Rebecca Quinn, you amaze me."

"Why is that, dear?"

"You know more about the people in this town than we do about ourselves."

"Nobody pays any attention to little old ladies in book-shops, dear. That's our burden—and our strength."

She sounded so smug about it that Claire laughed again. "Go forth and conquer, O intrepid one. Meantime, I've got calls to make and letters to prepare returning all these checks. I might as well do something constructive while I'm grounded."

It took just as long to return a check as it did to thank a listener for one. While she filled in database fields on au-topilot and got the mail merge ready, she called Margot at home and asked her to stop payment on the Good Shepherd Church's check. Then, after forty or fifty letters, Claire real-ized that the eerie silence in the station had been going on for some time.

Dead air.

The tapes had stopped playing.

With a gasp, she leaped to her feet and ran into the stu-dio, where the phone console was lit up like Main Street at Christmas with people calling in, no doubt wondering what had happened.

Oh dear. Oh dear. What was she going to do? Start the tapes over? No, the station was going to be in enough trou-ble when all of this broke without adding the fact that they'd all been fooled by a two-dollar tape. She sat at the console. She'd seen him do this often enough. Blindly, she reached for the nearest CD sitting in the caddy and popped it into the player. Okay. Slide the lever up to route sound to the mic. Headphones on. Now, talk.

"This is Claire Montoya, coming to you live from 98.5 KGHM, where we—" *Are the biggest fools God ever put on the planet.* "—rock for Jesus!"

She punched the Play button on the CD, slid the lever back down, and while the studio filled with the rapid-fire swing of Five Wise, she slumped back in the chair and burst into tears.

It didn't last long. Her eyes already stung from crying so much, and besides, she had only three minutes while the song played. So, when the digital counter told her she had thirty seconds to get the next song started, she put another CD in the tray. She'd figure out how to back-call them in a minute. While the second CD played, she ran back into her office and got the stack of letters.

She glanced around her desk. Oops, better take the contents of the inbox, too. Back in the studio, she let the CD go to the next track while she got herself organized, then decided she'd do that for all of them.

"This is a Two-Track Weekend," she announced to five counties when the song ended. "Today you'll get not one, but two songs from each album. If you have any requests, just give us a call."

Whew. That would give her six or even twelve minutes in which to get some work done. Unless the phone rang, which it did, a couple of minutes later.

"KGHM, this is Claire. What can I play for you?"

"Miss Montoya, I thought we made it clear that you were in Investigator Harper's custody."

It took Claire a second to place the voice. "Um—"

"This is your attorney, Miss Montoya. Spencer Rodriguez. Is the investigator at the station with you?"

"No," she said.

"Do you have an explanation as to why you are suddenly a DJ and he is not there?"

Dead air probably wasn't the explanation he was looking for. "Ray believes Luke Fisher may have gone to Idaho to collect a check I sent to one of his false names. So, he's gone after him, and since I can't leave town and no one is here to run the station, here I am."

"You realize you are breaking the terms of your temporary release."

"I know," Claire said. "But I don't have a choice. I'm hoping Toby will be here any minute, and then I'll come to your office." She glanced at the clock. Past two, and Toby's shift usually started at noon. What on earth was going on? Had everyone fallen into an alternate universe, where nothing was where it was supposed to be? "I'm not going anywhere, Spencer. I promise."

"You'd better hope no one at the police station is listening to the radio."

She was hoping that, as a matter of fact. "Oops. Song's ending. I have to go."

TWO HOURS LATER, Claire had exhausted the contents of the CD caddy and had had to raid the library. She wasn't familiar enough with popular music to know what she was doing, but she recognized enough of the artists' names to fake it fairly well. Luke had a list of the prayer requests in an open document on his computer, so every fifteen minutes she read one of them, feeling like a complete fraud.

Well, the listeners had paid to have their prayers read, hadn't they? Despite what had happened to their money, she could at least give them what they'd paid for.

The exterior door slammed around four o'clock, and Claire looked up from her play list as her heart jumped in her chest.

Ray?

But it wasn't.

Toby Henzig opened the studio door and closed it behind him, collapsing into the plastic guest chair as if he'd just expended his last reserve of strength. Claire finished back-calling the last fifteen minutes of songs, announced the next band, and started the CD player. Only then did he speak.

"I thought you didn't want to have anything to do with this," he gestured around the booth.

"I didn't have a choice. And you wouldn't believe what changed my mind." She yanked the headphones off and tossed them on the turntable that no one seemed to use. "Where on earth have you been?"

"You wouldn't believe me, either."

"I'd believe a lot of things today that I wouldn't have believed yesterday. You heard I was arrested, right?"

"Oh, I heard. Luke told me the whole thing in great detail last night before his show, with a lot of hand-wringing and crocodile tears over how misled he was about you. I told him that was impossible and a huge mistake, which I assume the police have now realized, since you're sitting here."

"It's a mistake, all right. Everything that guy has done or said since he got here has been a complete lie. He's been embezzling the listener donations for weeks and set me up to take the blame for it."

Toby stared at her with a lot less astonishment than she would have expected. "So your friend Derrick told me."

"He called you, then?" Bless Rebecca for getting her messages through. That made two people in the world that Claire could count on.

"Oh yes, he called. That's where I've been all this time— at an emergency assembly of your folks down at the mission hall. You have a very efficient phone-tree system, I must say."

"You?" After they learned they'd been duped by Luke Fisher, Claire wouldn't have been surprised if the Elect had risen up and stoned any Outsider who would have dared set foot in the mission hall. "What happened?"

"It seems Derrick has had his suspicions about Luke from the beginning. I had reservations myself, but he seemed so sincere and so—let's face it—successful that I thought I was just being narrow-minded and maybe a little jealous. So, when Derrick got your message to come and talk to me and we both realized we'd had the same misgivings, it didn't take much to decide that the whole church needed to know. I'll be speaking to Hamilton Falls Community Church tonight."

"So, everyone knows it wasn't me, right?" If she could come out of this a free woman, that's all she would ask. She'd never think badly of her mom again. She'd never roll her eyes at her dad because he loved to watch *Seinfeld* late at night. They'd had it right all along and she'd been an insufferable, self-righteous prig who thought she was better than they were because of how she looked. As soon as this was over, she'd have her parents over for dinner and beg their forgiveness.

"Not many people knew you had been arrested, and when they heard about it, no one believed that you did it anyway," Toby assured her. "Some still can't quite believe Luke could have done it. Owen Blanchard took it as quite a blow. I understand he and Luke had become friendly."

"Together they were our leadership team. So, then what happened?"

Toby smiled his gentle smile. It held neither malice nor triumph, only a tired kind of satisfaction.

"I invited them to church."

Chapter 15

CLAIRE BLINKED and stared at Toby, not certain she'd heard correctly. "You what?"

His gaze was direct, though there were lines of exhaustion around his eyes. He lifted a hand, palm up on his knee, and let it fall. "Let's be honest, Claire. Your group is not going to survive in the form it has been all these years. The leadership is faulty, the doctrine is unsound, and now that people see they've been mistaken in their faith a second time, it might be the wake-up call God has been trying to give them."

Claire tried to feel a little indignant, to defend the community in which she'd grown up, but there was no getting around the fact that he was right. She'd come to the same conclusions herself, some time ago.

"I proposed that the people of the Elect be our guests at our Sunday-evening service tomorrow. I don't know if any of them will come. But this town needs healing, and if the members of the body of Christ don't reach out to each other, it won't happen."

Claire couldn't imagine the Elect going to a service in a "worldly" church. But then, she couldn't imagine herself being arrested for larceny, either—or imagine falling for a cop who didn't believe in God. But she had. And who was to say God's hand wasn't working in all this, leading the Elect away from the mess they'd made with all their rules and regulations, and bringing them, despite themselves, to a knowledge of the truth?

"Toby," she said with complete sincerity, "if I'm not back in jail, I'll be there."

His smile was the tired grin of an old friend as he slumped in the hard plastic chair. "I hoped you would be. And bring your friend Ray, as well."

"That'll be up to him, but I'll give it a try."

"Ready to hand the headphones over to me? Probably no one in Hamilton Falls is interested in the stock reports right now, but it's my job to read them anyway."

She held the headphones out with the air of someone trying to hand over a crate of tarantulas. "Here. Take them. If I never have to do this again I'll be a happy woman."

He slid them over his ears and took her seat behind the console. "Oh, I don't know about that. You sounded great—as if you'd been doing it for years. I'll bet you a doughnut that you start getting fan mail."

Laughing, she gathered up her piles of paperwork and took them back into her office with a huge sense of relief. Toby was back. Ray was on the job. She had her paperwork. If you didn't count the fact that she was illegally at large, all was right with the world.

As she dumped the pile on her desk, her phone rang—the

office line, not the studio line, which meant it was station business and not a fan making a request or someone calling in to rant about the discount store going in.

"KGHM, this is—"

"Claire, it's me." Ray's voice was exhausted, with anger and frustration making the edges a little ragged.

"Ray! What's going on? You're never going to believe what I've been doing all—"

"I've lost him."

She stopped, a cold feeling prickling over her shoulders. "Lost him?"

"Yeah. He emptied his post-office box and closed his account, about two hours before I got here."

"What about the bank?"

"He was there. Made himself real memorable when he tried to cash the check and the teller told him about the fifteen-day hold."

"What happened?"

"He's getting frustrated. Had a shouting match with the teller, and they finally escorted him off the premises. He took the check with him."

"I had Margot put a stop payment on it," Claire said. "He'll look for a bigger town now. Somewhere he can blend in while he waits his fifteen days. And then he'll find he can't cash it anyway."

"A bigger town in which direction? Boise? Spokane? I'm sitting here at a gas-station pay phone on the interstate because I forgot to charge my stupid cell phone during all the excitement last night. There are freeways going in four directions and I have no idea which one he took."

Defeat hung heavily in his voice. She couldn't stand it. Luke Fisher had destroyed her church's faith in itself and had broken the trust of countless people in five counties. She absolutely would not allow him to destroy Ray's irrepressible spirit.

"There has to be something we can do," she said desperately. "Don't give up."

"Maybe you should ask God to give us a clue."

She blinked against the sudden prick of tears. "Ray, please don't be sarcastic with me. I can't deal with it. Not now."

"Honey, I'm not being sarcastic. What I am is out of gas. In a metaphorical sense."

"You're asking me to pray for a—what do you call them? A lead?"

"Why not?"

"Because God doesn't care about things like leads in fraud investigations."

"Why shouldn't He? He cares about you and me, doesn't He?"

There was a note in Ray's voice she had never heard before. "What's going on?" she asked again, meaning something different this time.

"There are a lot of miles between us right now, and a lot of room for thinking. So, I've been doing just that."

"And what did you conclude?"

"I've concluded that I need help."

"I've concluded that myself." Propping her elbows on her letters, she rubbed her gritty eyes.

"I thought you already had a direct line to help."

"I used to think I did, until last night. Then I realized I

really don't know much about anything. I think I have to start over."

"Yeah, me, too."

Claire could do nothing but sit with the receiver pressed to her ear, marveling at the circumstances that had brought them to this point, connected to each other by the fragile means of a phone line, making the same discovery from completely different points of origin.

"Claire?"

"I'm here."

"About that prayer?"

"What, you want me to pray now? Over the phone?"

"I don't know about you, but I think I need to hear it. You know how I am. Reading about it in the papers later just won't do it for me."

She smiled, despite the fact that her throat was a little closed up. She stared at the invoice on the top of her inbox pile without really seeing it. Instead, she saw Ray in the late-afternoon light, standing in a phone booth at a nameless gas station, someplace where two roads met.

"Father, Ray and I have come to the end of ourselves in more ways than one." She hesitated, then cleared her throat. "We need help, Lord. You know our hearts, what's inside us, better than we do. Thank You for showing us that we can't go on like this, him depending on himself, and me depending on the Elect, instead of depending on You.

"If it's Your will that we find Luke and bring him to justice, we pray that You'll show us that, too. And if it isn't, help us to focus on You anyway, Lord, so our lives can please You." She paused, but Ray said nothing. "We ask these things in

Jesus' name, who gave His life that we could come to You this way without fear. Amen."

"Amen," Ray breathed.

A little silence fell, punctuated by a growl in the distance as a diesel rig went past where Ray was standing.

Claire's gaze fell again on the invoice on the top of her stack. Brandon Brothers, for fifty thousand. A lot of concrete that was never poured and a lot of pipe that had never been laid.

"I never paid it," she said suddenly.

"Paid what?"

"This invoice sitting here. Luke yelled at me to pay the balance to Brandon Brothers the day it came, and I got so mad at him I chucked it in my inbox and never did it."

"Brandon . . . Brothers?" Ray said carefully.

Oh. My. Stars. Claire, you idiot.

"*That's* where I heard that name," she said. "It's the general contractor in Spokane that we hired to build the worship center."

"We did, did we?"

"Luke did. Ray?"

"Yes?"

"It's laser printed, just like the church thank-you letter. And they have a post-office box, too."

"In Spokane, you said? What are the odds they really exist?"

"Not very good." Excitement and hope blossomed inside her. "When I called them, a really unprofessional woman answered the phone. It sounded as though I woke her up. I was trying to get better terms for payment, and she told me I had to pay the invoice on receipt."

"Ten to one it was some lady friend of his and he paid her to say a few lines if anyone ever called. What's the box number?"

She told him, then said, "Ray, I bet he's going to go west. He didn't have any success in Idaho and now he's heading for the check in Spokane. Except there isn't going to be any check there because I didn't pay the bill."

"So, not only can he not cash the one he has, he's going to drive all the way down there and find an empty box. That might push him over the edge and he might come after you. We can't risk it. I'll call the OCTF and have whatever investigator is closest pick him up. Even if I doubled the speed limit I'd never make it in time to do it myself. I'll alert the postmaster there, too, so they can stall him until my guys get there."

"Then what?" She was practically trembling with excitement. Maybe God really had been in that little temper tantrum that had prevented her from paying the invoice and thus making it easy for Luke to get what he wanted. Maybe He really did work in people's lives in this day and age, contrary to what she'd been taught. Maybe prayer really was for something other than continually asking for the willingness to wear black.

"Ray?" she asked when he didn't answer right away.

"I need you to go someplace where I know you're safe," he said.

"I'm going to Spencer Rodriguez's office as soon as I hang up."

"Good plan." He paused. "And while you're there . . . keep on praying."

THE INISH COUNTY lockup in Pitchford, where the OCTF operative had escorted Luke Fisher, had old-fashioned views about incarceration. The doors were made of multiple layers of alloy steel and bulletproof glass, and they clashed closed behind Ray with the kind of sound that would echo in a felon's dreams for years.

At least, Ray hoped so.

Maybe Fisher was even in the cell Phinehas had occupied before they'd transported him to the state pen. In any case, as the only jail facility in the county where Fisher had committed his felonies, it was familiar territory to Ray.

The interview room was dim and quiet. Even though they would be videotaped, Ray took his personal tape recorder out of his backpack and put it on the table, as was his habit. Then he leaned back in the metal folding chair, glanced at the clock, which said nine P.M., and took a sip of his vending-machine coffee while he waited.

He didn't have to wait long before Fisher was escorted in by a uniformed officer. He wore wrinkled khaki pants and a shirt whose right sleeve had been torn away at the shoulder. Sweat had made rings under his arms, and his hair, which Ray had never seen other than fashionably styled, was oily and raked straight back from his forehead.

Fisher collapsed into the chair and extended both hands. "Ray, thank God you're here. I don't know what kind of mix-up this is, but I've told them I've done nothing wrong until I'm blue in the face, and it hasn't done a bit of good. How soon can you get me out of here?"

Ray glanced at the outstretched hands, then reached past them and turned on the tape recorder. "You don't mind if this is running while we talk, do you?"

"Of course not. This is only a formality, right? They don't seem to understand I've got a show to do, people whose salvation may hang on a word in season. But then, cops are notorious for being ungodly. You should have seen the one that dragged me in here. Built like a gorilla, complete with do-rag and greasy leather vest."

Ray pressed his lips together and reminded himself that every word out of the guy's mouth (a) was a lie, (b) had an ulterior motive, and (c) was all of the above. Well, except for his very accurate description of OCTF Investigator Paul Kowalski, who could bench press three-fifty without even breathing hard and did tend to favor cotton scarves under his motorcycle helmet.

No, Luke Fisher was like a chameleon, changing to suit his environment. He'd say what he thought Ray wanted to hear, whether it happened to be the truth or not, if it would get him his way. For a sociopath like Fisher, his own way was all that mattered.

He was about to find out that the rest of the world might not agree.

"Tell me what's been happening, Luke," he suggested in a tone that could be sympathetic or completely expressionless, depending on how desperate—or delusional—you were.

"Well, to start with, if you're back in these parts, you must have heard about the Claire debacle. How she's been diverting the gifts from KGHM's programs into dummy accounts of her own instead of to the worship center where they belong." Luke spread his hands wide. "I couldn't believe it when I found out. I trusted her. Gave her a job. Treated her like my sister in Christ—and what did I get in return? Stabbed in the back. And my injury was the smallest. She might as well have crucified Christ all over again. She's betrayed all the Elect and every listener who ever cast his two mites into the treasury for the glory of God."

"Sounds pretty serious," he said.

"It is serious. As soon as I get out of here, I'm going to recommend to the leadership that she be Silenced or even cast Out. We can't allow a viper like that in our bosom. And for sure she's out of a job. Willetts has probably already fired her."

"I don't know about that. Someone told me they'd heard her on KGHM today. It sounds like she's taken over your show."

Dead silence fell in the room as Fisher goggled at him. Under the fluorescent lighting, his skin paled to a shade somewhere between white and green. "What did you say?" The sound was leached out of his melodious voice by shock—or maybe rage.

Ray shrugged. "Just what I heard."

"But she was arrested! I saw them take her away myself!"

"Apparently a little misdirection of the truth occurred."

"Misdirection! Miscarriage of justice, you mean. This is an outrage." He sat back in his chair, as if the moral indignation was too much to bear.

"Yeah, it was pretty outrageous," Ray said mildly, "especially when it turns out her story is exactly the same as yours, only without the preaching. Apparently everything you accused her of was true—she did take in large amounts of money and deposit them without a countersignature. She did write checks to these bogus ministries and send them off, again without a countersignature. But she mentioned a few additional facts that you forgot to tell the Hamilton Falls PD."

"Mentioned—or made up?"

"Well, that remains to be determined in court. She said that all the checks she sent away were at your direction, to charities you specified, and to addresses you gave her."

"All lies."

"If it's a lie, then why did you travel up to Idaho to empty the post office box there? A box number that, again, you specified for her?"

Fisher looked at him as if he were crazy. "I didn't. I've been in Spokane, having the station's mobile unit outfitted, as I told Claire before I left. If she says anything different, she's lying."

"I suppose the postmaster in Miller's Ferry was lying, too, then, when I showed him your picture and asked if you'd been there. He recognized you right away. And the teller at the bank where you tried to cash the check—she was probably lying about the fuss you kicked up, too, was she?"

"All right, all right, so I took the van for a test drive and went to see my friend in Miller's Ferry. He's the pastor at a church there. There's no crime in that."

"There's no pastor there named Richard Myers, either. But that's not surprising, is it, Ricky?"

Fisher looked behind him, as if expecting to see the other person whom Ray was addressing.

"Your real name is Richard Brandon Myers," Ray said. "You were born in West Hollywood on April 13, 1974. In Seattle you went under the name of Brandon Boanerges, and in Hamilton Falls you took the name Luke Fisher. I have people in each location who will testify to this, so don't even try to deny it."

Fisher stared at him, and Ray could practically see the wheels spinning in his mind as he tried to come up with a plausible story that would fit, get turned inside out, and be fashioned into something that would help him weasel out of this fix.

But Ray had made sure the facts were watertight. Fisher wasn't going to get out of this one.

"It's really true, isn't it?" Fisher said, shaking his head sadly. "The armies of Satan don't want God's work to succeed, so they come in droves to fight against it. The Elect will vouch for me. Owen Blanchard is a good man. He'll testify in my behalf."

"That probably depends on whether he gets his house out of hock or not."

"Why would he want to do that? The worship center is too important to the economy in Hamilton Falls."

"There isn't going to be any worship center. No loan, no land, no center. No listener donations, either. I'd be careful about showing my face around Hamilton Falls right now if I were you."

Fisher's face crumpled in an expression that was part disgust, part contempt. Then it smoothed out and the smile returned. "They're my community. They'll back me up."

"You didn't really grow up Elect, did you, Luke?" Ray said quietly. "I did some checking around. Your home church was Second Congregational in West Hollywood. Mrs. Paulson still remembers you."

"I came to the Elect after that."

"Sure, you did. Right around the time you came to Hamilton Falls."

"Hey, God works in the Elect as well as any other group."

"You mean, you could work on them better than you could on most groups. There they were, leaderless and vulnerable, their belief in themselves a little shaky. Perfect pickings for a . . . leader like you."

"It was easy, too." Fisher leaned forward eagerly, his need for admiration clearly outpacing his good sense. "I did some asking around about their customs and stuff, and the rest I pulled out of Owen Blanchard. That guy is desperate for someone to talk to, what with his wife in prison and all."

"So, you let him talk. And built yourself a whole history out of what he said, huh?"

Fisher shrugged modestly, evidently pleased that Ray appeared to understand him so well. "They wanted a celebrity. I gave them one. They wanted a leader. I gave them that, too. Hey, they were happy. They got what they wanted. No crime in that."

"Too bad you didn't leave it at that."

"If that snide comment was about the money, they gave it freely and willingly. I read their prayers, I played what they wanted. They got their money's worth. A laborer is worthy of his hire, you know?"

"I don't think a laborer is worth a hundred thousand bucks, a swamp, and a couple of mortgages."

Fisher grinned the charming grin that had always annoyed Ray. "Like I said, they gave it willingly. I hardly had to say a thing."

"It's not the giving we have an issue with. It's the taking afterward. Not to mention mail fraud, exceeding treasury limits with a bank transaction, and larceny. Did I mention that the Feds are in line to talk to you after I'm done?"

Like a salmon running with a hook and desperate to get away from the line that dogged him, Fisher juked in another direction and took off.

"Speaking of giving willingly, I see you fell for her, too," he said with a man-to-man grin. "She took you in and hosed you, just like she did to me. I'd pity you if I didn't feel so sympathetic."

The sociopath is a glib liar. Ray's psychology tape replayed in his memory. *He can create and believe a complex structure of lies, to the point where he can pass a lie-detector test. He will change his story in response to the interviewer's reactions, whether the details are true or not. In fact, he doesn't even care if they are true. He only wants to manipulate.*

"Who would that be, Luke?" Ray asked. He was beginning to get a little tired of this. "Teresa White, your girlfriend in Hollywood? Barbara Corelli, the lady you were romancing in Seattle? Or the bank teller in Miller's Ferry? You've used so many women in your career that you're going to have to be a little more specific for me."

"You know who I mean. Claire Montoya."

Ray said nothing, just frowned slightly, as if inviting Fisher to go on.

"She's so pretty that you'd never believe the kind of mind she has. Take it from me, you don't want to know."

"Probably not."

"She's like this—this pit you fall into and before you know it, you're doing whatever she wants. Of course, the bait is pretty good. She has a beautiful body and she knows how to use it."

Ray clamped his teeth together so hard he thought he'd bend his fillings. *He only wants to manipulate.*

"Take it from me, Ray. I got in deeper with her than I ever thought possible. You've heard the expression *white-washed sepulcher*? Well, that defines her perfectly. Gorgeous on the outside and filthy inside. Why, what she knows about sexual positions alone would turn your—"

"This interview is terminated at twenty-one forty-five hours on Saturday night, the thirtieth of September," Ray told the tape recorder. His skin was cold with disgust, but his hand was absolutely steady as he reached over, turned off the recorder, and slid it into his backpack. With a nod at the uniform standing by the door, he slung the backpack over his shoulder as Fisher was hauled to his feet and re-cuffed in preparation for his walk back to his cell.

"Don't say I didn't warn you, Ray," Luke called as Ray reached the door. "If you go anywhere near Claire Montoya, she'll bite you like a spider."

But the clang of the steel door crashing shut between them was the only reply Ray bothered to make.

Chapter 16

CLAIRE HAD NEVER smelled anything as sweet as the scent of lake weed and sand at the tail end of the day. She and Ray strolled down the beach past the concession stand, closed now for the season, late Sunday afternoon with no particular direction in mind. Claire dragged in breath after breath of freedom.

"Have I told you lately how glad I am that you ever came to this town?" she asked him.

"Only about twenty times. I'm beginning to think my only attractions are my badge and my ability to get charges dropped."

She laughed, and when he took her hand, she didn't pull away or change the subject or run, all of which she might have done before they'd both been through the fiery trials of this week.

"Both very admirable qualities in a man, I think." They walked a few steps in companionable silence, and then she said, "But then, you have a lot of those."

"What, admirable qualities?"

"Yes. Not to mention a nice truck."

"Uh-huh. Trust a woman to get right down to brass tacks. But you forgot the most important one of all."

"What's that? No criminal record?"

He smiled and squeezed her hand. "How about the ability to pray? Or admit a need for God? How about those?"

A rush of hope and love silenced her for a moment. "You're right. Those are the most important qualities I could find in a man."

"I'm tired of this silence inside myself, Claire. When you prayed on the phone last night, I heard this voice inside me telling me this was right. Prayer was right." His voice cracked, and he cleared his throat. "I learn by hearing. Maybe if I'm going to be a Christian, I should spend a little time listening to what God has to tell me, huh?"

Her throat ached with joy and the need to sing out in praises to God. "I think that would be a great place to start," she said instead, her voice as soft as his. "For both of us."

They reached the concrete steps that wound up the river rock to the little park above. It overlooked the waterfall for which the town was named and was a popular make-out spot for the teenage crowd. But at the end of the day, most people were at home eating supper, and Ray and Claire had the cool, weed-scented twilight to themselves.

The steps were only wide enough for one person, so Claire had time to get her emotions under control before Ray saw the traces of tears on her cheeks. At the overlook, she leaned on the parapet made out of round river stones. Ray leaned a hip on the wall and followed her gaze out over the lake. "So, do you think Toby will follow through and show up at Gathering tonight?"

"I can't imagine he wouldn't. He strikes me as the kind of guy who stands behind what he says. Unlike certain people we know."

"Well, certain people won't be bothering the folks around here for a long time, if I have anything to say about it. Nice job getting that check looked after."

"It was easy. I called Margot at home. She connected to the bank interface from there and did it on the spot. Not without a whole bunch of editorial comments on my religion and its tendency to harbor crooks, however."

"It harbors decent, well-meaning people, too."

"Yes, but those aren't the ones who make headlines. Just imagine what the papers are going to say tomorrow."

"There was already a news van outside the county jail when I left Pitchford last night. I suppose they picked it up on their scanners."

"It's right that people know, despite what they'll probably say about the Elect. I'm sure they'll find a way to tie it back to Phinehas, too. But with all the money that poured into the station, you've got to believe a lot of people in five counties are going to feel they were involved." She made a face. "I just hope no one feels inclined to file a lawsuit."

"Let's jump off that bridge when we get to it. In the meantime, Gathering is going to start in half an hour, right? This ought to be interesting."

Claire pushed away from the wall and walked down the footpath to the road at Ray's side. "To start with, think of all the gossip that will start up when we arrive together."

"That going to bother you?" Again, he took her hand, and she marveled at the strength and calm assurance of the gesture. Here she'd always thought holding hands was for teenagers.

"After spending a night in jail? We have more important things to think about now."

"Good thing. I was starting to get a complex about it." They crossed the road fronting the beach and walked up the block. The Mission Hall was just on the other side of the cross street. "I figured you were ashamed of me or something."

"Not ashamed." Claire tried to find the words to explain what was obvious to an Elect girl and a mystery to an Outsider. "But so overly concerned about appearances that it almost overshadowed the fact that you were trying to be my friend." She shook her head at herself. "Boy, were my priorities messed up."

"Just your friend?"

But they had arrived at the hall, and in the flurry of shaking hands with people and finding a seat, Claire chose not to answer. She was almost afraid to say anything aloud, and yet they had to discuss it. Ray was due to go back to Seattle in the morning and knowing him, he'd want something settled between them.

Yet what could she say? She loved him, but her sister had loved Andrew, and look how that had turned out. There were no guarantees in relationships.

There are no guarantees in religion, either.

Well, she'd argue that one. Maybe not religion as the Elect saw it—she'd proven that herself. But what about faith?

Both she and Ray had done something they'd never done before—stepped out into the dark with only the power of prayer, and God had stayed faithful to His promise that he'd be with them. Could she make that a starting point? Could she and Ray both make a new start, like a pair of babies just learning how to walk? After a lifetime of thinking she was a Christian and being so concerned about every jot and tittle of the Elect law, it was a simple fact that she knew next to nothing about grace or faith or the things that really mattered. She knew a lot about the Bible, but it had all been filtered through the Shepherds' teachings to support the Elect way of life. Who knew what the Scriptures actually said? She'd be looking at them with new eyes, the same as Ray.

She'd look at people differently, too, without that sense of superiority ingrained in a person who had been told they were part of a peculiar people, chosen of God and singled out from the people of the world to bear His name. The fact was, she was just as clumsy and in need of help from God as anyone on the street. There was nothing special about her. Her parents were the special ones, to have put up with her for this long.

She needed to buff the layers of complacency off herself and discover what was really there underneath. The experience of helping to capture Luke Fisher had shown her there was good, solid steel somewhere under there. She just had to find a way to bring it out and get used to the person she could become if she gave herself a chance.

Maybe Ray wouldn't love that person as much as he loved the one he saw now. But she had to find out. She had to try. With God's help and by earnestly seeking His will for her life, maybe she could do it. She'd start by standing on her own two feet and moving to Seattle to be close to Ray. No more waiting for men to tell her what to do. The important thing was to find out what God wanted her to do.

Owen Blanchard mounted the platform with his hymn-book in one hand. His step was slower than she remembered it, and she realized suddenly that Owen, on whom many of the teenagers had had a crush when he'd first married Madeleine, was a middle-aged man. She imagined that the last few days had probably been pretty hard on him, too.

He announced the hymn, and when they had sung it and Mark McNeill had given a prayer, Owen returned to the microphone.

"Folks," he said in a voice that reflected his exhaustion and disappointment, "you've probably heard what has happened, but in case you haven't, let me tell you. Luke Fisher, whom we had welcomed among our number a few weeks ago, has been arrested for fraud and embezzlement, among other things. He has been stealing the money that this community has been sending to KGHM for the worship center." A collective gasp went up. "I want to apologize publicly for vouching for him and putting him in a position to defraud so many of you. If it hadn't been for the skill and vigilance of our own Claire Montoya and Investigator Ray Harper of the Organized Crime Task Force, Mark and I would have lost our homes and our folks would have had such a mountain of debt and legal issues to deal with that it makes me sick to think about it. Claire especially has gone through the fire on this one. Luke blamed all of his crimes on her, and she was arrested instead of him. I want to declare here and now that she is innocent of all charges, and in fact, she used her knowledge to trace him and help bring him down."

The audience murmured and craned their necks to see where Claire was sitting. She resisted the temptation to slouch and disappear, and instead straightened her spine against the metal back of her chair. *Steel*, she reminded herself.

"Folks," Owen went on, "it's clear to me that the way we're organized and led is flawed, and has been from the beginning. It has made it all too easy for someone to come in and fool us with a golden statue, as it were, so that we're blinded to its feet of clay. Any flock needs leadership, it's true, but it also needs accountability, openness, and corrected vision. To speak to that, I'd like to invite Toby Henzig, assistant pastor at Hamilton Falls Community Church, up to the front."

People buzzed and whispered as Toby made his way out of his row and up to the microphone.

"Lord, be with him," Claire whispered, and next to her, Ray murmured, "Second that." Whether they knew it or not, this was a turning point for the Elect. Either they'd go forward in faith, or they'd go back to the old ways and pull the blanket of tradition and habit over their heads, warding off the cold of the unknown in the only way they knew.

"Thanks, Owen." Toby took a breath and spoke into the microphone. "Folks, I know you're hurting and maybe even angry at what's been happening lately. It's a lot of public scrutiny, and maybe some of you haven't been treated very well by people who associate you with Phinehas and now Luke. But folks, I'm here to tell you that not everyone is like that. There are those who have been praying for you all, those who have been asking that God will send you comfort throughout all this. One of the ways He can do that is for you to let the folks at Hamilton Falls Community help you. We'd like to invite you to our evening service tonight at eight o'clock.

"Now, I know you've been told that churches other than the Elect are worldly and deceived. But you've been told that the Shepherds are the anointed of God, too, and that turned out to be . . . well, an overstatement. We're all on this planet together. Christ died for all of us. We're brothers and sisters in the body of believers, and folks, I'd like to see this false separation between us dissolved.

"Humans are funny, aren't they?" Toby went on with a smile as people looked at one another uncertainly. "They want to feel special, like they have a lock on eternity that no one else has. But you know what? Only Christ has that. This is all about each one of us as individuals and Jesus. That's it. It's not about this church or that church or who's right and who's deceived. It's about Jesus and what He did for us so that we could approach God clean and sinless.

"I want that for all of us, no matter what we call ourselves. Please come and join us. It's only a few steps down the street. We're looking forward to meeting you and calling you our friends, too."

Toby stepped down, shook Owen's hand, and walked down the aisle and out the door. People moved restlessly in their chairs. They looked at Owen. They looked at the door, standing open where Toby had left it.

Derrick Wilkinson stood up. "I don't know about anyone else," he announced defiantly, "but I think he's right."

"I do, too." Rebecca's voice rang out in the uncomfortable silence. She got to her feet, small and slender and indomitable. "Derrick, will you escort an old lady down the street, please?"

They made their way out of their respective rows, and Derrick offered her his arm. Owen watched them go, then picked up his Bible from his chair. "Ryan, Hannah," he said to his children, "come on. We're going, too."

"Well, I'm not." Elizabeth McNeill, Julia Malcolm's mother, folded her arms and stayed planted in her chair, which groaned in protest.

"I'll tell you about it when I get home, then," her husband, their former Elder, said as he stood to leave.

Elizabeth's mouth dropped open, and she gathered up her coat and handbag. "Mark, Owen, wait for me." She rushed to catch him, her son-in-law, and her grandchildren before they reached the parking lot and left without her.

Claire glanced at Ray as some of the people—including her parents—filed out, and some—including Alma Woods—stayed in their seats, immobilized by the clash between tradition and discovery, between the known and the unknown. "Well?" she said.

"This is new to me." His gaze held hers.

"I know. To me, too."

"I'm probably not going to be very good at it."

"It's not a contest. And there's plenty of help."

"Can we do it together?"

She wasn't sure if he was referring to learning to believe or learning to love. In the end, maybe it was the same thing.

"I'd like to try," she said, and stood up. She held out her hand, and he stood and took it, looking down into her eyes.

"He said it was only a couple of steps."

"Didn't you know?" She grinned at him, her lower lip trembling just the tiniest bit. "All the best journeys start that way."

His hand remained sure around hers as they walked outside, where the biggest harvest moon Claire had ever seen had begun to rise, lighting the way before them.

1. Have you ever heard the expression *toxic church*? What do you think it means? Were the Elect a toxic church? Have you yourself ever been involved with a toxic church? If so, what was your experience?

2. First Corinthians 13 tells us that without charity, no matter how eloquent a person may be, he or she becomes like a sounding brass or a crashing cymbal. Did Luke Fisher convince the Elect that he was a "real" evangelist possessing the love of God? Or does he? If so, how did he do it? Were the people simply starstruck?

3. When he introduced Luke to the congregation, Owen Blanchard urged them to "try the spirits and see if they are of God." With their history, were the Elect able to do this? How might you yourself do so?

4. Claire Montoya struggled with self-image issues. In a toxic church, many women find that decisions are made for them under the guise of a "womanly example." Do you think such practices are valid? What are the advantages and disadvantages of such an example?

5. The toxic church can impose restrictions on its members in any aspect of their lives. Would you allow such restrictions in your own church? Do you think it was reasonable for Claire to stay in Hamilton Falls at the Shepherd's request when she wanted to move away? If

you had had her background, what would you have done?

6. At what point did Claire realize she had let the Elect leadership make all of her decisions for her? Do you consider the needs of your church before making your own life decisions?

7. Claire's relationship with her parents was strained because their views on living up to the church's expectations differed from hers. Is this reasonable or realistic? Do your own views on behavior and dress differ from those of your parents' generation?

8. One of the themes of *A Sounding Brass* is that "faith comes by hearing." Investigator Ray Harper was an auditory learner, as opposed to a visual learner. In what way do you learn the best? Was Ray's experience realistic?

9. Have you ever heard the voice of God audibly? If so, what was it like? Do you think God speaks to people in this day and age?

COMING IN MAY 2007

IF YOU ENJOY THE NOVELS OF
SHELLEY BATES, LOOK FOR. . .

Over My Head
by Shelley Bates

Even in November, when the trees were bare and skeletal
and the ground wet, the jogging trail by the river was still
Lamorna Hale's favorite place to run. Not that she was wild
about jogging, mind you. But something had to be done
about her flabby stomach and wobbly thighs, because she
was simply not going up to a size sixteen on her next trip to
the mall, and that was that.

There are barriers in every woman's life beyond which
she will not go, and a size sixteen was one of them.

Besides, jogging got her out of the house. Going to
Curves would do the same, but she'd still be in a gym with
people she knew from church and Anna and Tim's schools.
What Lamorna liked best about running by the river was
simply that she was alone.

When you had a ten-year-old son and a fourteen-year-
old daughter, who could blame you for taking extreme
measures by resorting to jogging in order to get a little peace
and quiet?

So what if her sweats were a shrunken pair of Robert's
and her shoes were from the local discount store? No one

was out here at seven on a winter morning. The executive types had already come and gone, taking the commuter train from the station in Glendale into Pittsburgh and leaving the trails to the winter birds, squirrels, and slightly chunky moms.

Lamorna's legs were beginning to ache, though, at the end of her mile. She wasn't much of a goal setter, but if she had to set one, it would be getting back to the bridge without keeling over and dying of oxygen deprivation. She was about to the halfway point where she turned around—where the Susquanny River widened a little and a sandbar had built up. Often the herons would gather there to pick over what the river had tossed up, or to spear minnows on their way past in the shallows. In the summer, the kids had loved to play here. Someone had tied a rope swing into a tree, and they'd drop off it into the deep pools closer to the bank. But now the swing was as frozen and lifeless as the tree that supported it, waiting for the sun and the return of the children.

There must have been some high water recently. A log had washed up on the sandbar, and crows were walking around it like car salesmen sizing up a new deal. There were clothes draped over it, too. Good grief. Surely someone hadn't been swimming? It had to be forty-five degrees out here.

Lamorna jogged a little closer, taking one of the offshoot trails closer to the bank. Maybe it wasn't a log, after all. Maybe someone had tossed a bag of old clothes off the bridge instead of taking them to the Salvation Army like normal people did. But weren't there branches sticking out? And was that an animal trapped under it? With brown fur?

The river trail, though beautiful and scenic, didn't change much. That was why Lamorna liked it. She didn't have to watch out for hazards because she knew where they all were, and she could pay attention to seasonal changes in the scenery without worrying about falling flat on her face.

So, anything different meant a little investigation was in order. Maybe there would be identifying marks among the clothes to tell her who the litterbug was. And then she'd march right down to the Glendale police station and wake up one of the—

Good heavens.

Lamorna slid down the bank and landed upright by sheer luck. She squinted against the sparkle of the sun on the water and focused on the pile on the sandbar.

Not fur. Hair. Dark brown, short-cropped hair, drying and rimed with sand.

A green jacket. Jeans.

Bare feet. Slender, pale feet, so cold they were gray.

The bundle on the sand was a girl.

Had been. Had been a girl.

Because even Lamorna could tell she was dead.

ABOUT THE AUTHOR

Shelley Bates has been writing novels since the age of thirteen. After writing five Harlequin romances, her first CBA novel—the RITA Award winning *Grounds to Believe*—debuted from Steeple Hill in 2004. The critically acclaimed *Pocketful of Pearls* followed from Warner Faith in 2005. Shelley has a B.A. in creative writing from the University of California at Santa Cruz and an M.A. in writing popular fiction from Seton Hill University in Pennsylvania. She is currently a freelance editor in the high-tech industry in Silicon Valley.